MR. TEA AND THE TRAVELING TEACUP

A Madeline's Teahouse Mystery

by

Leslie Matthews Stansfield

Copyright © 2012 by Leslie Matthews Stansfield

For information, email **Cozy Cat Press**, cozycatpress@aol.com or visit our website at: www.cozycatpress.com

COZY CAT
PRESS

ISBN: 978-0-9881943-2-8
Printed in the United States of America

Cover design by Scarlett Rugers
http://www.scarlettrugers.com/

1 2 3 4 5 6 7 8 9 10

This book is dedicated to Becky Niles Letko, my first and lifelong friend, and to our childhood companions who lived on and around Kenaware Avenue. It was with you that I learned a good imagination is the key to adventure! Also, to my husband and children who knew I would rather write than clean!

CHAPTER 1

The hum of the bedroom's air conditioner was not enough to drown out the sound of the shattering glass. Terry's eyes sprung open, her body reeling from that groggy, spinning feeling that comes from being suddenly awakened from sleep. She knew it was, once again, the sound of a crashing teacup that had so rudely intruded on her sleep. The first time this happened, she was confused about the sound, the second time concerned, and now—time number three—fear encompassed her. Actually, that was the odd part. Why be afraid? She was in no danger, not that she could tell anyway. Tomorrow, her older sister, Karen, would arrive. That should make things better…maybe.

She sat up, feeling another wave of exhaustion. How many more nights of this could she take? She was so tired, and she just wanted to blot the incident out of her mind and go back to sleep. Her head began to pound. Dang it! In a woozy fury, she threw back the covers. Terry knew she would not sleep until she went downstairs and swept up. The first time, she didn't know what the sound was and decided to figure it out in the morning. The second time, she just didn't want to deal with it. Now, she wondered what the heck was going on. This was getting ridiculous.

Yanking on her bathrobe and stuffing her feet into her slippers, she flipped on the hallway light and trudged down the stairs. As she reached the bottom step, her grogginess abated, and the realization of what she was doing snapped into her brain. Whoa there,

Nelly, she cautioned herself. Get a grip. Someone could be down here. Just because no one was before doesn't mean… Her stomach flipped as a new wave of fear almost brought her to her knees. Shaking, she debated which way to turn. Her first instinct was to check the tearoom where the shelf holding the ever toppling teacups was. However, that would leave her back exposed to the parlor. She stood still, wanting to listen, but her pounding heart was making such a racket that she could barely hear herself think. Her back against the wall beneath the stairs, she slid herself stealthily along to the broom closet. Carefully cracking open the door, she reached in and grabbed a broom. She inched her way back. Easy, girlie, she told herself. She quickly turned around so she was against the wall next to the doorway of the tearoom and she could see into the dark parlor. She stared hard, looking for any sign of movement. Nothing. Adrenaline raced to every nerve. In a flash, she reached her hand around the doorway, flipped on the light switch, jumped, broom at the ready, into the room screaming, "Hiiiiyyyyaaaa!" Then she twirled around so she faced the parlor for a moment and twirled back with a grunt. Her eyes carefully scanned the tearoom for anything amiss. All was in order except for a shattered teacup lying just below the shelf on the wall. Just like before. Only the teacup from the middle shelf was broken. The top and bottom shelves still possessed their fragile cargo. As she glanced out the window toward the street, she thought, I must look like an ass, jumpin' around like an uncoordinated ninja! Thank God no one saw me!

Wearily, she trudged back to the broom closet and retrieved the dustpan. As she swept the pieces of the broken cup onto the dustpan, emotional overload took over. She plunked down to the floor, put her head in her hands and sobbed.

It was less than seven months since her mother, Madeline Sutter, died, leaving their childhood home to Terry and Karen. The sisters always planned to one day turn the house into a teahouse. Terry left her job as an art teacher in Connecticut and came back to Maine. It was harder than she ever thought to redo the house. So many memories lingered like friendly phantoms. Redoing each room was like demolishing the past, her childhood, all her wonderful memories. Her parents' faces and voices were like dandelion seeds on a spring breeze, gently floating by and dancing in the rooms. The tea parties she and Karen enjoyed on the front porch with their mother beckoned to her, calling her back to times she could not ever touch again. Her grief, mingled with her current fear, overwhelmed her. The tears flowed.

After a few minutes, she gasped for air as she looked up at the ceiling. What was going on? Why did any cup she put on the middle shelf keep falling? Was it a prank? How could anyone possibly get in? Was it a ghost? What happened to her mother's cup, a blue lace pattern teacup, missing since her death? The delicate white cup covered with blue vines and flowers always sat on the middle shelf.

"Mom, I can't do this," she whispered into the empty room. "I miss you so much. You and Karen were the strong ones; I was the wimpy artist. Look around," she cried, her arm sweeping the room. "I've done all this. I used my talents to transform this place and I don't even know if Karen will like it. Do you like it? Why is this happening? Mom, is it you knocking the teacup off the shelf?" Then another thought hit her. If it wasn't her mother, but some other lurking entity, did that specter mean any harm? Perhaps a much bigger ally was needed. "God, I need some help here. Make this stop. Make whoever or whatever this is go away."

Terry leaned against the wall and closed her eyes. How she wished she could once again feel her mother's gentle kiss on her forehead, but that would never happen again, ever. Her mother was gone, buried next to Daddy. Large quiet tears rolled once again down her cheeks. She stood and picked up the dustpan and broom. In the kitchen, she emptied the dustpan into the trash. She sat down at the kitchen table and gazed through the pickup window into the tearoom. Her eyes glanced up at the clock, 2:00 a.m. Her thoughts turned back to Karen. She would be here in twenty hours. Maybe things *would* seem better, then. Of course, Karen would initially think Terry was off her rocker. However, if this kept up, Karen would see for herself. Yeah, Karen's presence would give Terry strength; misery loves company.

She trudged back upstairs. Once in bed, she giggled as she pictured herself playing ninja with the broom. Silly fool, she thought as she drifted off to sleep.

The next night, Terry stood in the middle of the teahouse with its lace-adorned tables. She ran her fingers through her long brown hair, then looked at her watch. It was eleven-fifteen at night, almost time to leave to pick up Karen from the airport. Terry glanced around and wondered, for what seemed like the millionth time that day, if Karen would like the décor Terry put her heart and soul into creating. Taking a sip of her chamomile tea, Terry heaved a sigh.

Of course, Karen's reaction wasn't the only thing bothering her. There was also that blasted shelf. Terry walked over to the three-tier white corner shelf and glided her fingers along the empty middle tier. Sitting down at the nearest table, she massaged her temples and pondered the question of the day: should she just take the whole shelf down? The top and bottom shelves still held bone china teacups. The middle shelf that always held her mother's teacup was empty. It glared at her like a corpse. That small corner shelf was the bane of her existence, despite all the work she spent on the walls surrounding it.

Terry spent months painting and stenciling. Her sketchbook, in her bedroom upstairs, contained hundreds of drawings that she created since returning home to run the teahouse. She began with templates and books on stenciling she bought in a craft store. One day, as she rummaged through the attic, she came across her Beatrix Potter books from childhood. Ideas began to swirl in her head. She pondered and revised hundreds of drawings until she felt the designs for the walls were just right.

She checked her watch again and debated putting another cup on the shelf. Would she be able to take the cup down before she went to bed without Karen noticing? What would that solve? Nothing. There would be the next night, and the next, and the next. Terry would forget to take the cup down eventually. If she left the shelf empty, how would she explain that to Karen? The truth was too bizarre.

Closing her eyes, she tilted her head back and, with another deep sigh, pulled the blue elastic band off of her wrist and put her hair into a ponytail. Jumping up and heading out the door, she yelled out to a seemingly empty house, "I really wish I understood your problem." That was the real issue; she wasn't sure if the house was empty.   Was it a ghost or just coincidence? If it was a ghost, could it be her mother? What was the point of knocking a cup off a shelf...that special shelf? Getting into her car, Terry gave an involuntary shudder.

CHAPTER 2

Karen looked at her watch for probably the sixtieth time since the plane took off. She didn't care what time it was. It was just something to do. Something that would keep her mind off of what she left behind in California. Deep inside, Karen knew that you couldn't run from yourself, but she was giving it her best shot. Left behind was Todd, a now ex-husband, whom she caught celebrating a big win in court by screwing his secretary right there in his office on his big fat mahogany desk. How cliché, she mused. She walked in, saw the dynamic duo going at it, screamed, slammed the door, opened it again, stepped inside and yelled, "I hope the cleaning crew is gonna sterilize that desk by morning!" and stormed back out the door. Slamming the door felt so good, she opened and slammed it another five times before she roared out of the office. She smiled as she remembered catching a glimpse of their stunned faces on the final grand slam—both buck naked with their mouths hanging open in a mixture of fear and confusion.

He claimed it was just a "sex thing," that he loved Karen and didn't want their marriage to end. This happened only a month before her mother's death. Madeline's death made her want to start all over, to put the past behind her. She filed for divorce, told Terry she was ready to commit to opening the teahouse, gave a few months notice at her job as a CPA and planned her new life. The problem, she discovered, was that she assumed the pain would end the moment she left

California. It hadn't. Again, she looked at her watch and wondered…how long?

An hour later, Terry pulled the car into the driveway, unlocked the trunk and lifted out Karen's suitcases.

"Ya know, I don't think I will ever adjust to those stores being across the street," Karen said, taking a suitcase from her sister. "I miss the woods that were there. I know we're too old to build secret forts, but dang, it would be nice to have the option."

"I hear ya," Terry said, leaning against the trunk of the car. "I think about it every time I go out the front door, but we should count our blessings. If the town hadn't rezoned that area, we couldn't have gotten the permit for the teahouse. At least the builders kept the Victorian architectural theme from the other houses on the street. Besides, I have to admit, I think those stores being there has helped business. People go there and then wander over here. I guess now would be a bad time to tell you the town is considering putting in street lights." Terry smiled at her sister and headed toward the house.

"Hey, you added more rockers to the front porch! Wow, window boxes too," Karen said as she walked up the three stairs to the porch.

"I really hope you like what I did inside," Terry said as her shaking hands unlocked the front door.

Karen walked inside and set her suitcase down. The silence that followed engulfed Terry as she watched her sister look around. "Oh, my gosh! It's gorgeous," Karen whispered, wide-eyed. "You did an incredible job! Mom would be so pleased! I can't believe how well it all turned out."

"Wait 'til you see the whole thing. I can't wait to show you around," Terry said, taking her sister into the room to the right of the front hall. "Voila! The parlor!" Terry entered the room and spread her arms open wide.

She watched in relief as her sister stood, mouth open, taking in the Victorian couch done in a cream fabric covered in small pink and yellow roses. Two high-back chairs done in a soft pink were on each side of the couch. They formed a conversational grouping in front of a large stone fireplace. There was a lounger done in the same fabric as the sofa by a window with two small chairs in the same soft pink as the high-back chairs. To the right of the doorway was the cash register and along the walls were wooden hutches holding teapots, cozies, cups, and teas for sale. To the left of the doorway stood a brass coat rack, adorned with large hats and some boas.

Karen turned slowly around, "This is…the bee's knees, as Mom used to say. Ter, I'm speechless. Never in my wildest dreams did I picture this. Holy Toledo! Where did you find this stuff? I'm afraid to ask about the cost."

"Well, you can relax. I went to an auction with Uncle Henry and bought the furniture. He and Aunt Rose helped me strip and reupholster. The furniture is apparently from an estate in Kennebunkport. Okay, c'mon, there's more! Close your eyes, I want to take you to the kitchen first." Terry turned her sister around and dragged her back past the suitcases, through the main tearoom, flipping on the main light switch as they went by, and into the kitchen. "Ta da!"

Karen stood speechless again, staring at the immense kitchen with a professional stove, a new large refrigerator and a butcher-block table in the center. There was a window that normally looked out on the tearoom, but Terry closed the shutters so Karen wouldn't see the main room until the end of the tour. In the back of the kitchen was a table with six chairs. Behind that, a door to another room was slightly ajar. Her mouth open in awe, Karen walked to the door and pushed it open to peek inside. She drew her breath. "Oh, Terry, this office is…wow!   The kitchen is amazing as well. I know we talked about it, but this is beyond anything I imagined. I can't even take it all in. I'm overwhelmed by what you've accomplished in the few months you've been here. I feel like such a heel. I've been in California while you've worked your butt off here."

"Karen, it was much easier for me to leave my job than for you to leave yours. Besides, we needed that extra money you've been sending," Terry replied. "Ready for the main room?"

"You bet your boots, sister. Lead on!"

"Close your eyes, no peeking! Remember, the walls are gone between the old living room and dining room. Get ready!" She gently led Karen out to the center of the main room. "Okay…" Terry held her breath, still nervous about what Karen would think.

"Holy shi—" Karen turned around slowly, her eyes wide. "I love the lavender tablecloths with the soft yellow trim. The flowers stenciled on the walls are great. Oh my…" Karen walked slowly over to the wall. "Those birds are drinking tea in their nest!" She looked around carefully again. "How cute, the squirrels over there and the rabbits in the corner are all having tea! You're so creative. I admit I'm jealous. I can't paint my nails, let alone do something as incredible as this. Wow."

As Karen sat in a chair with her hands on her knees and continued to look at the artwork, Terry felt her body relax and she heaved a deep sigh. Karen really loved it.

"Oh look," continued Karen, "over here are rabbits napping by some lettuce…this one is holding a teacup. And here, a mouse is peeking out of this cup." Karen got up and walked along the wall a bit. "Here's a baby rabbit napping in a yellow canopy bed and his mother is bringing him tea. Oh, for heavens sake! This squirrel is sitting in a rocker with her feet in a bucket of hot water while she drinks tea.   This is so unbelievably clever. I love the picture of the badger and the fox having tea while the mouse peeks around the corner! How did you get this all done in time to open?"

"It was pretty close. There are some details I still want to add here and there. Luckily, the handyman Mom always used, Carl Despard—I'm sure you remember him—was willing to do a lot of the lifting and moving of furniture which left more time for me to do the artwork."

"How's Carl's mother? I was so sad when I heard about the stroke. I used to love it when she babysat for us. I feel guilty I didn't stop in to see her the last time I was home."

"I wouldn't feel guilty. There was so much goin' on. According to Aunt Rose, she's doing well. Her speech is clear and she can just about walk on her own. Rose volunteers at the convalescent home a few afternoons a week now. It gives her something to do and it gives Uncle Henry a break."

Karen turned her attention back to the artwork. "I can't believe you painted such incredible details on those teeny-tiny cups the animals are drinking out of. Little sister, I really envy the talent you have!"

"I wouldn't be too jealous. You're a CPA and I can't even balance my checkbook. I'd be sunk if you didn't do the accounting for this place," Terry said as she leaned against one of the walls, her arms crossed in front of her. "By the way, tons of paperwork is already in a folder on the desk in the office waiting for you. C'mon upstairs and let me show you the sitting room I put up there. I used the guestroom. When we go to the Bed and Breakfast phase and add on over the garage, we can decide if we want to keep the room as a sitting room or make it back into a bedroom and put the sitting room someplace else. I left Mom's bedroom alone. I couldn't deal with touching that, not yet." Terry turned on the light to the stairs, picked up one of Karen's suitcases and started up. Her sister followed suit.

Terry walked into Karen's bedroom and realized her sister was not behind her. "Hey, where'd ya go?"

"Oh, Ter, this is…" Terry heard Karen's voice coming from the sitting room. Terry put the suitcase down and ran to the sitting room as Karen continued.

"Oh my gosh, new couch, new entertainment center. I love the pastel blue color. It's not the southwest décor I'm used to, but I love it." Karen put her other suitcase in her bedroom and as the two of them walked back downstairs, Terry said, "My talent without your business and accounting knowledge wouldn't get me a cup of tea."

"That's probably why Mom left the house to both of us. She knew we always wanted to open a teahouse and Bed and Breakfast. We balance each other out," Karen said, walking into the tearoom and sitting down at the nearest table.

Terry looked out the window and sighed as she thought of her mother. Madeline died suddenly. She was seventy-two. Her health was excellent up until a few weeks before she died. She started feeling tired and worn out. Before she could go to the doctor, she fell down the cellar stairs, hit her head and died. Her older sister, Rose, found her a few hours later. Rose called an ambulance, but it was too late. The tearoom, Madeline's Tearoom, was named after their mother. Turning her attention back to Karen, Terry said, "Hey, I want to see your tattoo. I think you're the first one around here to have one."

Karen stood up and slid down the waist of her pants to expose a butterfly tattoo on her hip. "That's not all," she said, pulling up her shirt.

"You got a bellybutton ring! Mom would have flipped. The neighbors *will* flip. You always were the bold and daring one. I was the careful, plodding child and you were always off like a shot! " Terry said, staring amazed at Karen's belly.

"Well, after Mom died and my divorce was finalized, I went out drinking with some of my friends. I wanted to do something wild that would help me to feel young again."

"Feel young again! You're only forty-two. Give me a break!"

"Mom's death made me feel old and the divorce from Todd didn't help any. I regret all the years I wasted on my career. I wish I'd had kids."

Terry sighed, unsure of what to say. She was forty and never married. She struggled with her own biological clock issues.

"Terry, do you remember the tea parties we had as kids?" Karen asked, changing the subject.

"Of course. We dressed up in Mom's clothes, high heels, jewelry, hats, the whole nine yards. Mom set the table with tea and cakes. We pretended we were having tea with the queen at Buckingham Palace." Terry laughed out loud. "I remember when Melissa Barlow came over and told you she thought it was a stupid game. You decked her...broke her tooth, as I remember."

Karen started to laugh as well. "Oh, yeah. Mom stomped out and said that ladies having tea at Buckingham Palace would never deck anyone, let alone a commoner! What a riot. She never did like Melissa. Mom called her a commoner..." Both sisters wiped tears from their eyes and took deep breaths.

"So, business has been good," Karen said, standing up.

"Yeah, I was surprised. I knew that during the summer and early fall, tourists flocked to the lakes and antique shops nearby. So I put flyers in hotel lobbies and advertised in the local paper. For the two weeks I've been open, business is already booming. I thought it would take longer. I told you to wait a few weeks before coming because I thought you'd be bored. Now I'm glad you're here. I've been on the run constantly."

"I can't wait to jump in and help out. Looking at all you've done...I told you, it makes me feel guilty," Karen said with a yawn.

"There's already a load of receipts on the desk in the office. You definitely won't be bored. I think this place will keep you busier than the job you left at Weinstein, Gold, and Green! In a few months, we should have the money to begin the Bed and Breakfast phase. I have a list of contractors that people recommended. You can start getting bids whenever you're ready. The man who did the initial work on the house is great, but feel free to get other bids as well."

Karen nodded and walked over to the large handmade quilt that hung on another wall. Slowly, she reached out and slid her hand along its yellow gingham border. "I'm amazed at how perfectly you coordinated the color scheme to Mom's quilt. Remember, Grandma Tyler made it for her as a wedding present. I think it's fifty-two years old, isn't it?"

"You're the accountant." Terry laughed. "You're much quicker at math than I am, but yeah, I think it is fifty-two years old."

Turning, Karen looked at the corner shelf. "Oh...you left the shelf empty where Mom kept her cup. Did you do that on purpose?"

"No, I never did find Mom's cup. I searched through the house again when I moved back. I rechecked the places we looked after she died and then took the house apart, looking for it. Every other cup I put on that shelf seems to fall and break," Terry said, thinking how creepy that sounded.

"Ooooo, maybe this is a haunted tearoom." Karen chuckled. "Mom never had any problems. Her cup sat on that shelf as long as I can remember. Remember, she kept her teapot on a small table underneath with a tea cozy over it."

"Of course, I remember, but I'm tellin' ya, every cup falls off that shelf. It's possible the problem started before Mom died. Maybe her cup fell off the shelf and broke. Perhaps you'll have better luck. Why don't you go into the kitchen and get a cup?" Terry suggested, wishing she took the shelf down. "I've gotten a lot of teacups at tag sales. Just pick any one. There's a bunch of them in the cabinet over the sink."

Karen walked into the kitchen and returned with a teacup decorated with yellow roses. She placed it triumphantly on the shelf. Stepping back, she looked at it. She took another step backwards. "Looks pretty sturdy from here."

"So it does," said Terry. "You must have the magic touch." She decided not to tell her sister that the cups seemed to topple only at night. Terry knew from experience that Karen would find the cup broken into pieces on the floor in the morning. Karen wouldn't think it was so amusing after a day or two. The phenomena certainly had Terry unnerved. The pile of receipts wasn't the only reason she was glad Karen was there. If the teahouse was haunted, Terry didn't want to deal with it alone.

"Well, I don't know about you, but I'm bushed," Karen said, giving Terry a hug.

"Absolutely. You'll be surprised how tired you'll be tomorrow after only a day of work. I think you'll be more tired than you are at tax season." Terry smiled, feeling satisfied at Karen's reaction. As she relaxed, she realized how tired she was as well. She'd run out that afternoon and bought a white noise machine. She didn't want to hear any breaking glass and she hoped combining the air conditioner with the machine would do the trick. Maybe all the cups would stay put. She'd look a little silly after all she told Karen, but she'd gladly trade looking silly for feeling unnerved.

Karen sat in bed with her usual four pillows propping her up. She reached for her journal. Every Christmas since they were sixteen, Mom bought them journals. She wasn't sure where Terry kept hers, but all of Karen's were in a locked box. All her thoughts, hopes and dreams from the last twenty-six years were locked securely away. As she took her pen and opened the book, her hands began to shake. The emptiness, locked away like her journals, seeped in.

Being home again is…hard. I love what Terry did to create the teahouse, but it was somehow painful to see everything different. I guess I sort of believed that coming back home would erase time. How silly. Mom is gone. Todd is a jerk. Man, Mom's death seems so real now…so final. It's tough not having her here. I need her hugs and her comfort. I needed to hear her voice tell me, once again, that Todd is a "doo doo head," a real slime ball. Hearing my mother say it seemed to make things better. I miss her voice. No voice can ever replace it. I'm feeling confused because my gut still aches. I want to feel safe and pain free again without the use of alcohol. I think I've been drinking a bit too much lately. It stops the pain. Right now, I could really use a margarita! Thankfully, I still have a few sleeping pills left. I sure hope I get over this inner yuck before I run out of pills. If not, I'm gonna have to spike the tea!

Smiling, she envisioned herself staggering around the teahouse. With a fluff of her pillows, she drifted off into a pill-induced sleep.

CHAPTER 3

It was the sound of the shower that woke Terry the next morning. Rather than get up and go downstairs to put on water for tea, she turned off her alarm clock. There was still fifteen minutes before it was due to go off. She put the pillow over her head. She was not going to go downstairs first. No way!   Just as she began to drift off to sleep again, she heard her bedroom door open for a moment and then shut as Karen peeked in. She felt the vibrations as her sister trotted down the stairs. Tossing the pillow aside, she lay in bed…waiting. Creak went the floor at the bottom of the stairs. A moan from the floorboards in the hallway signaled Karen's approach to the room where the teacup shelf hung. Silence. Another groan from the hallway floorboard, a creak from the floor by the stairs, feet running up the stairs…3, 2, 1…

"Terry!" Karen said, panting as she plunged through Terry's bedroom door. "Have you been downstairs this morning?"

"Nope," was Terry's calm reply. With a sense of satisfaction, she asked, "Why?"

"The teacup, the one I put on the shelf yesterday, is on the floor…smashed."

"Well, I'll be darned, no kidding," Terry said with the tone of a sister who is holding back an "I told you so."

"Is that when it always happens? In the morning, I mean?" Karen came and sat on Terry's bed.

"Yup."

"Why didn't you tell me that yesterday?"

"Oooo, maybe it's a haunted teahouse," Terry said in a voice three octaves higher than normal. "You were gonna have to see it for yourself. You don't think it's so funny now, do you?"

"I'm sure there must be a logical explanation," Karen said, standing up. "Although, running a haunted teahouse would be kinda cool!"

There was the faint sound of a knock at the back door, followed by the fainter sound of a key in the lock and finally, "Yoooooohooooooo, my darlings, it's Aunt Rose. Yoooooooohoooooooo!"

Terry scrunched her face up and sighed. "Gotta get that key back." Putting on her bathrobe, Terry trudged downstairs just far enough behind her sister to see Karen's five-foot four inch frame engulfed in a hug by the five-foot nine Aunt Rose. Karen's head was lost somewhere in Rose's ample bosom. Terry often thought that her own five-foot nine frame greatly increased her life expectancy. It just couldn't be good for one's health to be suffocated by Aunt Rose on a frequent basis.

Rose let go of Karen who staggered backward a bit. "My sweet darling, it is so good to have you home again. The Maine air is much healthier than that smog in California, I'm sure! Look at how thin you've gotten. What did that accounting firm do to my girl? You're as thin as your poor sister here. She's been so busy, I don't think she eats. The two of you are running a teahouse and I'm gonna wind up cooking for you so you don't faint from hunger! Thank God, I live next door! Why don't you girls sit down and let me make you breakfast?"

Terry's breath was momentarily stolen by panic. Regaining her composure, she blurted out, "Aunt Rose, that's so sweet of you, but we really have a lot to do before we open at eleven-thirty. My stars, look at the time, it's already eight-thirty and I still need to shower!" She loved her aunt, but she was not up for a long visit. Rose, always mothering and hovering, was best appreciated in small doses.

Rose looked disappointed as she said, "Well, why don't we plan on dinner tonight then?"

"That would be great!" the sisters said in unison.

Karen opened the pantry door and removed the broom and dustpan. As she turned to go, Rose asked, "Oh dear, did another cup fall and break? I kept forgetting to mention to you, Terry dear, that I couldn't keep a cup on that middle shelf when I watched the house for you those few weeks after Maddy died. God rest her soul. I meant to give you money to replace the cups. I really don't know what the problem is. Henry thinks it's the roadwork two blocks down. All that jackhammering is probably knocking the cups off. Things at my house are fine and I haven't heard of other people having that problem, but this house is over one hundred years old and its foundation is older. I don't think the cup she used got broken. Actually, I don't recall seeing it at all. Well, I should go. Ta ta for now. Perhaps tomorrow morning, I can find some lovely teacups at a tag sale. See you this evening, my darlings." With a wave of her hand, Rose's ample bottom waddled out the door, leaving both sisters looking at each other, speechless.

By eleven-fifteen, the tables were set, the various scones baked, and the teas steeping. "My gosh, how did you do this all?" Karen asked Terry with more than just a hint of admiration in her voice. "We haven't opened for the day and I already need a nap!"

"Shannon usually helps me. I told her to come in later this morning because you were going to be here. She's been busting butt with me twenty-four seven for the last month." The back door opened and Shannon Dindle, the sisters' next door neighbor and lifelong friend, walked in.

"Your ears must have been burning, I was just talking about you," Terry said as she wiped down the counter. "Karen thought I pulled the daily prep work off by myself. Ha! I gave credit where credit was due!"

Karen and Shannon shrieked and hugged each other.

"You look so good! You still have the perfect figure and mesmerizing auburn hair that we all loved to hate," Karen said, holding Shannon at arm's length.

"Yup, and I work out so my boobs and buns are still perky, too! Not!" Shannon laughed. "You're so nice and tan! Terry and I are still white. We haven't even stopped long enough to see much daylight. By the time things are done around here, the sun is heading down behind the mountains. The only sand we've seen is what the tourists drag in here on their feet. This place will make your fancy CPA job look like a picnic. I can't complain, though. Terry and I have really had a lot of fun. I bet she's told you the money's been rollin' in."

"Yeah, she did. I haven't had a chance to look at the books yet. I can't wait. We'll be in the Bed and Breakfast phase before we know it."

Shannon stood in the middle of the kitchen, tying the strings of her lavender apron in a bow behind her. "So, what still needs to be done? Oh, by the way, my mother, a.k.a. Ms. Etiquette, is coming today. Let's make sure all utensils are in their proper places. Let's not give her indigestion. Karen, did Terry tell you about my mother's little age issue?" Shannon remarked with a smirk.

"No..." Karen said as Terry and Shannon giggled.

"Well, get this.   My mother, the one we all nicknamed Ms. Etiquette, has developed…this problem. Now, remember, her hearing is going."

"Yeah?" said Karen, frowning with curiosity.

"Ms. Etiquette," Terry giggled, "has developed a…flatulence problem!"   Terry and Shannon burst out laughing.

"You mean she…farts?" Karen asked in amazement.

"Like a truck driver!   Almost every time she stands up," roared Shannon.

"And she can't hear it!" Terry chimed in.

"How long has this been going on?" Karen said, giggling.

"Long enough for Uncle Henry to figure it out. He's constantly thinking of reasons for her to stand up…sit down….stand up…" Terry and Shannon could barely stand.

"Your mom? No kidding? Well, life certainly takes unexpected turns!" Karen said, chuckling and shaking her head.

"Oh, gosh, look at the time!" Terry said, rushing to unlock the front door and turn the sign on the door from "closed" to "open."

Within half an hour, every seat in Madeline's Tearoom was full and people were waiting on the benches outside.   The two other waitresses, Sara and Jen, came in at twelve.   It was go, go, go until around four o'clock.   Silver serving trays with china tea pots and cups, scones and tea sandwiches were held high above their heads as they gracefully hustled from one table to another. The drone of the chatter was punctuated with the ding, ding, beep and rattle of the cash register.   From her front row seat at the serving window in the kitchen, Terry thought of it as the dance of the tea fairies

"My goodness," sighed Karen, walking into the kitchen. "You weren't kidding when you said it's busy. I can't believe it's almost four o'clock already."

"This is just the calm before the final storm. At about four-fifteen, business picks up again until we close at five-thirty. Some people like to have a late tea and then a late dinner," Terry explained over her shoulder as she prepared for the next onslaught. Shannon, Sara and Jen were tidying up tables, straightening chairs, and filling teacups for the few customers still there. Karen headed out to help.

The door opened and Terry watched as Shannon Dindle's mom—"Ms. Etiquette," dressed in a soft purple dress with a purse, hat and shoes to match, walked in slowly with Mrs. Hardy, her companion du jour. Mrs. Hardy, a widow like Mrs. Dindle, carried herself with perfect posture and a no nonsense expression on her face. Her light pink ensemble perfectly complemented her companion's outfit. Terry smirked as she thought, good gracious, it's the waddle of the sourpuss fairies. Mrs. Dindle still carried herself with perfect posture too, but, to be fair, Terry and Shannon noticed that lately she seemed to have a tiredness about her and a definite mellowing with age. Instead of shooing a stray cat away, she put out a bowl of milk. She sat out on her porch and, instead of looking at her watch and remarking about the time, she thanked the papergirl for the paper and tipped her at the end of the week.

"Oh, Karen! Shannon said you were coming home. It's so good to see you again. I'm so pleased you're moving back. Doesn't she look wonderful, Marge?"

Mrs. Hardy looked Karen up and down, remarking, "You know, too much sun leads to skin cancer. Watch yourself."

Terry, still watching the scene from the kitchen, was shocked to see Mrs. Dindle, alias Ms. Etiquette, give her companion a disgusted look.

"Would you ladies like a table by the window?" Karen asked, offering her arm to Mrs. Dindle.

Before Mrs. Dindle could open her mouth, Mrs. Hardy said, "It's a bit cool in here. Seat us by a window that gets sun. Perhaps over here." Mrs. Hardy skirted around Karen and led the way to a table that overlooked the garden and got the afternoon sun.

Just then, the kitchen door opened and in waltzed Uncle Henry, wearing his tan gardening pants, green shirt and a look of mischief on his face. "Hey, kiddo," he whispered, dashing to the kitchen window and peering out. "I thought I saw Dottie Dindle come in with Margaret Hardy. Hot diggity! "

He strolled out of the kitchen just as the women took their seats. "Karen, it's good to see you," he cooed, giving her a hug.

Terry smirked and rolled her eyes. What a con artist, she thought.

"Good afternoon ladies," he said with a bow. "I apologize for the interruption, but I just wanted to tell my niece a quick hello." Turning to Karen, he said, "I hear you'll be having dinner with us. Can't wait." Then, he turned to Mrs. Dindle and remarked, "Dottie, what a lovely dress you have on. I swear I saw it in the window of Town and Tweed last week."

Mrs. Dindle beamed. "Why, yes, Henry, I purchased this outfit just a few days ago. Thank you for noticing."

Uncle Henry took her hand in his. He said, "I think it looks better on you than on the mannequin in the window. May I see the back?"

Mrs. Dindle blushed and began to stand up. "No!" snapped Mrs. Hardy. Terry assumed that Mrs. Hardy, who was not at all hard of hearing, knew of Mrs. Dindle's flatulence troubles. Mrs. Hardy and Uncle Henry locked eyes. Terry could tell they declared war. Everyone stared at Mrs. Hardy.

"Henry, there is no need for this poor woman to stand up in the middle of a public establishment and model for you! You have a wife, go ask her to model dresses for you, you old coot!"

Henry put his hand to his chest and looked taken aback. With another bow, he said, "Dottie, I apologize if I offended you. I simply wanted to pay you a well-deserved compliment. Again, my apologies if I was out of line." He looked out the window and remarked, "I would like to get your opinion on the new water garden I put in the back. Yours is so lovely. I'm surprised you didn't want to sit over there where you can see it."

Wow, he's good! Terry thought from her spy window in the kitchen. Mrs. Dindle had the nicest water garden in town. It was her pride and joy. Henry clearly had her attention.

"I wasn't aware the girls had you put one in. I would love to see it," said Dottie Dindle. "Karen, would it be an imposition for us to switch tables?"

"We're staying here!" Mrs. Hardy said, her voice truculent. "No need to move. We can see it next time, or perhaps after tea."

Terry, who had a sense of humor much like her uncle's, came rushing out of the kitchen. "Mrs. Dindle, would you really be interested in advising us on the water garden? Yours is truly magnificent." Terry eyed Mrs. Hardy.

Mrs. Hardy gritted her teeth and seethed, "I don't think that is appropriate now. Let Mrs. Dindle...stay put!" Terry almost giggled as she thought, is that stay put or say putt?

Terry looked around. "Oh, we have a bit of a lull now. Here, Mrs. Dindle, let me escort you to a table with a better view." Uncle Henry moved in quickly to help Mrs. Dindle push back her chair. Terry put out her hand and helped her up. Pppppppppuuuttttttt came the sound as Ms. Etiquette stood. Mrs. Hardy threw down her napkin in disgust.

A young child of about five in a pink and white dress with matching bows in her hair looked up from her plate with hopeful inquisitiveness. Her big blue eyes conveyed to Terry that Mrs. Dindle was the highlight of her visit to the teahouse. Terry saw Karen wink at the child and cover her mouth in mock surprise. The little girl grinned from ear-to-ear.

Once reseated, Mrs. Dindle gushed over the new view. She and Uncle Henry made a date to discuss what enhancements could be made to it. Terry returned to the kitchen with Henry in tow.

As Henry was about to go, Terry said, "Marge Hardy is on to you, ya know."

Henry's face lit up like a rich lady's diamond ring. "Oh, Dottie Dindle was such a prissy thing in school. Well, I guess there were a bunch of prissy girls back then, Margaret included. However, I thought Dottie was the prettiest girl in town. The only way I could get her attention was to put frogs in her desk, spiders in her pockets, dip her pigtails in paint, and put worms in her lunch box. In time, I realized that she was too prissy for me. I don't like to feel guilty if I put my elbows on a table or be afraid of the gas I get from some good, ol' fashioned, hot chili. Rose accepted me as I was. So bugging Dottie makes me feel young again. Of course, she doesn't know she makes funny sounds when she stands up, but it still makes me feel good. Today, watching Margaret Hardy was an extra treat. Made my day. Of course, I'll have to gussy-up the water garden under Dottie's supervision, but it'll be worth it. See you tonight, kiddo, gotta go. I'm supposed to be working in my own garden."

As she filled a few more teapots, Terry giggled. It really is the little things in life that keep us going, she thought. She wondered how her mother would have reacted to Henry's prank. Madeline would have conniptions when her father asked Terry and Karen to pull his finger. "Harold, for heaven's sake, don't teach little girls things like that. It's rude!" Terry smiled at the memory. However, there was the time after their father died that Madeline rushed into the kitchen and said breathlessly to Terry, "Quick, pull my finger!" Terry had and the two of them roared with laughter. Terry knew her mother was brought up to have good manners and never, *ever* swear. Still, her mother had a good sense of humor. Terry remembered her parents and Rose often laughing over one of Henry's latest pranks. Funny, you never really take the time to ponder people until they're gone, then it's too late to ask them. How many times did Terry want to ask her mother something when she was alive, but Terry didn't pick up the phone and call her? It seemed there would always be a later. Now there was no later and so many questions would go unanswered. Terry blinked back the tears as she prepared another plate of scones.

CHAPTER 4

About seven o'clock, Terry and Karen made their way next door to Uncle Henry's and Aunt Rose's house. It was a perfect summer night, so they lingered a bit in their garden. Terry noticed she was more relaxed because Karen was home. It's amazing, she thought, that having my big sister around still makes me feel safe. You'd think that after all the times she ripped my hair out, roots and all, I'd have an aversion to her. Spontaneously, she hugged Karen.

"Ooof," Karen said, "what brought that on?"

"It just feels great to have you here," Terry said, smiling at her sister.

"I can't believe how tired I am," Karen remarked as she leaned against the white picket fence that separated the two homes and their gardens. "What a perfect night. The sound of the ocean just a few blocks away, the crickets chirping, the gentle breeze, I'd forgotten the wonderful sounds, feelings and smells of summer here. I'm really glad to be home. Leaving California was a big decision for me, but this feels so right. How about you?"

"It was hard to leave my teaching job in Connecticut. But, like you, this feels right. I don't think my soul really ever left here. This is truly home." Terry put her hand on her sister's arm. "Karen, was it hard to leave Todd behind?"

"I'd like to kick Todd in the behind," Karen said, smiling, but Terry saw the pain flash across her face. "I think it would have been harder to stay. I never thought he would do that to me. I don't know if I'll ever be able to trust someone again. It made me feel...old, unattractive, unwanted. Honey, let's change the subject. It's a bit of a raw nerve right now." Karen hugged Terry and they both hung on for an extra moment.

Opening the gate and walking into the garden next door, Karen said, "I wonder if people ever emotionally leave the homes they grew up in."

"There you are!" exclaimed Rose, opening the sliding glass door to her porch and coming outside. "We've been waiting. Would you like to sit outside or inside while we have drinks and chat?"

"Outside would be great," Karen answered. "I was just saying how wonderful it is to be back here."

"I'm so thrilled to have you both back," Rose said. "Henry and I have missed you so much. Of course," her voice caught a bit, "the circumstances...Maddy's death..." She looked up at the mountains in the background, collecting herself. Terry felt her heart wrench. Rose and Mom were so close. There was an emptiness without Mom here, a void impossible to fill. Rose and Henry were in their seventies. Who could tell how much longer they would be here? Terry wished she could stop time and hold on to the remaining few years forever. A lump rose in her throat and the ache in her heart seemed to merge with it to make her chest feel like a cavern overflowing with the heavy dark ooze of pain.

Uncle Henry broke the silence. "What can I get people to drink?"

Terry smiled weakly, thinking, typical male, heaven forbid we get emotional.

Rose's head jerked in Henry's direction and she said, "I made some fresh iced tea, would you like some, girls?"

"Tea!" snapped Henry. "Good gracious, Rose, these poor girls have probably had it up to their eyeballs with tea! How about letting me make you gals some strawberry margaritas?"

"Perfect, perfect, perfect," said Karen. "I haven't had one of your famous margaritas since last summer. Bring 'em on!"

"Be back in a jiffy," called Henry over his shoulder as he headed inside to mix the drinks.

"Girls, let me show you the treasures I found while tag saling today." Rose reached for a shopping bag next to her chair. Carefully, she pulled out a few wads of newspaper. Slowly and gently, she began to unroll the newspaper, revealing bone china teacups.

"Where did you find those? They're lovely," Terry said as she reached out and picked up a teacup with drawings of lilacs and ivy. She turned it around in her hand, delighted at the beauty of the delicate cup.

"No Harley Davidson mugs?" Karen said with a smile. "I confess that I need to readjust to all this Normal Rockwell New England quaintness. I've gotten used to cups with Indian designs and cacti."

"Oh...dear...you don't like these cups?" Rose frowned.

"No, no, I do like them. It's just odd not to see any with that southwestern flavor I've surrounded myself with for the past twenty years in California. I've dreamed of this teahouse for years. These are perfect, really. I'm just going through...culture shock. So, where did you find them? How many did you get...looks like ten or more."

"I found thirteen total. So many seniors moving south these days and they're weeding things out before they move. Lucky us!" Rose beamed and clapped her hands. Terry felt another wave of emotion as she realized how excited Rose was with her treasures for the teahouse. Terry remembered her art students used to excitedly present her with their hand-made birthday cards.

"And, I've saved the greatest treasure for last. Who would like to open it?" Rose held up a pink gift bag with pink and white tissue paper poking out of the top.

"Let Terry open it. She's been busting her aaa...umm...butt for the past few weeks. She deserves to open it."

Terry reached for the bag and smiled. Rose may have accepted Uncle Henry with all his faults, but she, like Madeline, detested swearing. Rose's father, Grandpa Charles, told his daughters that people used vulgarity because they were too uneducated to think of better words. Terry never really minded the "no swearing" rule, but Karen, who always gravitated towards the earthier things in life, always tripped herself up. Karen swore that she ate a truckload of soap by the time she turned eighteen. Carefully, Terry reached inside the bag and removed an item wrapped in tissue paper. As she began to catch a glimpse of its hidden treasure, her hands began to shake. She involuntarily held her breath as bits of a blue design became visible. Could it be...it was...a perfect copy of her mother's teacup, the blue design of vines and flowers on a white background. "Oh, heavens," gasped Terry. "Where on earth did you find this?"

Rose's eyes gleamed. "At the Goodwill store. I couldn't believe it when I saw it. Just like Maddy's."

Terry cradled the cup as if it was a priceless artifact. Her eyes began to tear as she pictured her mother sitting at the kitchen table, drinking her tea. Then, Terry's eyes caught something and her heart began to pound. She opened her mouth and no sound came out.

"What is it, dear?"

Rose and Karen both leaned forward, staring at her, confusion in their eyes.

"The cup," Terry whispered. "The cup is cracked on the handle exactly like Mom's. I think this *is* Mom's."

"Let me see it, dear." Rose reached for the cup. "It can't be Maddy's. Look, Maddy's had…Oh, God."

"What, for heaven's sake? Mom's cup had what?" Karen looked unnerved. "What do you see?"

"Maddy bought her cup when she was ten years old," Rose croaked. "She saved a few pennies and we went to the general store. Mr. Witherspoon, the storekeeper, told her she could have this cup because it was irregular. The blue design wasn't perfect. The ink was smudged on the flower, just like it is here." Rose's face became pale.

Karen, it seemed to Terry, attempted to be the voice of reason. "Whoa, ladies. Let's get a grip here. There has to be an explanation…"

"Explanation for what?" Henry asked as he stepped onto the porch with a pitcher and glasses on a tray. "Rose, honey, what's wrong?"

"This cup," whispered Rose. "I think it's Maddy's cup."

"Maddy's cup, that's impossible!" said Henry as he set the tray down on the table.

Terry and Rose began to yammer simultaneously, each showing Henry the telltale signs.

Henry sat quietly, thinking for a moment. Then he asked, "Now Rose, I remember that Carl helped you pack up some of Madeline's things to take to the church for the bazaar. Isn't it possible that he took the cup and gave it away?"

"No, it is absolutely *impossible*," Rose snapped. "Do you honestly think I would let him give away anything before I checked the box carefully? I went through every box, item by item, before I let him take anything out of that house. Besides, I would have noticed the cup, Henry. I knew it was missing."

"Any chance that Mom gave it away?" Karen asked, her voice flat from shock.

"Oh no, dear," Rose said, wide eyed. "She often joked that I should have her buried with the cup. She had it for nearly sixty years. No, no, no, Maddy did not give that cup away."

"Well," said Henry with a sigh. "It looks as if there might be another mystery in that house."

"Another mystery?" asked the girls in unison.

"Oh...sure, don't you know the history of that house? I'm sure I told you," Henry said emphatically.

'Uh, no," Karen said. "I would have remembered that. Any chance that Terry's idea about the house being haunted is valid?"

"Haunted?" It was Henry's and Rose's turn to talk in unison.

Karen and Terry explained the smashing teacup problem to them.

"Well, could be," Henry said as he poured another round of margaritas into glasses. "When I was a kid, that house stood alone on acres and acres. None of these other houses were built. The house was owned by a man named Beauregard Hamilton. The rumor was that Mr. Hamilton made his money robbing banks and the money was hidden on his property. 'Course, the rumor was probably started because he detested having anyone on his property. Anyway, a story like that is too good to let pass. Me and my friends would sneak out of our houses in the middle of the night and try and scout the property for treasure. Any soft spot or sag in the dirt was suspect. Old man Hamilton let his dogs out a few times during the night. We had a few close calls, as I remember. Anyway, when he died, another rumor sprang up that he haunted the property, guarding his treasure. He was so tight that he never told his wife or their only child, Beauregard Hamilton, Jr., where the money was.

"When I was about twelve years old, the younger Mr. Hamilton married and they had a son, Thurston. Now that kid was bad news. By the time I was about twenty, some of the surrounding property was sold and houses were being built. 'Course, we all half-expected Old Man Hamilton's treasure to pop up, but it never did. Anyway, as I said, Thurston was bad news. People's dogs and cats were being hung, the builder's equipment was damaged, equipment taken and it was all said to be the work of Thurston Hamilton. Well, what is now Mrs. Dindle's house was built. Two wealthy spinster sisters, Eloise and Mary...what was their last name? Oh yeah, Gutherie. Eloise and Mary Gutherie moved in. Why the house was built so close to the Hamilton's, I'm not sure. Anyway, Thurston and two of his buddies, one of which was Carl Despard, harassed those two ladies constantly. I remember hearing Eloise tell someone one Sunday in church that she was sure the property was haunted. She swore uphill and down that Old Man Hamilton was having a fit about his property being built up. The rest of us thought it was Thurston playing tricks. Anyway, Eloise and Mary put the house up for sale, but before the house was sold, they disappeared...vanished without one word to anyone. However, their car was left behind. Now here's another interesting thing. None of their money was ever found. They seemed to have no bank accounts anywhere. No money, no bodies, no note, nothing. People in town were convinced that Thurston Hamilton was involved in their disappearance, but before anyone could prove anything, Thurston was killed. His body was found down by the shore, a bullet in his head. Thurston's parents sold the house to your parents and the Hamiltons moved away from here. That was that. No problems until now. But if you're lookin' for ghosts, could be Old Man Hamilton, Thurston Hamilton, or maybe even the Gutherie sisters." Henry sat back and took a sip of his margarita. "Of course, I'm sure your parents never had reason to think the house was haunted or they would have said something to Rose and me. We built our house the year Karen was born. We've never had reason to think there were ghosts either."

"So could it be...Mom?" Terry asked as she swirled the red liquid around in her glass.

"Oh, my goodness gracious, I should hope not." Rose's voice quivered. "Why would she want to haunt the house? This is just too much for me." Rose gave an involuntary shudder and wrung her hands.

"I don't think it's Mom's cup or a ghost. Sometimes weird coincidences happen," Karen stated matter-of-factly.

"Let's not talk about this anymore," Rose said weakly. "I made a lovely roast and I'm losing my appetite."

"I don't suppose you made your wild blueberry pie," Terry said, very willing to change the subject. Something in her stomach was doing the rhumba. The idea of pie seemed to be so apropos. Terry remembered sitting at the kitchen table with her mother and Karen, eating pie, drinking tea and gossiping about events in town or the boys Karen and Terry liked. Mom, as always, used her teacup. Could she possibly miss the cup? That just didn't seem to make sense. Perhaps she was trying to tell them something. Rose's voice interrupted Terry's thoughts.

"Yes, dear, I even made *two* pies!" Rose beamed. "I made homemade mashed potatoes and broccoli casserole as well." Rose looked at her watch.

"Actually, dinner should be just about ready. Let's eat inside, just in case some nasty mosquitoes decide to crash our party."

Rose, like the pied piper, took the lead and they began to file inside. Terry caught a glimpse of Karen holding out her glass to Henry for a margarita refill. Yeah, right, Terry thought, just coincidence, my foot. You believe that like I believe in Santa Claus.

Rose noticed Karen getting a refill as well. Rose remembered Madeline telling her that she was concerned Karen was drinking too much after she found Todd with his secretary. Madeline called Karen a few times during the evening and thought her voice seemed slurred. Rose decided to keep quiet and just watch things for a bit.

As she put dinner on the table, Rose thought about the teacup. Madeline did say she wanted to be buried with it, but Rose assumed it was a joke. Madeline was a kind and thoughtful person; it would be totally out of character for her to frighten the girls over a teacup. Still, there was a part of her that wanted it to be Maddy. That would mean Maddy was near and Rose missed her terribly. No, it couldn't be her. Terry was not one to make things up or jump to conclusions, so something odd was going on. Was the cup Maddy's? How did it get to Goodwill? Rose saw Karen take another swig of her margarita and thought, Maddy, I hope I'm up for this. Ghosts; broken, aching hearts; a new business venture, yours are some pretty tough shoes to fill. Couldn't I have started with something easier like…how to cook a pot roast?

The cricket orchestra was playing a piece in fortissimo as Karen and Terry walked back home through their garden. Terry was feeling the sleepy fogginess caused by second helpings at dinner as well as wild blueberry pie ala mode. Karen seemed to be weaving a bit and Terry assumed it was from at least five strawberry margaritas.

"I can't believe we have to be up early for church in the morning." Karen moaned. "If God is so merciful, why does He allow services to start earlier then noon?"

"Ooo, you hussy heathen!" Terry said, laughing. "Besides, you won't mind it so much when you see the new pastor. He's so hot, it's sinful and he's single."

Karen raised one eyebrow and looked at her sister. "You talk that way about a pastor and I'm a hussy heathen? People in glass houses...should wash windows, or whatever the expression is!" Karen said as she weaved her way inside the kitchen door and toward the stairs to bed.

Terry watched her go, but remained behind. The question of what to do with the teacup was weighing on her mind.

Karen stopped halfway up the stairs and turned to look at her sister. "You're not thinking of putting that cup out tonight, are you?"

"Yup. I'm just afraid it will break."

Indicating that the last margarita she consumed a half hour before they left was just kicking in, Karen sat down on the stairs and slid down to the bottom step. Terry smiled and looked at her sister whose elbow was on her knee and her chin rested on her palm. "Whaddaya think?" Terry asked.

Karen sighed as she regarded Terry through eyes at half-mast. "Since cups only fall off the middle shelf, I suggest you put it on the top shelf."

"Hey, that's a very good thought from a fairly drunk woman. Nice work!"

"Thanks, it comes from years of practice. I have gotten pretty good at thinking in a fog." Karen smiled.

"However, that still leaves a gap on the middle shelf," Terry said with a yawn.

"Oh, just try any other cup. What's one more broken cup? Did ya ever think of gluing a cup to that shelf?"

"Wow, you're a genius when you're cocked! I'll leave the middle shelf empty for now and get glue tomorrow." Terry removed the teacup from the top shelf and put the blue and white teacup in its place. Then she helped her sister to her feet and the two of them trudged up to bed.

CHAPTER 5

As the alarm clock rang on Sunday morning, Terry reached out and batted it into silence. A moment later, she heard the muffled ring of Karen's alarm clock. One thought consumed Terry's mind...coffee. Half asleep, she plodded down the stairs, tying her robe as she went. Out of habit more than a conscious decision, her eyes wandered to the shelf.   The cup was gone.   Her stomach knotted as she looked down, no cup. Scanning the room in a state of panic and confusion, Terry spun around in a circle. The cup sat unbroken on the table next to her. She opened her mouth to scream, but terror gripped her throat, preventing any sound from escaping. Her feet seemed glued in place and Terry's whole body shook, upsetting her stomach even more. What in the world is going on? she thought.   How could this happen?   There *is* a ghost in this house. Does Mom disapprove? Is that really her cup? How the heck did her cup get to Goodwill? It *can't* be her cup. She would never have given it away. Who is doing this? Why?

The sound of a key in the kitchen door snapped her into action. Terry ran full bore into the kitchen just as Uncle Henry stepped in, carrying a coffee carafe. His bright smile turned to shock as he looked at Terry. "Kiddo, what happened?"

Terry's eyes filled with tears as she pointed wordlessly towards the room where the shelf hung. Henry peered into the room through the window and looked around. Karen came down the stairs and entered the room, fluffing her hair as she walked. She and Henry stared at each other. Realizing they were unsure of the problem, Terry forced a whisper. "The cup, the cup, the cup, I left it on the top shelf last night."

Karen's eyes focused on the cup sitting unbroken on the table. "Holy...what the h...?" Uncle Henry led Terry into the kitchen and over to the round kitchen table and pulled out a chair for her. Karen came in and sat on one side of her while Henry sat on the other. No one spoke as tears streamed down Terry's cheeks. Uncle Henry got up and poured them all some coffee, then he sat back down and put the carafe on the table. They sat quietly for a few more minutes and then Rose burst through the door. "Henry, what is taking you so...?" She frowned at the group sitting around the table.

"Terry and Karen apparently left the cup like Madeline's on the top shelf last night. This morning, Terry found it sitting unbroken on the table across from the shelf," Henry explained to Rose, his voice just above a whisper.

Rose walked over to the window adjoining the two rooms and looked around. "Oh my," she muttered as she joined the crew at the table.

As Rose sat down, there was a brief knock at the door and Shannon Dindle walked in, dressed in shorts, a tee shirt and her hair obviously pre-shower. "Hey, do you guys have any cof...?" She stared at them, her mouth still open in mid-sentence. Karen pulled out the chair next to her and Shannon sat down, looking quizzically around the room. The others all began to explain the strange events of the past few weeks as Terry poured Shannon a cup of coffee.

"Wow, pretty eerie!" Shannon said, staring into her coffee cup. "I'm sure nothing has fallen off shelves at our house. Mom has knick-knacks all over the place and I know she'd mention it if something fell. Besides, I do a lot of the house cleaning and I would have noticed it. Terry, you poor thing, why didn't you say something the past few weeks? I would have stayed overnight so you didn't have to be in the house alone."

Terry fidgeted and stretched a bit. "At first, I thought I was being silly. By the time I was starting to get creeped out, it was only a day or two before Karen got here. I really was too embarrassed to say anything. It sounds too weird."

Henry looked down at his watch. "Ladies, if we're going to make church, we're going to have to hustle. What's the verdict?"

"I'm going to church. Sitting around here is only going to creep me out more," Terry stated, glad to have a reason to get out of the house. Everyone stood and followed suit.

"We can discuss this more after church," Rose said as she headed out the door. "I'm sure there must be a logical explanation. There usually is."

At the coffee hour after church, Terry stood quietly next to Karen as she chatted with a number of people she hadn't seen since before Madeline died. In addition, Karen made sure she met the new minister. Terry half-listened to bits of the conversations. "So nice to see you"; "How wonderful you look, dear!"; "I can't wait to have tea…"; "Your mother would be so proud", blah, blah, blah. She was glad that Karen was the center of attention since Terry was not in the mood to chat. She simply smiled and nodded her head occasionally.

Rose and Henry joined them. "I really enjoyed that sermon," Henry said. "I can't tell you how many times I've wondered if I can forgive myself for mistakes I've made. It's nice to consider that forgiveness is God's department. To say 'I can't forgive myself' is silly. It kinda lifts a weight off one's chest." He put his arm around Rose and smiled. "Well, we should be going. You girls almost ready?"

Phew, thought Terry. I got through that without having to have a big conversation with someone. Today, she needed that reprieve!

Terry and Karen arrived back home later than expected and rushed to get things ready in time to open. To Terry's relief, the day flew by, giving her very little chance to think. They closed at four o'clock on Sundays so it seemed she no sooner opened the teahouse and it was already time to close. Terry locked the front door as the last customers left and then she wandered into the kitchen where Shannon and Karen were just finishing cleaning up. Terry noticed a book on the kitchen table and went over to look at it.

"My mom dropped that off a few minutes ago," Shannon said, looking over her shoulder at Terry as Shannon put the last few cups in the dishwasher. "It's a book on water gardens. She thought you might want to look through it to get some ideas. Henry is going to have his work cut out for him."

"Speaking of Henry," Karen said as Uncle Henry walked in through the kitchen door.

"Hey, kiddos, Rose sent me over to insist you all come over for drinks and I'll grill some burgers. Shannon, you and your mom are invited as well. Rose just loves a chance to get in a tizzy. She's been baking and fussing all afternoon. I thought she was in her glory when a snowstorm hit, but apparently a good mystery involving the possibility of a ghost is even better. I'm surprised she hasn't sent me shopping for a month's worth of groceries. Let's hope we can find an explanation tonight for this teacup business or Rose is gonna cook and clean me out of house and home!"

Just then, the door opened and in came Dottie Dindle. "Hello, everyone. Henry, I thought I saw you come in here. I wanted to let you know I gave the girls a book on water gardens to look over. It will help them get some good ideas."

"Good, good," said Henry, a bit distracted. "I was just inviting everyone, including you and Shannon, over to our house this evening around four-thirty. Dot, we seem to have a bit of a mystery going on. I'll let you ladies fill her in. I need to get back and fire up the grill." With a wave, he darted out the door, leaving Dottie Dindle, Terry thought, looking around, puzzled. Terry gestured to the kitchen table and they all sat down. "Well," she began, "after my mother died, we couldn't find her teacup so..." On and on she went as Karen and Shannon interjected here and there. As they talked, Terry decided that Aunt Rose might love all the excitement, but Terry was exhausted by it. She just wanted life to go back to normal.

It was almost four-thirty by the time they were done explaining the happenings of the past few weeks. "Mom," Shannon said, "do you want to go home and change or just go next door to Henry and Rose's?"

"Oh, I'm fine just the way I am. I'm too tired to fuss," Dottie Dindle said, to Terry's surprise. The Mrs. Dindle Terry used to know would have wanted to run home and gussy up. The group was already walking up the stairs to Henry's back porch before Terry realized that they were all so engrossed in the discussion of the mystery that no one noticed Mrs. Dindle's getting up noises.

After lemonade and strawberry margaritas were served, along with some cheese and crackers, Rose settled down in her big white wicker rocker and said, "Okay, let's see if we can find an explanation for all this teacup nonsense. I can't imagine Madeline wanting to come back and upset her girls over a teacup."

"Maybe it's not Mom," Karen said, taking a long sip of her margarita. "It could be one of those ghosts that like to annoy people. I forget what they're called. Por..? Pul?"

"Poltergeists," Shannon jumped in.

"Yeah, poltergeists. Uncle Henry, you said it yourself. There was Mr. Hamilton or his grandson or those ladies who lived next door. Couldn't it be one of them?" Karen asked, swatting at a mosquito.

"Oh my. What a good memory you have, Henry. I'd forgotten all about that. What was the rumor about Mr. Hamilton?" asked Dottie Dindle, who seemed to be loving her strawberry margarita. Rose smiled as she noticed Dottie was keeping right up with Karen.

"He made his money robbing banks," Henry said as he got up to check the coals on the grill.

"Oh, yes. Then those poor old women disappeared from the house I live in. However, if it was them, one would think that I'd have had a problem and I haven't. Bob and I once thought someone was taking the lunch money he left out each night for Shannon when she was in grade school. Each night, he would put it out and every morning, it was gone. We made extra sure all the windows and doors were locked at night, but still it would disappear. Oddly enough, Bob found it in the garden when he went to weed it one Saturday. Never had another problem. A few months later, we discovered Shannon was sleep-walking . It must have been her. No mystery, just Shannon."

"Would you like me to refill your drink, Dottie?" Rose asked, unable to help herself. She'd been quietly keeping score between Karen and Dottie. Maybe Karen didn't drink as much as she thought? Maybe Dottie drank more than she thought. Hmm.

"Well, we're closed tomorrow," Terry said, refilling her glass with lemonade as Rose refilled Dottie's with margarita. "I've decided it would be best to take the shelf down. I'll take a look at my sketches and just paint in a few scenes where the shelf is now. I hope that's okay with everyone. Karen suggested gluing cups to the shelf, but I'd rather just take the shelf down."

"Good idea!" Henry hollered over his shoulder as he put hamburgers on the grill. Terry looked relieved, but Rose felt sad. That shelf was always there. She remembered Maddy taking her cup down along with another one so she and Rose could have tea. It would be nice for the girls to no longer need to worry about the shelf and the cups, but Rose would miss that shelf. The house was so different now that it was the teahouse. That shelf was a way to touch the past, to keep *something* the same. Change stinks and so does aging, thought Rose.

After dinner, as she prepared to go home, Terry couldn't help thinking about the shelf. The idea of taking it down was depressing. Terry saw Rose frown a bit when they discussed it. Somehow, taking down that shelf seemed to make the void of her mother's absence bigger. It wasn't *just* a shelf. It was the shelf where Mom kept her special cup. Of course, the cup was a whole other issue altogether. How could such a tiny cup cause such a big problem? Was the problem the shelf, as she originally thought, or was it the cup? She felt as if the weight of all the teacups in the world were on her.

Her voice shaking, she said, "I don't think I'm ready to take down that shelf. I know this may sound silly, and I know what I said before, but I just don't want to do it. I feel exhausted, and I admit I don't want to deal with crashing teacups. However, I just don't want to take the shelf down. Does it sound like I've lost my mind?"

Rose jumped right in. "No. It does *not* sound like you've lost your mind. I don't think I could do it either. Why don't you and Karen stay here? You can get a good night's sleep that way."

Terry felt a wave of panic. She didn't want to stay at Rose's house. She loved Rose, but she needed some space. Rose would mother her and smother her. What a choice, Rose or toppling teacups. Hmmmm "Oh...no...that's not necessary. I'll be okay at the house," she hedged.

"There's our house," jumped in Shannon.

Rats. Thanks, Shannon, that helps...not, thought Terry. Now I can rip my aunt's heart out by telling her I'd rather sleep at your house. Ugh!

Seeming to sense her dilemma, Karen piped up. "How about we split up? I can have Aunt Rose and Uncle Henry to myself, and Terry can relax with Shannon."

"Oh, I'd love that!" Henry jumped in, as if he too sensed Terry's dilemma. Phew, thought Terry. Uncle Henry to the rescue!

"Settled," said Karen decisively, and, grabbing Terry's arm, headed toward the house. "I'll grab my things and be back, Aunt Rose," she hollered over her shoulder.

A warm breeze rustled the leaves as Uncle Henry, holding a flashlight, accompanied Terry, Karen and the Dindles home. Normally, this was not necessary, however, the Dindle's floodlight, which illuminated their backyard and kitchen door, was hit recently by a falling branch and shattered.

"I keep wondering if I should have that oak tree taken down," remarked Dottie Dindle as the group trooped along. "It's so old and huge; I worry about it damaging my house during a storm. I'm lucky all I lost was that light bulb. I do love watching the squirrels, though. Also, to get rid of the stump, my whole garden would have to be ripped up."

"Dottie, do what Rose and I did a few years ago. Have a professional come and cut it back a bit. That tree's been around longer than you or me. I for one would hate to see it go."

The little party stopped at Karen's and Terry's house and Terry unlocked the door. She'd left the kitchen light on to ease her fears when they returned from dinner. Terry felt exhausted from the day's events. It was weeks since she had a good night's sleep. All she wanted to do grab her things and go over to Shannon's and sleep. Leaving the others chatting at the kitchen door, she walked into the adjoining room. Better take the cups down, just in case, she thought and she began to remove the cups from the shelf. An emptiness followed by a fresh wave of grief flooded through her. It was the end of an era. Images of her and Karen flashed in her mind as she remembered helping put out Christmas teacups, the memory so vivid that she could almost smell the gingerbread baking.

A breeze from the stairwell caught her attention. Terry went to the foot of the stairs, turned on the light and looked up toward the bedrooms. The stairs to the attic were down and a tiny river of what appeared to be blood trickled over them. Her scream filled the house before her throat closed up from horror.

Shannon and Karen reached her a moment or two before Uncle Henry, while Dottie Dindle brought up the rear. They ran over to her, clamoring, but she couldn't move or speak. She felt Karen grab her arm.

"Ter, what the? Oh...my...God!" Karen remained still with her hand on Terry's arm. Terry heard the others gasp in unison.

"Ladies, turn right around and run to my house. Tell Rose to call the police," Uncle Henry shouted at them. Terry knew his shouting indicated his own fear and it snapped her out of her horror. "Run!" Uncle Henry shouted again, shoving them gently in the direction of the door. "Just go, I'll wait outside for the police."

Karen was out the door and already at Rose's house while Terry and Shannon helped Mrs. Dindle. Karen's shouts of "Aunt Rose, call the police," echoed through the neighborhood.

"Oh, my! This is all so dreadful!" Mrs. Dindle fretted as they made their way back across the yard. Holding one arm while Shannon held the other, Terry could feel the woman shaking so hard, her bones rattled. Please, God, thought Terry, don't let her have a heart attack. Terry looked back over her shoulder and watched Uncle Henry pace back and forth in the yard. Terry withheld a nervous giggle as she realized she and Shannon were shaking as hard as Mrs. Dindle. She had a mental vision of poor Mrs. Dindle being shaken violently by both girls as if electric current pulsated through her. Terry imagined a doctor saying, "Poor woman would have lived if she hadn't been shaken to death!"

Karen and Rose emerged on the porch just as Terry and Shannon helped Mrs. Dindle up the stairs. Mrs. Dindle sat in the nearest wicker chair.

"Oh, Dottie," gasped Rose. "Come inside, dear, the mosquitoes are just awful." Like a sheepdog, Rose tried to herd them into the house.

"The heck with the mosquitoes," barked Mrs. Dindle. "I need to catch my breath! How awful, how dreadfully awful."

Karen and Rose sat down on the wicker loveseat while Terry and Shannon plopped down on the porch steps. "Please explain to me exactly what happened," whispered Rose, wringing her hands.

"I thought I felt a breeze coming down the hall stairs," Terry said, trying to muster patience because she did not feel like discussing the details. "Since we have central air, the breeze seemed odd. I went to the stairs to take a look. I turned on the light and saw the stairs to the attic had been pulled down and there was blood running down the stairs and onto the floor in the upstairs hall."

"Whose blood?" Rose asked with a puzzled look.

The four women looked at each other. Whose blood, indeed. "I...I don't know...I didn't see... Did any of you see?" Terry asked. The others shook their heads just as the sound of sirens screamed into the night air.

CHAPTER 6

State Police Detective Greg Mullins was on his way home after a long sixteen hour day when he heard the call over the police radio.

"....teahouse, Madeline's Tearoom, on Willow Street....break-in....possible homicide."

He grabbed the radio. "Dispatch, this is Detective Mullins, I'm in the area and will respond, over."

His thoughts raced. He couldn't ever remember a murder in this town. He had helped investigate homicides in other local areas, but somehow he never thought one could happen here...in his town. Wasn't that the teahouse his mother and sister were nagging him to take them to? The one opened by the Sutter girls he went to high school with? Yeah, it had to be the one. Terry Sutter...I wonder if she's still as talented and mesmerizing as she was in high school. I wonder if she's okay.

Greg pulled his car over in front of the teahouse. The front door was open and an elderly, balding gentleman stood in the doorway. He stepped to the side as the other policemen ran, guns drawn, from their squad cars and into the house. As Greg approached the house, he looked through the open door and saw the stairs, leading to what was probably the attic, covered in...blood. If it was blood, where was the body? He saw Officers Tom O'Hara and Rusty Peterson go up the stairs. Greg drew his own gun and stepped quickly inside the doorway.

At last, Tom O'Hara appeared at the top of the stairs, holding a small paint can in his gloved hand. "Attic's empty. The red on the stairs is paint from this can, Greg. C'mon up and have a look around."

Taking the foyer stairs two at a time, Greg approached the attic stairs. Carefully avoiding the red paint, he entered the attic. He noticed immediately that a window that sat diagonally from the entrance was open. A few splatters of red led to the window.

Aiming his flashlight out the window, Tom said, "See there...a small smudge of red. I think the perp used the window and the tree to exit. No sign of forced entry at the window. Though, we haven't checked the rest of the house."

Greg stepped back to the light at the center of the room and stared into each corner of the attic. "See the scrape marks in the dust over there?" he said, pointing. "Looks like whoever it was moved some boxes around. Don't let anyone else up here; I want to take another look around, but first, I want to talk to the people who discovered this. Where are they?"

"They're next door. The uncle and aunt live there. Dennis went to talk to them," Tom said, checking his notebook.

"House is clear," one of the officers yelled from downstairs. "The family's on their way back."

"By the way, who made the call?" Greg asked

"Dispatch said an elderly woman called it in. Probably the aunt," Rusty Peterson chimed in. "Greg, I also noticed there are footprints around the edge here. I think the boxes were moved to reach the perimeter."

Greg gave a last look around. "Okay, let's see what the family has to say. Could be a nasty prank." Greg headed back down the stairs shaking his head. What a horrible prank to play, he thought

Terry, Karen, Uncle Henry, Shannon and Mrs. Dindle already told their story to Officer Burdick and were coming into the house by the front door when they heard footsteps descending from the attic. Terry was shocked to see Greg Mullins. She had a crush on him the first two years of high school. She felt Karen's and Shannon's eyes boring into her. She couldn't look at them.

"Well, Greg Mullins! How are you? Fancy seeing you her," Karen said. Terry, although she knew it was silly, was mortified.

"Hey, ladies! Sorry to see you under these circumstances." Greg smiled at them.

He still had the curly light brown hair and deep blue eyes that Terry remembered. She was sure he remembered Karen and Shannon, but did he remember her? They served on student council together, but she was two years behind him and certainly not part of the "in" crowd. Greg was the high school football star and, from what Terry could see, he was still a hunk. That thought was confirmed as he came down the stairs and led them into the parlor.

"Hey, Greg, I think I have the facts down," Officer Andrew Burdick said.

"Okay, let's go over them." Greg glanced around the room. "Let's start with introductions. I'm Detective Greg Mullins." He looked directly at Uncle Henry.

"Henry Sanders, Detective, I live next door." Henry pointed in the direction of his house. "I'm the uncle of these two women here whom you seem to know." He gestured towards Terry and Karen.

"Dorothy Dindle. I live next door," Mrs. Dindle said, pointing in the opposite direction. "I think you know my daughter, Shannon Dindle. She lives with me." Shannon raised her hand in a small wave.

"Well, you know Terry and me," Karen said. "We live here and run the teahouse. I was in California until a few days ago. My sister has been here for the past few months, getting the teahouse ready to open." Karen took a deep breath and continued. "Our mother died suddenly a few months ago and left us the house. We are turning our childhood home into the teahouse."

"Well, it appears what you all thought was blood is red paint," Greg said. "That's the good news."

"Red paint?" the group said in unison.

"Why would anyone dump red paint down the stairs?" Karen asked. "Terry, you didn't have paint up there, did you?"

"No. I didn't use red paint at all. This makes no sense. I don't get it." Terry looked up at Greg. For the past hour, she'd been chilly, but suddenly, her palms were sweaty. She casually ran her palms over her jeans.

"Okay, then, let's go over what happened tonight."

Officer Burdick repeated the happenings of the evening to Greg and the group interjected when needed. As they were winding up, Officers O'Hara and Peterson entered.

"No sign of forced entry that we can see," Peterson said with a shrug.

"Was the window in the attic always left unlocked?" Greg asked, looking at Terry and Karen.

"Unlocked? Heck, I don't even remember it ever being opened, do you, Karen?"

"Nope, to be honest, I didn't even know there was a window up there. It's been years, like probably ten years, since I was up there."

"I was up there a month or so ago, looking through boxes for some children's picture books. I'm sure the window was closed...but locked? All I remember is that it was really dirty…dusty." Terry ran her fingers through her hair.

"Officers, if you don't mind, I would like to call my wife, Rose. She's holding down the fort next door and I'm sure she's frantic with worry. She might know if her sister, Madeline, the girls' mother, ever opened the window. Rose took care of the house and got rid of some things after Madeline died. She might have gone up there for some reason."

"Actually, Mr. Sanders, would you mind having her come over? I know it's late, but she might know some things the others don't. Can any of you think of something someone would have wanted in the attic? Is there a safe up there?"

As Henry headed for the kitchen to call Rose, Karen gave a chuckle. "A safe! No, there's no safe, or valuables, for that matter, in the attic. The only jewelry my mother owned was her engagement ring, wedding ring and a strand of pearls. Terry, do you know where those are?"

"As far as I know, they're in her jewelry box in her bedroom. I took the engagement and wedding rings from the funeral home. I think I put them all together. I can go check." Terry looked questioningly at the officers.

"Please, let's make sure nothing of value was taken." Greg moved to the nearest chair and sat down. As she headed up the stairs, Terry couldn't help but notice how nice Greg Mullins looked sitting in her teahouse!

As Terry came back downstairs with the rings and pearls, Rose was coming in the front door.

"Oh, dear, such a terrible scare! Who would do such a thing? Now, who wanted to know about the attic window?"

"That would be me, Mrs. Sanders. I'm Detective Greg Mullins. I understand you may have had occasion to go into the attic in the past few months."

"Well, no, sir, I didn't. After Maddy died— Maddy's my sister—I did pack up a few things with the help of Carl Despard, the handyman Maddy often used. One day, I did start to go up in the attic, but I knew Maddy didn't keep much up there. She stored things in the basement rather then the attic." While she was still talking, Henry got a chair for her and she sat down. "I looked around and decided to leave it for Karen and Terry. I can't say for sure if the window was locked, but I know it was closed. I imagine it was locked. Maddy was pretty safety conscious. I can't say for sure, though."

"Do any of you know where the red paint can came from?" Greg scratched his head and looked around.

"I don't think we *ever* painted anything red." Karen scowled.

"I think you're right, Karen dear. Maddy hated red. She certainly wouldn't have painted anything in her house red. Ever since I can remember, she just never cared for that color."

"I remember some paint in the attic," Terry said, squinting her eyes as she thought. "It was in an old wooden crate. The tops of the cans were rusted. I think it came from the original owners of the house. Yes, the crate was over to the side. I looked at it briefly. I remember thinking that the box was really old...eighteen-hundreds kind of old. By the way, here's my mother's jewelry. Nothing seems to be missing."

"Hmm. Back to the paint can. Did you move the crate, Ms. Sutter?"

"No, Gr— Detective Mullins. I left it where it was. Like I said, I was looking for a specific group of books.

Aunt Rose is right, though. We didn't store a lot in the attic. I knew the books were up there because I put them up there when I went away to college."

"Hmm," Greg said, running his hand over his curly hair as he looked back over his notes. "It appears at the moment that the open window in the attic is how the person or persons left. The large oak between the two houses is tall enough and wide enough for someone to use to gain access to or escape from the attic. There are clumps of dirt on the stairs leading to the second floor and the stairs to the attic, indicating that someone may have entered from the kitchen and gone upstairs. However, we can't say for sure since you all entered from kitchen and went to the base of the stairs. Finally, there is the paint can. Whether it was pried open and then dropped or purposely dumped on the stairs to frighten people is uncertain. However, it does look like the box the paint was in was moved across the floor. This fits with what Terry said."

"Oh, my," said Dottie Dindle. "I wonder if my house could've been broken into. That tree is smack in the middle between both of our houses. Greg turned to look at her. He eyed her for a moment and then called into the kitchen where a group of detectives were still poking around. "Tom, please check the house next door. The perp could have broken in there, too." Then turning to Mrs. Dindle, he asked, "Ma'am, can we have your house keys so we can check your house as well?"

Mrs. Dindle looked at Shannon who took a bunch of keys out of her pants pocket and handed them to Greg.

"Thanks," Greg said as he handed them to Tom O'Hara.

Looking back at the small band, he said, "Okay, I want to make sure I have the facts in order." Greg read from his note pad. "All of you were together this evening, having dinner next door. When you returned home, you unlocked the door and entered. Are you sure the door was locked?"

"Absolutely," Terry stated, nodding. "I locked it when we left and then unlocked it when we came home. I heard the deadbolt click both times and I turned the door handle to make sure it was locked."

"Okay," sighed Greg, pushing his cap back a bit on his head. "You went into the room next to the kitchen to…take down a shelf?"

"Yes, it's been…um…loose lately." Terry looked at the others briefly.

"So, it was then you felt a breeze and went to the stairs to see where it was coming from. Is that correct?"

Terry nodded again.

"How long until the others joined you by the stairs?"

"About ten seconds or less."

"Greg, it's all clear next door. No signs of a break-in," Tom O'Hara said as he entered the parlor. "Actually, it looks like we're done here. Can you think of anything else?"

Greg thumbed through his note pad. "Nope, I'm going to take another look in the attic. I'll talk you to tomorrow."

With a brief touch of his cap, Tom O'Hara left by the front door, followed by the other officers.

"Okay," Greg said after they left. "I want to have you, Terry, come up in the attic with me and take a look around. Something may look different to you since the last time you were up there." Greg nodded toward the stairs.

"Is it okay for me to take my mother home?" Shannon Dindle asked as she stood up.

"Absolutely, thank you for your patience and cooperation. Mr. and Mrs. Sanders, you are free to go as well, unless, Mrs. Sanders, you would like to take a look at the attic?"

"I think I would like to, if you don't mind," Rose said as Shannon helped Mrs. Dindle out the front door.

"Terry, I assume you're still staying over, especially now. I'll wait up for you. Just c'mon over when you're done here," Shannon called over her shoulder.

"Thanks, I'll see you in a bit. Take care, Mrs. Dindle. Sorry to keep you up so late!"

"Oh my goodness, it's not a problem at all. At my age, a little excitement is a good thing. Keeps me on my toes," Dottie Dindle said with a big grin. "Thank you again, Greg, for having the police check out my house as well. Bye, bye, Henry, Rose. I'll probably see you tomorrow." Everyone waved as Shannon and her mom headed across the front yard for home.

The remaining group slowly made their way up to the attic, being careful to avoid the paint. For a few moments, no one said a word as they gazed around.

Terry was stunned at the change in the appearance of things in the attic. She really hadn't thought about what to expect. She said, "Most of the boxes have been moved. All of those," she pointed to a cluster of three boxes, "were along the edge. There was hardly anything in the center here. And that piece of wood was...on the window. Not actually on, more like across."

Everyone looked as she pointed to a bit of wood that sat on the floor by the window. Greg walked over and, with gloved hands, picked it up. "Like this?" he asked, holding the wood just above the metal latch for the window.

"Yeah, just like that. I guess that means the window was locked or at least blocked so it wouldn't slide open from the outside, huh?" Terry said, suddenly realizing that whoever broke in did not come in through the attic window. She knew Greg must realize it, too, because he put it in a bag from his scene kit.

"Hey, will ya look at this!" Uncle Henry said, kneeling down by the old wooden crate that contained the paint. "This is from an old bank! I'll be darned. Hey, kiddo, you were right, it says 'bank property, 1890.' Hmmm, maybe there was something to that bank robbing legend. Wait just one minute. Come over here, Detective Greg. I think there's something under this paint."

Greg went over and helped Henry remove the paint from the box. Under the paint was a wooden board. Everyone watched as Uncle Henry lifted the board from the box. "Hmmm, what have we here?" Henry said as he lifted an old photo album out from the box.

Everyone crowded around. Rose stood behind Henry, leaning over his shoulder, Terry and Karen sat on the floor on each side of the box and Greg knelt behind Terry. "It's leather, old, cracked and worn leather," Henry whispered, opening it carefully as if he held a priceless artifact.

No one spoke for a moment as the first picture was revealed. "Henry, isn't that Beauregard Hamilton?" Rose asked, peering intently at the old photo. "Who's that man with him?"

"Well, Rosey, I believe that's Beauregard there on the right and his father standing next to him. It looks like they're hunting, or just returned. Look, see they have guns with them."

"Who's Beauregard Hamilton?" Greg asked.

"The man who used to own this property many years ago. He had a son named Beauregard Jr. Eventually, Beauregard Jr. had a son named Thurston. He was killed in a hunting accident, I think. After that, the Hamiltons moved away."

"Any idea where they went?" Greg asked.

"Not really. I believe they went to live in their home by the shore, but I could be wrong. The Sutters bought the house and we bought the lot next door and built our house," Henry said as he turned a few of the pages of the album. "Here, right here is Thurston Hamilton. I was tellin' the girls last night that the boy was trouble, one hundred percent trouble. He must have been about eight, hmm, maybe ten in this picture."

"Hey, who's that kid with him, Uncle Henry? He looks sort of familiar." Terry pointed to the figure in question.

"Well...I believe it's Carl Despard." Looking up at Greg, Henry said, "Despard is a handyman here in town. Ever met him?"

"Yeah, I think I have. I believe he did some odd jobs at the police station. About six feet, thin, probably in his early sixties, is that him?"

"Yup, sounds like him. Nice guy. Hard worker." Henry turned another page.

"Wow, that has to be Samuel Brinker, my old math teacher!" Karen said, pointing to a boy with Thurston and Carl standing on a pier, holding a fishing pole.

"Sure looks like 'im," Henry added. "Did you know the poor guy had some kind of a breakdown? He's in the same nursing home as Carl's mom. Some days, he's clear as a bell, others...he don't know where he is." A few more pages were turned and regarded in silence.

"Man, they sure like squirrels!" said Karen. There must be at least ten pages of them. They do look cute looking in the windows, but, geeze, they went overboard with the snapshots. "

"Wait, go back a page!" Greg called out. "Isn't that this attic?"

"Yup, seems to be," Henry said, looking at the picture and then looking around him. "Looks like the

Hamiltons were putting the floor and walls in. Here's Thurston and Samuel Brinker hammering away. See, here's the window. Looks like they got a squirrel watching them. See, there's one in the window."

"Do you think I could take those pictures to the nursing home tomorrow? I bet Mrs. Despard and Samuel Brinker would get a kick out of seeing them." Rose said.

"Oh, I think that's a neat idea!" Terry said, standing up to stretch. "I think they'd love them!"

"Anything else, Greg?" Karen asked. "It's almost two-thirty. I'm exhausted."

"Man, yeah, I guess that's it. Anything else, Terry?"

She glanced around again. "Nope, the boxes and the wooden bar, that's it."

Greg walked Henry, Rose and Karen next door and made Terry go with them. She protested, but he said he could tell she was still shaken up. Terry couldn't help thinking how sweet that was. Then she mentally kicked herself for thinking like a high schooler.

When they returned, Greg helped Terry secure all the doors and windows. Finally, he walked her over to the Dindle's. True to her word, Shannon waited in the kitchen for Terry.

"Wow," Shannon said, opening the kitchen door. "Service with a smile."

Terry couldn't tell in the glaring light of the backyard spot light, but she thought she saw Greg blush.

"Andy Griffith has nothin' on me. Of course, don't tell my mother I said that. She may not like the idea of bein' Aunt Bea," Greg said as he took hold of the kitchen door. He waved goodnight as Shannon and Terry retreated to the kitchen.

"My stars, you must be dying!" Shannon gushed once Greg was gone. "He's still gorgeous. I'm sorry, really, about the break in, but hunka, dabba do!"

Terry blushed and whacked Shannon in the arm. "Don't be silly. I'm sure he's that way with every person he deals with, but, yeah, he is a looker." She blushed again and followed Shannon upstairs to the bedrooms.

As she lay in bed, exhausted and still a bit shaky, Terry realized she left the teacup sitting on the table nearest the shelf. She fell asleep, wondering if she should tell Greg about the teacup.

CHAPTER 7

Before Greg even got in the car to drive to the police station for work, his mind was twisting, turning and dissecting the events from the night before. In fact, he was so distracted that he drank over half of his coffee before he realized he never put milk and sugar in it. He hated black coffee! Leaning up against the kitchen counter, he stared into the cup, realized he was disgusted by the taste and, lost again in the recesses of his own mind, reached out and poured orange juice into his cup. It took him another four swallows to realize what he'd done. He dumped the nasty liquid into the sink, thinking that he would be safer stopping at the coffee shop on the way to work. He smiled to himself and mused that if he drove the way he made his coffee, he'd be dead before he reached the coffee shop.

He couldn't stop seeing Terry in his mind. He walked through the events of the evening over and over again, only to have his thoughts interrupted by her smiling face. The window was, according to Terry, locked before the break in. Someone came in through the kitchen. No sign of a forced entry. They swore no one in town had a key. Someone had to. Of course, assuming the locks weren't changed, the Hamiltons could, but that didn't make sense. The Hamiltons sold the house over forty years ago. No, they wouldn't still have a key. Perhaps Mrs. Sutter had a male friend the daughters didn't know about. Surely, she would have told her sister Rose. Then again....

When he got to his desk at the police station, he was quite surprised to find a report detailing the events of the night before already on his desk. He picked it up just as Tom O'Hara stopped by. "I wrote that up and put it on your desk about ten minutes ago. I came in early, couldn't sleep. That whole set up last night nagged at me, Greg. Nothing seems to fit. I thought that if I wrote it all down, something might jump out at me. No such luck. Do you think there's any chance they staged that as a publicity stunt?"

"No way, Tom. Too many people involved in the story, some of whom are elderly. I can't see them all pulling it off without a hitch. No...it can't be a publicity stunt, but it is a weird set of circumstances, that's for sure! No one outside the immediate group has a key, but there's no sign of forced entry. Nothing in the attic seems to be worth stealing, but someone was up there looking around, someone who was familiar with it. Remember the paint cans? Those suckers were old as the hills. I stayed for a bit last night after you guys left. None of the people involved think the Sutters bought the paint. It was probably in the attic since before the Sutters bought the house. Yet, someone knew enough about the attic to dump the paint. My first thought was that it was a scare tactic, but that doesn't seem to fit. Who'd want to scare them like that and, besides that, why move boxes around if all you wanted was to scare the heck out of a couple of young women? The perp probably knew about the tree outside the window as well. Oh yeah, Terry Sutter remembered a scrap of wood being across the window. We found the scrap right by the window. I want to send a couple of guys out there to dust for prints. I bagged the scrap last night. I'll take it down to the lab."

Greg sat at his desk in silence while Tom O'Hara leaned against it, arms folded across his chest. Finally,

Tom broke the silence. "You're right, nothing fits. Every possible scenario I come up with doesn't fit because a stranger wouldn't know the contents of the attic and those familiar with the house were all together and have no reason to lie about what happened. I guess we could ask around at the shops across the street, see if they've had anything odd happen. It's a long shot, but it seems to be the only avenue left. Whatta ya think?"

"Tom, it's worth a try. You know the game, keep turning over rocks until you find something to poke at. Right now, all we can do is hunt and poke."

Tom nodded. "Do you wanna ask the people at the shops, or do you want me to do it?"

"I guess I'll do it. I don't have anything pressing at the moment. I'll touch base with you this afternoon or first thing tomorrow and let you know what I find. Fair enough?"

"Fair enough," Tom said as he walked away.

Terry sat in the Dindle's kitchen, gazing out the window at the large water garden Mrs. Dindle built from scratch. It amazed her that the prissy woman Terry knew growing up blossomed into such a fun and interesting senior citizen. Terry's thoughts drifted to her own mother, after Terry's father died ten years before. Madeline told Terry and Karen that, once their father died, there was no choice but to stand up and face the challenges of life. It was either that or drown. She'd volunteered at the church, joined a bowling league, took an exercise class and even a class for finances for women. Still, Terry and Karen were flabbergasted when their mother told them she enrolled in a home repair class in the adult education program in town. Their mother, the woman who had trouble changing a light bulb, was taking a home repair class!

Did wonders ever cease? Then, just a few weeks later, she became too exhausted to do things. It was as if someone threw a switch. One day, she was perky and the next day, totally drained of energy. As she studied the water garden, Terry wondered what her mother would have accomplished if she hadn't died.

"More coffee, dear?" Mrs. Dindle asked, interrupting Terry's thoughts.

"Oh, no thanks, I'm fine. I'm just getting my thoughts together. I actually took a break from thinking about last night's break in and was appreciating your water garden. Mrs. Dindle, you amaze me! How did you manage all the lifting and toting that was needed?"

"Well, Carl helped me a bit with that. I picked out what I wanted and then Carl took me to pick it up. He brought it out to the backyard and installed the basic pond. I took it from there. I've always loved digging in the dirt. It pained my heart a bit to dig up some of the original garden to make room for the water garden. The big garden was here when we bought the house. I felt as if I was removing a part of history, a monument to the hard work that went into creating that garden. I know it's silly, we've lived here over forty years. I guess I'm just sentimental. Until Henry brought it up the other night, I forgot the original owners disappeared without a trace. When we bought the house, I used to lie in bed at night and imagine that they eloped with two wealthy brothers, leaving this life behind. It was nicer than thinking they were lying murdered somewhere. I half-expected them to turn up someday, but time went by and I pretty much forgot about them."

"What happened to all their things? Did they have any relatives?" Terry was enjoying the momentary diversion from thinking about her own troubles.

Mrs. Dindle sat down and looked out the window, her eyes seeming to focus on the past rather than the scenery outside. "Well...let me see now. Hmm, I think we were offered the furniture in the house, yes, that's right. We could have bought the house fully furnished, but we chose not to. There was a relative somewhere, a niece, I believe, who inherited everything. She must have disposed of the furniture because it was all gone when we moved in. The curtains were still here. I remember thinking that they smelled of roses. It seemed fitting because of all the rose bushes around the house. When I put in the water garden, I moved one of the rose bushes, see that one right over there?" She pointed to a large bush that contained the last remnant of yellow roses.

"Wow, that's huge! Carl helped you move it, didn't he?"

"No, no...I think he was away on one of his fishing trips. I hired Rudy's Landscaping to help. It took four men and a large truck, but they got it moved and nestled safely in its new spot. I couldn't bring myself to destroy it. The bush was the only thing I found a new spot for. I did feel guilty about doing away with those other plants that were my pride and joy for years and years." Mrs. Dindle looked at Terry and let out a big sigh. "Oh, well, I guess a little change is a good thing. I'm so looking forward to helping with your water garden. I was feeling a bit bored. A new project is just what I needed! Maybe this afternoon, we can look through the book I gave you."

"Absolutely! I think we all need a diversion. I'm dreading going back home. It seems creepy now. I'm going to call the police station in a few minutes. If they have no objections, I think I'll go visit Mrs. Despard at the nursing home. It will be good to get away for a few hours."

"I'm sure Mrs. Despard will love it!" Mrs. Dindle's face brightened. "I think Carl is away on another

fishing trip. I haven't seen him around for a few weeks.
He's been doing some work at the shops across the
street, adding shelves, sanding floors, moving some
antique furniture around, that type of thing. He came
by about a month ago and asked me if I needed
anything done. I told him that, in the fall, he could
touch up the paint around the windows and freshen up
the shutters."   Dotty Dindle stood with a small
ahhhhuuuga sound, which, as usual, she didn't notice.
She took the coffee pot and refreshed her coffee and
offered some to Terry, who shook her head. Sitting
back down, Mrs. Dindle continued. "He's such a nice
man, but I get the feeling that he and his mother are at
odds. I don't know why, though. His brothers all live
down south. Carl is the only local family she has. But
when I go to the nursing home to visit some friends, if I
ask how Carl is, she flips her hand in disgust when she
answers. I stopped asking her about him. If I don't
bring him up, she's as pleasant as can be. My, my, it's
already ten-thirty. I'm going to wake Shannon. Help
yourself to anything in the kitchen!"

Terry stood as Mrs. Dindle rose and headed for the
stairs. "I'm fine. I think I'll just check in with the
police and get dressed." Picking up her purse that sat
by the kitchen door, Terry fished out Greg Mullin's
business card. Although he still made her heart pound
every time he walked into the room, given the
circumstances, she wished she could forget about
calling him. Besides, he probably never gave her a
second thought, anyway. He was just another thing to
make her heart hurt, and she'd had too much of that this
year already. She decided she'd call Mrs. Despard first,
just to make sure it was okay to visit. Then, of course,
she needed to check with Aunt Rose and Karen to see if
they wanted to go, too. She'd invite Mrs. Dindle, too.
She looked down at the card in her hand just as

Shannon walked into the kitchen, still wearing her pink baby doll pajamas. Terry groaned inwardly. Even with no make-up, Shannon still looked good.

Shannon looked at Terry and smiled. "Thinking up a reason to call your high school heartthrob?" Shannon wiggled her eyebrows.

"More like trying to avoid calling him. I'm into avoiding pain these days." Terry pulled out her cell phone to look up Mrs. Despard's number. She knew her mother's death took a lot out of her. She most certainly did not need a broken heart at this point in time.

"Terry," Shannon said, rolling her eyes, "his face lit up last night when he saw you. I think you're both trying to play it cool. Karen and I thought he liked you in high school. Remember, we used to call him 'chicken boy' because we thought he was just too chicken to ask you out." Shannon poured herself a cup of coffee and sat down at the kitchen table, looking up as Terry took the phone off its cradle by the door and began punching numbers.

Terry humphed. "Oh, for crying out loud, you're nuts. He dated other girls back then. He wasn't too scared to ask them out. You and Kar— Hello, Mrs. Despard? This is Terry Sutter. I'm calling to see if I can stop by and visit you this afternoon?"

Mrs. Dindle's statement about Mrs. Despard being thrilled was an understatement. Terry's whole outlook brightened, just knowing that Mrs. Despard adored her and couldn't wait to see her. Terry called Rose. Both Rose and Karen were up for a visit to the nursing home. Mrs. Dindle said she would love to go as well. Terry's day was looking up.

"Do you want to come with us?" Terry asked Shannon who was now eating toast and jelly.

"No, but thanks anyway. I have a lot to do here. You still have to call him, ya know."

Terry, her heart pounding, looked at the card and began to punch the numbers on the phone. Maybe he would be out and she could just leave a message. As the phone began to ring, she silently prayed for voicemail.

"Detective Mullins."

"Greg, this is Terry Sutter. I'm calling because I'm planning to go to Fair Meadows Convalescent Home today. If there's anything you need, could it wait until about four o'clock?"

"Actually, I was just about to head out there myself. My grandmother is there. I have some clothes my mother asked me to drop off. I was planning to come by this afternoon and take a look at that big tree in the daylight. I also want to ask the storeowners across the street if they've had problems. So, I may run into you, but no, right now, I have no questions. Is there anything else you can think of that you forgot last night?"

Terry's stomach flipped as she thought about the cup. No need to mention it. They couldn't be related. Why make him think she was a nutcase? "Um, no, nothing. I guess that's it then." Terry's hands shook so hard that she almost dropped the phone. Shannon shook her head and chuckled.

"Okay, then. If I have any more questions, I'll contact you tonight. Okay?"

"Great. Have a good day." What a stupid thing to say! Ugh!

"Thanks, you too."

Terry hung up and looked sheepishly at Shannon. "Well...what did you want me to do? Say, 'Any more questions, Detective, and, oh, by the way, how about a movie?' Give me a break!"

Shannon exited the kitchen, mumbling, "Hopeless, absolutely hopeless. Chicken boy and chicken girl..."

Greg sat back, feet on his desk, pondering the conversation. She definitely hesitated when he asked her if she needed to tell him anything else. He thought again about the night before. All of them seemed to give honest answers, yet they kept looking at each other. What could they be holding back? He was sure they didn't stage the break-in. Had they seen something they were afraid to mention? Had someone threatened them? There was something missing in the story, Greg was sure of it. No, he didn't think they were lying...they were...omitting. What in blazes could it be? Maybe he'd pry it out of one of them tonight, but how? He glanced at his watch. He'd finish up some paperwork and then go visit his grandmother. She always made his day!

Terry and Karen tramped behind Aunt Rose and Mrs. Dindle as they entered the convalescent home. Aunt Rose brought the photo album found the night before. Rose seemed sure Mrs. Despard would enjoy seeing a young Carl, but, after Mrs. Dindle's comment, Terry wasn't so sure. She didn't say a word to Rose about Mrs. Dindle's observations. Terry wondered why Mrs. Dindle hadn't said anything to Aunt Rose about it. Terry decided it was best for Aunt Rose to see for herself. Besides, there was no arguing with Rose!

As they entered the large visiting area, there was a loud wolf-whistle and a high pitched call of "Aren't you a cutie! How's about a kiss?"

Terry and Karen stopped in their tracks. Rose giggled. "That's the new mascot." She pointed to a large mahogany framed cage. "He's a macaw that belonged to one of the residents. He says the darnedest things."

Terry and Karen walked over the cage. "Wow, he's a gorgeous bird," Terry said. "I love the colors on him."

"Howdie," squawked the macaw, "gonna be friends."

Karen and Terry smiled. "I hope so," Terry said with a giggle.

"Bet on it," came the bird's reply.

"You're awful sure of yourself," Karen said.

"Kiss me, toots," said the macaw.

Terry burst out laughing. "I love this guy. Whatta riot!" Terry turned to see where Rose and Mrs. Dindle went. She spotted them talking to Mrs. Despard. Terry and Karen trotted over to give their friend a hug.

"Nice legs, toots. C'mon, honey, kisses for peanuts," called the macaw.

"Isn't he just a dickens?" said Mrs. Despard with a wink. "I never know what he's going to come out with. His vocabulary is amazing. You'd swear he knows what he's saying. Anyway, girls, Rose, it's so wonderful to see you. I admit I'm getting a bit bored here. One can only play so much bingo and make so many crafts! However, good news, my therapy is coming along well. There's hope I can move to the assisted living section. I asked that handsome new minister to pray for me. Perhaps, by Christmas, I can have my own apartment."

Before Terry or Karen could answer, Rose chimed in. "Can't you go back to your own home? Couldn't Carl help look after you?"

"Bah!" said Mrs. Despard with a wave of her hand. "I'd rather be here. I feel much safer. Carl's never home. I never know what he's up to. Probably no good, that's what!"

Aunt Rose looked a bit taken aback. "Now, Maude, he's so much help to people. Look what I've got here. I found a picture of him as a kid. Wasn't he such a handsome fellow?"

She opened the photo album to show Mrs. Despard the picture. Terry and Karen eyed each other. Terry sensed Karen didn't think showing Mrs. Despard the picture was a good idea either.

"There! Just what I thought!" yipped Mrs. Despard, stabbing at the picture. "I told him that rich boy was no good, but he didn't listen to me! I knew he was slinking around with him. That boy was trouble…good riddance! That's what I thought when he was shot. Good riddance to bad garbage!"

"Bad, bad boy!" screamed the macaw.

Terry was stunned. She never saw Mrs. Despard like this. The woman Terry knew was sweet and kind. Mrs. Despard was the cheery plump woman who hugged Terry and Karen, made a big deal over all their accomplishments, and always seemed to have candy around to hand out. The venom in Mrs. Despard's voice concerning her own son shocked her.

Rose's mouth hung open as she looked sadly down at the picture. "I'm sorry, Maude. I thought you'd…well…never mind. I didn't realize…Anyway, that's wonderful news about the apartment. That would be truly an answer to prayer, then."

Mrs. Despard took a moment to collect herself. "I'm so very sorry. Carl was a good kid until he started hanging out with that hooligan. Since then, things haven't been the same with Carl. Oh, and that poor Samuel Brinker. Did you know he's here?" Without waiting for an answer, she continued. "He's Carl's age and the poor man had a breakdown. He's partially paralyzed, can't really walk. I hear there's nothing physically wrong with him. It's just part of the breakdown. They let him out of the hospital to come here. Now, there's another example. Carl came to see me and when Sam Brinker saw Carl, he turned pale. Looked like he saw a ghost. I asked Carl what happened between the two of them and Carl acted like he didn't know what I was talking about. He said it was probably the breakdown that made it look that way. Breakdown, my foot! Right after that lousy rich hooligan died, Sam stopped coming around. He and Carl were the closest of friends once. Sam turned out well. Show Sam that picture. He might enjoy it." She paused and looked up at the Rose and the girls.

Still feeling a bit awkward, Terry sat down on the couch by Mrs. Despard. Karen, Mrs. Dindle and Rose pulled up nearby chairs.

"I had Mr. Brinker as a high school math teacher," Karen said. "He was a great teacher. He was the first one to get me excited about math. I joined the math club where he was the advisor. He wrote me a letter of recommendation for college. I'm an accountant, remember, Mrs. Despard?"

"Oh, good gracious, yes! I'm so sorry about my lousy manners, girls. Terry, you look a bit pale, but Karen, you are as tan as a peanut. Terry, you need to get a little bit of sun! Karen, when did you get back?"

"I got back on Friday night. Actually, now that I'm back, maybe Terry can get some sun. She did such an incredible job on the teahouse. Have you seen it?"

"Not yet. Carl keeps saying he'll take me. Of course, he's been away for the past few weeks fishing. He's due back...today, I think. Before your poor mother died, he came almost every day, but lately, nothin'!"

"By the way, Maude," Mrs. Dindle interjected, "how've you been sleeping? The last time I saw you, I think you said they were trying to adjust your medication."

"It all seemed to work out. I was sleeping well, and then I wasn't. I was getting confused, thinking I hadn't taken pills when I had. Carl talked to the doctors and they adjusted the dose. Then I was too tired. It seems to be okay now. Thank you for asking, dear. So, Karen, how is it to be home?"

"It feels really nice. I don't miss my job yet. That's a good sign!"

"What's your husband doing? Is he here?"

"Ummm, no. He's in California with another woman. We're divorced. He decided he preferred a newer, younger model. I'm okay, though."

"Oh, my goodness! I'm so sorry, I didn't know that. Forgive me, dear. I didn't mean to bring up a sore subject."

Before Karen could speak, the macaw cried out, "Forget the loser! He's parrot poop!"

Karen turned toward the bird and cried out, "Ya got that right, Polly!"

They all laughed. "See what I mean?" said Mrs. Despard. "You'd swear he heard our conversation."

"I can't seem to remember," Rose said, frowning. "Where'd he come from?"

"He was Silvia Nitmeyer's bird. When she passed away a few weeks ago, she left him to the nursing home."

"Oh, that's right," Rose cried, slapping her leg. "I can't believe I forgot that!"

"Mrs. Nitmeyer, the lady who said she was psychic?" asked Karen.

"Yup, the one and only," Mrs. Despard said.

"My goodness, I didn't even know she passed," Terry said.

"Her brother didn't want it in the paper. He didn't even want a memorial service here. It was all sort of hush, hush. One day, the bird was just here. I've heard they want to find a home for him. I get a kick out of him, but some people don't like him." Mrs. Despard leaned forward in her chair. "I think he hits the nail on the head too often for the comfort of some. "Confidentially," Mrs. Despard lowered her voice to a whisper, "Mrs. Nitmeyer once told me that the bird was a psychic, too. She said he knew some things even before she did. Whattaya think of that!" She sat back with a look of satisfaction, seemingly proud to have the whole scoop on the bird.

"Oh, fiddlesticks!" said Rose, rolling her eyes. "That woman was a nut!"

"One never knows, Rose," Dottie said. "Why did her brother hush things up? Silvia had lots of friends here in town."

"I'm not really sure. I think he thought she was a nut. They weren't close. Her sister, Evelyn, as you may remember, stayed clear of Sylvia. Evelyn was embarrassed by Sylvia's...what shall I call them...idiosyncrasies."

Before anyone could say another word, the bird called out, "He's a hottie! Hunk alert! Hunk alert!"

Hearing the sliding doors open, Terry turned to see Greg walk in the door. She turned to Mrs. Despard, unable to say a word.

"How's that for proof! That's Hattie Mullins' grandson, Greg. You girls must know him from school. In my day, we would have called him 'the cat's meow!' He's a hunk, as you young people say. No doubt about it!" Mrs. Despard smiled broadly, pleased at the bird's "prediction." Terry felt herself blush. Karen started to laugh.

"Oh, yeah! The bird's right on the money. Huh, Terry?" Karen grinned at her sister.

"Why, that's the nice detective from last night! Of course! Now I know why he seemed so familiar. Yooohooo, Detective Mullins!" Rose called as she waved.

Terry wanted to crawl under the couch. Why, Rose, why? Lord, take me now! Terry prayed. Sure her face was the color of a lobster, Terry tried to collect herself as she saw Greg head in their direction. He was carrying two large plastic shopping bags. Terry assumed they contained the clothes he brought for his grandmother. Terry stole a glance at Karen who looked like the cat who ate the canary.

"Good day, ladies." Greg smiled broadly at the group. "How are you doing today, Mrs. Despard? Still making progress in the workout room?"

"Oh, yes! I'm getting stronger all the time. I was just telling these lovely young ladies that I may be able to get into assisted living by Christmas time. It was so nice of you to volunteer to come and help out in the workout room. You are such a dear! Now, what is this I just heard? Rose, what do you mean he's the detective from last night?"

"Oh, Maudy, listen to this!" Rose began the saga, obviously thrilled to have a good story to tell. Terry and Karen looked at each other and sighed. Greg waved goodbye and went looking for his grandmother.

As Rose finished her tale, Maude clapped her hands together. "Goodness sakes alive, what a terrible ordeal. Who would do such a thing?"

Terry shrugged, glad Rose omitted the part about the teacup. She glanced at her watch. She didn't want to talk about last night. Perhaps she could think of a reason to get going.

"I was scared to death, running to the stairway after hearing Terry scream," Karen said with a shiver. "I thought any second, a crazed madman was going to come down the stairs and kill us all. Aunt Rose, you should be so proud of Uncle Henry. He jumped right in and took charge."

"I'm glad no one was hurt and that Henry didn't have a heart attack on the spot!" Rose said, wringing her hands.

Mrs. Despard reached over and gently patted Rose's hand. "I don't blame you a bit, Rosey. You must have been a wreck while you waited at home. Terrible, terrible."

"Heeeeere's Granny," called the macaw as Greg wheeled his grandmother into the visiting room. He waved to the group. Right behind him, a nurse wheeled in Mr. Brinker.

Mrs. Despard motioned them both over. "Greg, bring Grandma over here. Hattie, please come join us. Oh, Sam, come see us. There's someone here who remembers you fondly. Come say hello!"

As Greg approached with his grandmother, the nurse brought Samuel Brinker over. He smiled broadly at the sight of Karen. "Oh, Miss Sutter, how wonderful to see you! What a treat, what a treat, indeed! Hello, ladies," he said, nodding toward the group.

Karen got up and gave Mr. Brinker a kiss on the cheek. Terry saw the look of love and admiration on her sister's face. Karen patted his hand and pulled up a chair next to his wheelchair. Terry never had Mr. Brinker in school, but she knew what an influence he was in Karen's life. Did Greg have him? she wondered.

"Mr. Brinker, it's so wonderful to see you. I'm back in the area, now. My sister and I have opened a teahouse. I'm doing all the accounting."

"I've heard some wonderful things from a few nurses and nurses' aides about the teahouse. I hope to get there sometime. I'd offer my accounting services, but I'm sure you could teach *me* these days! Hey, a friend of mine brought me some magazines filled with math puzzles. There's a couple real tough ones in there. If you have some time, maybe you could come help your old business math teacher." He grinned broadly. "I showed one to this smart guy here," he said, pointing to Greg. "It took him awhile, but the smart detective figured it out. Guess the town's safe in his hands."

Greg laughed. "I sure hope so. I just wish my job involved solving math puzzles more often."

"Well, young man," began Maude Despard, looking at Greg, "I hear you're helping out with the awful happenings at the teahouse. Such a love you are! Hattie, what would we do without brave young men like your grandson?"

Terry saw Greg blush. "It's just my job, Mrs. Despard, really."

Terry was momentarily distracted as Rose got up and headed toward Mr. Brinker with the photo album in her hands.

"Careful," cried the bird.

Terry turned back to the conversation with Mrs. Despard. She wanted to watch how Greg handled the situation. "...no braver than the other men I work with," Greg was saying.

"Oh, God!" yelled Samuel Brinker. "Forgive my sins! Oh, God!" The poor man was obviously unnerved. Karen yanked the photo album off his lap and sent it flying. Mr. Brinker sobbed. Karen was on her knees by his chair, trying to calm him, and a nurse came running over. "I didn't take it, I swear. I don't know where it is! He never told me, never!" Samuel

Brinker was becoming hysterical. He clutched at Karen, his eyes wild with fear. He seemed to be begging her to believe him. "I told them to let it be. I tried to stop them." He held his hands up in front of his face. "The blood, the blood, the blood, oh my God!"

The nurse got down on her knees in front of the chair and looked into Mr. Brinker's eyes. She gently cupped his face in her hands and asked him to look at her. His eyes seemed to focus on her face. He lowered his head, his body heaving with sobs. Everyone looked at each other with confusion on their faces. The nurse wheeled Mr. Brinker back toward his room.

Another nurse approached the group. "It's okay. That happens with him now and then."

"It was the picture," Karen said, her voice shaking. "It was this picture. He took one look at it and freaked."

"It may not have been the picture at all," said the nurse as she rubbed Karen's back. "He wakes up with nightmares, yelling like that. It happened once when he was in his room by himself, watching television."

"Why?" asked Karen, who looked devastated.

"I really don't know. It's part of the breakdown. I'm sure he'll calm down soon. I'll let his doctor know. Really, it wasn't your fault," she said. "Are you a friend of his?"

"An old student, he was my favorite teacher, my mentor. The poor man," sighed Karen.

Terry looked over at Karen and watched the nurse rub her back. It broke Terry's heart to see the pain on Karen's face. Terry hoped that seeing Mr. Brinker would give Karen an emotional boost. What Todd did really hurt Karen. Terry wanted Mr. Brinker to be a positive experience. Maybe she would suggest Karen come help him with some math puzzles. Perhaps the student and teacher could help each other.

The nurse left and the group sat quietly for a few moments. Maude Despard broke the silence. "Was that the picture of him with Carl and Thurston?" she asked in a whisper. No one said a word, Karen and Rose just nodded. Maude looked up at the ceiling and shook her head.

"Wow," said Greg, "it's hard to watch a brilliant man suffer like that. Once a woman saw her little boy get hit by a car. He'd run out in the road after a ball. She screamed out his name, but it was too late. As far as I know, she never spoke again. I can't help wondering what happened in his life. Poor man."

"I wonder if it was the picture," said Rose. "It's too bad there's no way to know for sure. I feel just terrible."

"Rose, the nurse is right, it probably wasn't the picture," Maude said. "I just hope and pray Carl wasn't involved in whatever it is that torments him so."

CHAPTER 8

It was raining buckets as the group left Fair Meadows. "I thought the weather was supposed to be nice today," Karen yelled as she and Terry made a dash for the car.

"It was. You know how fickle the weather is here. Give me a break! It'll probably be sunny in an hour," Terry replied as she jumped in the car. "It's just our luck that the downpour started as we were ready to leave. It's par-for-the-course with us."

She pulled the car up to the entrance way and Mrs. Dindle and Aunt Rose climbed in. They sat in silence for quite some time.

At last, Mrs. Dindle spoke up. "That poor, poor man. It's always puzzled me that some people can handle life's bumps while others crumble. I can't imagine what's upsetting him so. His parents were certainly wonderful people and he had a wonderful career as a teacher. So many of his students adored him! What a tragedy for him to be going through something like this! Such a shame, such a shame." She shook her head sadly.

"He was the reason I went into accounting," Karen added. "He was the one who encouraged me and told me I had an aptitude for numbers. If it wasn't for him, I would probably have floundered for my first few years of college, trying to decide what I wanted to do for a career. Terry, remember how I was always changing my mind the first two years of high school? I don't think there was career I didn't consider!"

"I'll second that!" Terry chimed in. "You were making us all dizzy, changing directions every few weeks. Nurse, circus clown, carpenter, veterinarian—we all wondered what you'd come up with next. You weren't the only one grateful for Mr. Brinker, trust me."

"Isn't that bird fun?" Rose said, chuckling from the front passenger seat. "Didn't you girls just adore him?"

"His vocabulary amazes me!" Karen said from the back seat. "I've never heard a bird use so many words and phrases. It's eerie how he started yelling, 'hunk alert' before Greg walked in."

"It's as if he really is psychic!" Terry said with a shudder.

Karen issued a stern warning to her sister. "Let's not get carried away there, toots. First the teacup stuff and now you're wondering about a psychic macaw. Pretty soon, we're going to have to have you evaluated psychologically! Mr. Brinker was hard enough on my nerves, let's not add you to the list!"

"Karen!" Aunt Rose snapped. "What a horrible thing to say! Besides, I think you girls should consider adopting the bird. I think he would make an excellent conversation piece in the parlor."

"Aunt Rose!" Karen sighed with exasperation. "He would probably say something that offended someone. Besides, I think we have enough going on right now."

No one spoke for a few minutes. Then Mrs. Dindle piped up. "You know, ladies, I think your Aunt Rose might be onto something. I agree with her, he would certainly be a conversation piece and on nice days, you could put his cage out by the water garden. Don't rule it out. He would be the crowning touch!"

The rain stopped as suddenly as it began. Terry gently steered the car to the side of the road. She looked at them all, one by one. Then she locked eyes with her sister. The two sisters stared at each other for a few moments.

"Birds are dirty and smelly," Karen said. "Let's not forget I had a parakeet. Mom made me clean that cage twice a week. I was a little relieved when he took off out the window."

"Whoa! Let's not change history, missy," Terry piped up. "You paid me to clean the cage."

"Not *all* the time," Karen said, folding her arms.

"Enough of it. I was crushed when Little Boy flew off. I swore you did it on purpose. You owe me a bird!" Terry said, only half-kidding.

"Oh, for heaven's sake! I did not let the bird out on purpose. It was almost thirty years ago. Let it go, Terry." Karen rolled her eyes upward as she spoke. "Okay, you win. Terry, turn the car around. We might as well get the blasted bird. A haunted teahouse *and* a psychic bird. What else could I want from life?"

"Hey, watch it!" Terry laughed. "You don't want people to think you're as odd as I am."

"Hmm, two odd sisters running a haunted teahouse with a psychic macaw…sounds like interesting publicity." Karen chuckled. "We might be on to something!"

"Oh, goodie!" chimed in Mrs. Dindle, clapping her hands. "I want to be the eccentric neighbor. I could dress like Mrs. Nitmeyer. I'm probably just as psychic as she was. I could pretend to read tea leaves."

"Now, wait just a minute there, Dottie. If anyone gets to be eccentric, it's me. After all, I am their aunt. It's more believable that oddities would run in the family. I think you should be…the naysayer. You could be the gossip that pooh-poohs the idea. Conflict always makes things more interesting, " Aunt Rose added with a smirk. Everyone laughed, but Terry wondered how far off the truth they were.

Greg climbed out of his unmarked police car and looked around. The dinette had a closed sign in the window, but the antique shop was open. There weren't any customers inside. This was convenient because it made it easier to ask questions without being interrupted. He sauntered in and approached a woman standing behind an antique cash register. She had shoulder-length, graying-brown hair and wore a yellow sundress.

"Hello, ma'am, I'm Detective Greg Mullins. It appears that the teahouse across the street was broken into last night. I'm stopping by to see if you've had any problems lately, any reason to think someone might have tried to break in here? Perhaps you noticed someone odd hanging around." He stopped and waited. The best way to get people to talk was to simply be quiet. People said the most amazing things just to fill a silence.

"I'm Carrie Pearson, the owner," said the woman, extending her hand. "Oh, those poor girls. You know their mother, Madeline, died suddenly a number of months ago. First their mother and now this! Of course, everyone was in shock over Madeline's death. She seemed so healthy! I guess one never can tell. Carl Despard, the local handyman, still blames himself for not being there when she fell. I keep telling him that it's silly to feel guilty over something like that. Now, the place gets broken into when he's away. I haven't had any problems whatsoever. Not even a missing tack!" She straightened some pamphlets behind the counter. "There are tourists here day in and day out, but I wouldn't say there was anyone who stood out. I can't imagine who would do such a thing. How did the person break in? Any idea what the burglar wanted? Was there any cash missing? Probably some wise guy teenager. Kids these days are always looking to make a quick buck." She stopped momentarily for air. It was obvious to Greg that Carrie Pearson was quite a talker. "I imagine that the girls will want Carl to help them make things more secure. He'll take good care of them, don't you worry, Detective Mullins. You know, when their mother got sick, it was Carl who helped her out in the afternoons. Yes siree, he'd go over there and do some housework so she could rest." Carrie folded her arms and looked out the front window toward the teahouse. " Madeline came over here one day and said she was so lucky to have him. You could tell the poor woman was exhausted. Such a shame, another day or two and she would have been to the doctor. I took a casserole over to Rose and Harry— Rose is Madeline's sister, you know." She shook her head. "Anyway, it was the least I could do. Rose, poor woman, was devastated for weeks after she found her sister dead at the bottom of the basement steps. Carl and I couldn't believe our eyes when the ambulance pulled up. I have a local college student who helps me out a few days a week. Well, she was here that day, so I left her to run things for a bit and Carl and I went across the street. The EMTs were thinking of calling another ambulance for Rose!" She pushed her hair behind her ears, took a deep breath and charged on. "Henry had all he could do to try and calm her down. Madeline wasn't just her sister, she was Rose's best friend as well."

Greg took advantage of Carrie's need for air and jumped in. "Why wasn't Carl over there that afternoon?"

"Well, that's the thing of it. Normally, he would have been, but I asked him to help me move some furniture around. He was planning to go over there after he helped me. That's why he felt so awful. Isn't life odd? One can never tell." She shook her head. "I told him that there are plenty of things in life we can't control. I suppose I *could* feel guilty that I asked him to come over here, but that would be silly. Why feel guilty over an incident I had no control over? My mother used to say, 'Don't waste time thinking about all the should haves and could haves in your life.' I think that's good advice."

"Was there anyone who would have had a key to the house? A housekeeper or Carl Despard, perhaps?"

"Madeline didn't have a housekeeper. Like I said before, she was perfectly healthy just a week or two before. She didn't need a housekeeper. I doubt Carl had a key. He wasn't there that often. He'd only been around frequently those few weeks because Madeline needed the help."

"You said she'd been sick a week or two. Why didn't she go to the doctor sooner?" Greg asked, shifting his weight a bit and rubbing his chin. Something didn't seem quite right.

"Well, at first, she thought it was the flu. When she didn't feel better after a day or so, she called the gas company. You see, there was a problem with her gas stove. She had Carl fix it. She told me she called the gas company to be sure there were no leaks There weren't. She trusted Carl, but one never knows. She couldn't understand why she felt so weak all of a sudden. She tried taking a vitamin with iron, but that didn't help cither. Only then did she make a doctor's appointment."

"How did Carl know she was sick? Was she feeling sick before he fixed the stove?"

"Oh, no, I'm sure of that. I'm sure Madeline felt fine until Carl fixed the stove. That's why she called the gas company. I'm not sure what was wrong with the stove, I just know he went over to fix it. He stopped over the next day, just to make sure it was working okay. He realized she was feeling awful and asked if he could get her anything. Never took money for it either. I guess he just kept checking up on her. He'd make her some tea and do some minor housekeeping or laundry, just so it wouldn't get backed up while she was sick. Then he'd stop in here for a bit to see if I needed anything. Such a nice guy. Why Madeline decided to try and go downstairs will forever be a mystery. The washer was down there, but Carl was doing the laundry for her. Now, what was it you asked me?" She looked at Greg for a moment. "Oh, yes, a key. No, I don't think anyone but family had keys. No one that I can think of, anyway."

"Well, Mrs. Pearson. Thank you for your help. Please let me know if you see anyone unusual hanging around or if you have any problems yourself. By the way, was an autopsy done on Mrs. Sutter?"

"No, the girls didn't want one. It would only serve to satisfy their curiosity about why she was so tired. They decided just to accept her death and let it be. I'm sorry I can't be more help, Detective. I do hope you catch whoever it was. Those girls have been through enough this year!"

Greg exited the antique shop and looked across the street. Something didn't sit right with him about Mrs. Sutter's death. She was probably in her sixties. Too bad they didn't have an autopsy done. Of course, he could be making mountains out of mole hills. Given the fact that Terry Sutter was the cutest thing he ever saw, he really couldn't be objective about her mother's death. Still…something bugged him. He gazed across the street and saw Henry pulling up in front of the teahouse. What was that in his car? It looked like a cage. Wait, was that the bird from the nursing home?

Why would Henry have the macaw? Greg jogged over to Henry's car.

"Mr. Sanders, what have you got there? Need any help?"

Henry, who'd been leaning over to get the cage out of his backseat, straightened up, looking startled. "Oh, hello, Detective. Can you believe these girls decided to adopt a macaw that was left at Fair Meadows when his owner died?"

"Mr. T, Mr. T, " called the bird.

"He says the strangest things, Detective. I walked in the convalescent home section to pick him up and the bird yelled, 'I'm a goner. See ya, folks!'" It was as if he knew I was there to get him. It's enough to give ya the willies!"

Greg smiled. "Yeah, my grandmother is there. I saw the bird this morning. He's quite the entertainer. I didn't know they were taking him."

"It was a last minute decision. Thought it would add to the ambiance. Apparently, some say the bird is psychic. Just what we need, first...." Henry stopped abruptly. Greg noticed that Henry looked down and cleared his throat. "First the break-in and now this silly bird. Never a dull moment here." Greg wondered what Henry started to say. He was sure it had nothing to do with the break-in.

"Let me give you a hand," Greg said, taking the cage from Henry.

The bird whistled. "Easy there, Studly. Don't rock the boat!"

Both men looked at each other and laughed. Greg headed for the door just as Terry came outside. "Well, Detective. I see you've met our new friend."

"I saw him at the nursing home. I was surprised to see him show up here. You're full of surprises, Terry Sutter."

Terry smiled. "Hello there. Welcome to Madeline's teahouse, Mr. Bird."

"Mr. T, Mr. T," said the macaw.

"Hey," said Terry. "What a great idea. I think we'll call him Mr. T spelled t-e-a. Is that too…silly?" she asked Greg.

Greg smiled. "Works for me. As long as I'm not cleaning the cage, I don't care what you call him. Now, where do you want Mr. Tea?"

"Oh, over in the corner there. See, we've set up a table for his cage."

Greg set the cage on the table and turned around to find Karen, Rose Sanders and the neighbor, Mrs. Dindle, all standing in the doorway and staring at the bird. "Wow," said Greg. "You've got an audience, Mr. Tea."

"Mr. T?" asked Karen.

Terry explained and everyone agreed it was a fitting name.

"Home sweet home," squawked Mr. Tea.

Greg looked at the small group. He wanted to try and press Terry for information. Henry Sander's hesitation outside gnawed at Greg's gut. Something was up, he could feel it. Greg decided to have another look around outside and see what happened from there.

"Terry, would you mind walking around outside with me? Perhaps you'll notice something in the daylight that didn't catch your attention last night." Greg, unusually nervous, put his hands in his pockets and rocked back and forth on the balls of his feet.

"Oh, um, okay," Terry stuttered as she and Greg went through the kitchen and out the back. Greg noticed that she was blushing. He wondered if he was the cause.

Although nothing seemed out of the ordinary in the back, the side of the house was another matter.

Looking up at the tree, it was clear that someone had recently climbed it. Up by the window, there were a few small broken branches and the wind from the rainstorm brought down leaves and branches that appeared trampled rather than windblown. Greg stood and stared up at the tree. The many trees he climbed as a child caused him to look at trees a bit differently. He crouched by the base of the tree. After staring for a moment, he pulled out his cell phone.

"I want to have guys look around here," he said to Terry as he pointed. "There seems to be an imprint of a boot there by the base. I don't suppose you or Karen climbed that tree in the last few days?" he said with a smile.

"No, actually, I think it was Rose," Terry said calmly.

Greg was stunned. He stared at her. Suddenly, she burst out laughing.

"I'm kidding, for heaven's sake!"

Greg laughed, too. "Duh! You had me there for a second. Good one." He dialed.

"Tom O'Hara."

"Tom, it's Greg. I'm over at the Sutter house. I'm having another look around. There's a very slight imprint at the base of the tree where someone dropped to the ground. I want some guys to come out here and take some photos, try and get a cast of the print, and get someone to climb up in the tree. There might be some fabric up there."

"I can grab a couple of guys and be there in….twenty minutes. Okay?"

"Okay, thanks." He flipped his phone closed and looked at Terry who was leaning against the house, staring wide-eyed at him. She wore a red print sundress and sandals that revealed her painted red toenails. A delicate gold cross hung from her neck. Greg wiped his palms on his pants, embarrassed that looking at her could still make him sweat.

"Is there a place we can sit and talk for a bit? I have just a few more questions," he asked, afraid his voice would crack. He hated being an adolescent the first time and he hated feeling like one now.

"Sure, come on the porch. Want some iced tea?"

"Yeah, that would be great, if it's not any trouble."

Terry smiled. "You've come to the right place. We have no meat or vegetables, but tea and scones we got!" As she headed for the front of the house, Greg couldn't help but notice that she looked as good going as she did coming.

Seated in a rocker on the front porch, Greg forced himself to concentrate on the matter at hand. "So, now you've got a guard bird," he said, smiling.

"Well, with everything going on, it certainly wouldn't hurt," Terry said. Greg saw her wince. She looked as if she said something wrong. Hmmm.

"What's everything?" Greg asked, sure he was onto something.

"Um, well, the break-in...um...we just opened...Karen just got here...you know." Terry blushed!

"Terry, I can't figure out who broke in if I don't know all the details. I got the impression a number of times that you and your family are holding something back. I want to know what it is. Has something similar happened before? Do you think you know who might have broken in?"

Terry looked at him wide-eyed. She looked panic-stricken. Then, heaving a big sigh, she began. "What I'm about to tell you is going to sound absurd. It probably is, but it's what we're holding back. Really, I know it's silly..." Over the next fifteen minutes, she told him the whole story. After she finished, she seemed too embarrassed to look at him. She sat, hands in her lap, looking at the floorboards on the porch.

Quietly, Greg responded. "My grandmother told me that when she was a teenager, her parents left her alone to go Christmas shopping one afternoon. My grandmother fell asleep, reading on the couch in the front room. Suddenly, she felt someone shaking her awake. She awoke with a start, but no one was there. She thought she heard something in the kitchen, so she got up to check it out. Just as she reached the kitchen, there was a loud crash. The farmer across the street hadn't parked his tractor correctly. It rolled down a hill, gaining speed as it went. It came crashing down through the front of the house and came to rest where my grandmother had been. She would have been killed. To this day, my grandmother swears that an angel woke her up to save her and made noise to get her out of the living room and into the kitchen. If I believe my grandmother, how could I not believe you? There may be another logical explanation, or there may not be. I guess we'll find out." He looked over at Terry and saw relief in her eyes. He smiled reassuringly. Greg was just about to reach for her hand when two police cruisers pulled up. Wiping his sweaty palms on his pants, he got up and walked across the front lawn to greet them. Dang it! he thought.

Although they couldn't get a good cast of the boot print, the agile Officer Andrew Burdick climbed the tree and found some bits of gray hair and a small patch of white fabric.

Henry Sanders looked at Greg. "Well, I'll be. I sure wish this head of gray hair could climb trees. I loved doing that as a kid. Ya know, kids used to climb trees all around this area. This tree is taller than the house now, but I remember when it barely reached the window sill there by the attic." He took Greg over to the other side of the tree and pointed at a dark spot on the tree. "This here was where a branch hung for a tire swing. I remember watching the kids, Karen and Terry, swing from it when they were little. About fifteen years ago, their father and I had to cut off the branch because it got damaged in a storm. See, here is where we put the tar over it to keep the bugs out. It was kinda sad. That tire swing was there ever since I was a kid. Cutting it off was kinda like the end of an era." Henry put his hands in his pockets, looked down and shook his head. "Life goes by just too fast. One day you're a kid and next...well, you're old, lookin' back."

"So," Greg said as he stared up at the attic window, "there are plenty of people who knew this tree was directly outside the attic window, correct?"

Thinking for a moment, Henry replied, "Well, yeah, I guess so. But anyone coming for tea could see there's a tree here. It wouldn't take a rocket scientist to realize that the window up there is to the attic."

"True, Mr. Sanders. However, I think whoever was up there last night was familiar with the house and the attic. A stranger looking for money or valuables would have hit other rooms, such as the bedrooms or office, before checking out the attic. I'm beginning to think that if we can figure out what the person was looking for, we can figure out who it was, not the other way around."

"Okay, perhaps that's true, young man, but there's nothing up in that attic. You saw for yourself last night. Nothing of value anyway. The whole incident makes no sense. Of course, not much going on here makes much sense these days." Henry shook his head and looked at Greg. "Terry mentioned to me that she told you about that blasted cup. It's the oddest thing. I can't say I believe in ghosts, but I do know my niece, Terry, and if she's certain something weird is going on, then, rest assured, it is.   Even Karen, who is as practical as a person gets, thinks something isn't right. Actually, I would say all of us involved, the Dindles included, don't jump to conclusions.   Yup, by gum, something odd is afoot, that's for sure."

Greg realized he liked Henry Sanders quite a bit. There was something avuncular about him.   Henry Sanders seemed to be the type of person people naturally felt comfortable around.   Greg pondered the break-in for a moment. He loved his job and cared a great deal about people, but there was something about *this* group that made him want to protect them.   The Sutter sisters, their aunt and uncle, and their neighbors had somehow wheedled their way into his heart.

CHAPTER 9

Terry sat with Greg, Karen, Aunt Rose and Uncle Henry in momentary silence in the parlor. Terry was relieved to know that Greg believed the business with the cup was real and not her imagination.

Greg ran his fingers through his hair and stood up. "It's possible, ya know, that whoever came in here last night is responsible for the problems with the teacup. I think we should begin by changing the locks, or at least adding a deadbolt to both the kitchen and front door."

"Sea shells, sea shells by the seashore," called Mr. Tea.

Terry, with a smirk on her face, glanced over at the bird. She really liked having him around. It felt to her as if he really belonged there. Karen's voice focused her attention back on the matters at hand.

"Greg, I don't see how anyone else can have a key to this place. Also, I think we would have heard the door if someone came in during the night to break the teacups. However, it certainly can't hurt." The tone of Karen's voice and the way she flipped her hair as she made the statement told Terry that Karen was feeling stressed after the events of the last few days.

Uncle Henry glanced at his watch. "It's only two-forty-five. Why don't I go over to the hardware store, get the locks and install them? At least we'll be doing something in the direction of putting an end to this nonsense."

"Plans of mice and men," Mr. Tea chimed in.

"Let's hope not, don't be such a pessimistic bird!" Aunt Rose snapped at Mr. Tea.

Mr. Tea blinked at her calmly.

Terry was stunned to hear Greg say, "I'm off duty now. Why don't I go with you and lend a hand?" Karen nudged Terry in the ribs and Terry forced herself not to react.

"I'd be much obliged, young fella. Let's take my car. I don't want the town gossips seeing me chauffeured around in a police car," Henry said with a chuckle.

"Oh, my!" added Rose. "The church ladies' group would have the telephone lines lit up quick-as-a-blink." Terry saw Rose wink at Greg. Terry sat on the couch with her heart racing as Greg and Uncle Henry headed out the door together.

"Hey, Carl," Terry heard Uncle Henry say before he could close the door. Terry got up and walked to the door. She liked Carl. He was always around to lend a hand to anyone in town who needed work done. Whenever he came over to help her father with a project, he had lollipops tucked in his shirt pocket for her and Karen. He always took a few minutes to push them on the tire swing on the side of the house.

"Well, are ya goin' outside or are you gonna watch traffic?" Karen asked, nudging her sister. The two of them joined the three men on the front lawn.

"Hello, ladies! Miss Karen, nice to see you! How do you like all the work your sister did to the place? Nice, huh?" Carl said, giving Karen a hug.

Karen smiled and gave an "oof" as Carl's hug lifted her off the ground. "I love it! She told me you did quite a bit of the lifting and toting so she could paint and decorate. I know my mom would have loved it. Any chance we can get your mom out here? We went to see her today. She seems to be doing pretty well.

From what she says, I gather she's going to be moving from the convalescent section to one of the apartments pretty soon. Terry and I would love it if you could bring her someday. "

"I'm sure she'd love it! I hope to do that soon. I think she's a little sore at me for suggesting she stay at Fair Meadows. It's not that I don't want her home, it's just that I would worry about her all the time. This way, help is always close by. The doctors said that because she had one stroke, her risk of having another one is high. I don't think she realizes she's better off there than at home. Anyway, I came over because I heard from Mrs. Pearson that there was a problem here last night. You all okay?"

Terry was touched by the look of concern on his face. It was obvious he cared about them.

Uncle Henry patted Carl on the back. "Don't you worry yourself about us. We've got this fine po-leese man lookin' after us." Uncle Henry smiled. "We're just on our way to get some deadbolts. That oughta help."

Carl frowned and seemed to think for a minute. "I think I have some back at the house. Can't remember now what I even had them for. I know they've never been used. Why don't you let me get them for you?"

"That's really nice of you, but I want to get a specific kind. There are some that are harder to bust than others. No offense, but I would feel better if we got some new ones," Greg said, looking a bit uncomfortable.

"No offense taken! Do you need help putting them in?"

"Naw, we got it covered," Uncle Henry said. "Gotta get goin', Carl. Hope to see you soon. Like the girls said, bring your mom over for tea." Henry and Greg headed to Henry's car as Carl waved goodbye and went across the street to his truck.

The door to the teahouse opened and Aunt Rose hollered out, "Terry, Karen, Mrs. Dindle wants to know if you'd like some plants for around the water garden. She said something about cutting some of hers back. She's on the phone, come talk to her."

As the girls headed back, Mr. Tea hollered, "Get a clue! Get a clue!"

"Quiet for a moment!" Aunt Rose snapped. "Or we'll plant you in the garden!"

"Give me a kiss, toots!" said the macaw.

The air was cooling off a bit as the late afternoon rolled around. Terry sat on a rock by the teahouse water garden. Encircling her were various pots with ferns and flowers from Mrs. Dindle's water garden. She heaved a sigh of contentment. Not only did Terry love to dig in the garden, but she had a wonderful view of Greg and Uncle Henry as they installed a deadbolt on the kitchen door. Terry was afraid to hope that Greg would see her as more than a friend, but whenever she looked at him, her stomach flopped like it was on a bungee cord. Karen, who despised worms and all other crawly things, was in the office, working on the books for the teahouse.

Grabbing the nearby spade, Terry stood up and looked at the plants. She wanted to wait until they decided on an actual design before she planted most of them. However, there was a bare spot just to the right of the waterfall, and she wanted to put the biggest fern there. She wiped her hands on her jeans, put on her gardening gloves and began to dig. It wasn't long before she was drenched in sweat. Painting is so much easier, she mused.

"Need some help?"

Terry, lost in her own thoughts, startled a bit at Greg's voice. "Are you done with the deadbolts already?" she asked Greg, wishing that he was still over at the kitchen door instead of right in front of her, seeing that she was a sweaty mess.

"Yes, ma'am. Henry is coming out with some tea. So, you want me to dig a bit? The roots on that sucker look big. You're gonna have to dig pretty deep."

"Yeah, it's been slow going because I keep hitting rock after rock after rock."

Henry emerged from the kitchen, carrying a tray with three big glasses of iced tea. Terry handed Greg the spade and took a glass. Greg took a few gulps, put his glass down on a rock and began to dig.

"Hey, give the young feller a break!" Henry said with a wink. "He's gonna be too tuckered out to fight crime."

Greg smiled. "Don't worry about me. This type of thing makes me relax. Takes my mind off of things for a bit...whoa!" The spade shook as he hit a rock. Terry and Henry watched in silence as he began to dig around to free it.

"Hey, go slow there," Henry said, bending down over the hole. "Sounds more like you're hitting metal than rock."

The three of them knelt down for a moment. Terry and Greg went flat on their stomachs as they dug around with their hands. Sure enough, a rectangular metal box began to emerge. It took them another fifteen minutes, but at last, it came free.

Terry held it in her hand. "That's odd. A buried metal box." She turned it around, looking for a design or some writing. There was too much rust and corrosion. She tried to open it, but the top wouldn't budge. She shrugged and handed it to Greg. Maybe he'd have better luck. She wiped her hand across the sweat on her face. Wonderful, she thought. I'm sitting here a dirty, sweaty mess and I just smeared mud on my face. I'm such a class act!

"Seems to be rusted shut," Greg said, tugging at the cover.   He tipped the box on its side, balancing it carefully. Henry and Terry stood up and moved out of the way. Taking the spade, Greg smashed it against the box. The top popped open, allowing an old yellow piece of paper to slide out. Greg reached down and picked it up.

"What's that?" Terry asked.

Slowly, Greg unfolded the paper and scowled. "Wow, it seems to be some kind of...poem. It's so faded, it's hard to read. Hmmm, let's see here."

Think carefully now
For the rumors are true
My treasure is hidden
To be found by you

"Holy cow!" said Henry. He and Terry went and looked over Greg's shoulder as he continued to read.

I've used enough
And lived quite well
And now it's time
My secret to tell

Greg stopped to decipher the next few words.

Beneath this house
My treasure awaits
Not mine but their
Quite worthy estate
These little tree gnomes

Will guard it quite well
And protect it daily
Under Heaven, above Hell
You might not see them
But watch you they will
They'll peep in each morning
At your window sill

It isn't that far
Just a hop, skip or two
Then dig it up
For it waits for you

Look quickly though
For you're against the clock
It's in a wooden box
And that can rot

Henry let out a whistle. "I'll be gosh-darned . If it isn't a joke, it could be there's something to the rumor about Mr. Hamilton's treasure. Hmmmm....I'll be..."

"What's this about a treasure?" Greg asked, turning the paper over a few times.

"I told you a bit last night. Let me put it all together." Henry told Greg more about the Hamiltons, the disappearance of the ladies next door and Thurston Hamilton's death. "You know what? I swear there's some old correspondence over at the historical society...I can't remember exactly what, but I think Old Man Hamilton's signature is there, maybe even more. I think I'll go over there tomorrow and check it out. It'll be interesting to see if the handwriting looks similar. Can't hurt, we might be going on a treasure hunt. Wouldn't that be a hoot?"

"I'm not sure I can stand another mystery," Terry said. "Although, I have to admit this is pretty cool. A rusted metal box with a poem that could lead to buried treasure. This is a once in a lifetime experience! Do you think it's real?"

"I dunno," Henry said, "but I'm gonna check what we got at the historical society. Hopefully, that'll tell us if Beauregard Hamilton, Sr. wrote it or not."

"Wow, let me know what you find out. The mysteries around this place get more and more fascinating," Greg said, handing the box and note to Terry. "Right now, I think I'll just finish digging the hole for this fern."

Terry smiled. "It's amazing to think this guy might have buried his treasure, thinking his son or grandson would eventually come across this. Maybe this property is haunted." She rubbed the goose bumps on her arms. "Oooo, I'm creeping myself out, just thinking about it!"

"Just relax there, darlin. Let's not jump to conclusions."

Terry could barely breathe. She glanced at Henry. Did he hear what she heard? She swore she heard Greg call her darlin'. He calls me darlin', the most romantic moment in my life, and here I stand with mud smeared across my face. Scarlet O'Hara, I ain't.

Greg continued to dig. "Why don't you wait and see what your uncle discovers tomorrow. Let's not say anything about this to anyone else. The best thing to do at this point is get some facts together before we tell anyone else what we found."

"That's a good idea," Henry said.

Stopping digging for a moment, Greg said, "By the way, Terry, would you mind if I spread out a sleeping bag in your main hallway tonight? Now that the new locks are in, I want to see what happens with the toppling teacup. Is that okay with you? I don't want to impose."

"Uh, uh, ummm," a tongue-tied Terry stuttered. Holy Moses, she thought. First the darlin' and now he wants to sleep over...well, on the floor, but that's gotta count. I gotta get inside and take a shower. I must smell like a wart hog! "Sure, that's really nice of you. You don't need to go to all that trouble, you know, now that the locks are in." Shut up, Terry. If he wants to sleep over, roll with it! she chastised herself. Wow, he called me darlin'! Does it mean they really like you if they call you darlin' when you look and smell like the swamp monster? she wondered.

"I know Rose and I would sleep better knowing you were watchin' out for the girls," Henry said. "We're a little rattled about last night."

Thank you, Uncle Henry. Thank you, thank you, thank you! Terry could've hugged him.

"No trouble. Me and Mr. Tea'll keep an eye out." Greg smiled and went back to his work.

"I, um, need to go inside for just a moment. I want to see how Karen is doing with the books," Terry said. And I hope I make it before I pee my pants, Terry thought.

Terry flew into Karen's office and shut the door behind her. Her legs crossed, she stared at Karen who was staring back at her with a frown on her face.

"Yes?" Karen asked. "Can I help you? What the heck, Terry. You're doin' the pee pee dance."

"I know, I really gotta pee, but Greg....Greg called me darlin' and...shoot. I'll be right back." Terry ran through the kitchen, skidded, turned around and ran back. "He wants to sleep over!" she said as she took off back across the kitchen.

"What?" Karen hollered behind her. "Oh, no. You are not leavin' me hangin' on that one, little sister."

Terry, not wanting to use the downstairs bathrooms for fear Greg or Henry might walk in, raced up the stairs two at a time with Karen right at her heels. She yanked open the bathroom door, sat down and stared up at Karen. "Do ya mind? I gotta pee," Terry said, starting to laugh.

"Go ahead. I'm not stoppin' ya. I'm your sister, for heaven's sake. Now, what was this about sleeping over? Actually, let's go back to the darlin' bit and work from there," Karen said, leaning against the door jamb.

"Okay, we were talking with Henry over by the water garden. I think the darlin' thing slipped out. He kinda blinked after he said it. BUT, the sleep-over thing is kinda cool. It's not like he wants to sleep with *me*."

"Well, he sure ain't sleepin' with *me*," Karen interjected.

Terry giggled. "Actually, he's kinda sleepin' with Mr. Tea."

"Now, I'm gonna puke," Karen said.

"Not like *that*! He wants to sleep downstairs and see if someone is coming in and messing with the teacups. It's not romantic, not at all, but…well, it's something!"

Karen grinned, put her right arm in the air and waved it around in circles as she sang, "Oh yeah, oh yeah, oh yeah." It was the dance the girls did whenever they conned their parents. It was a victory dance of sorts. This time, Karen added a few pelvic thrust moves to the dance. Then, Karen walked over to Terry, who was still in mid-pee, gave her a high five and left the bathroom, closing the door behind her.

CHAPTER 10

For Terry Sutter, the rest of the day seemed to drag on. She could hardly think. Terry desperately wanted to tell Karen about the note in the garden. The fact that the Dindles went shopping made keeping the secret a little bit easier. Terry thought that if she had to stop herself from blabbing to both Karen *and* Shannon, then she would have needed a tranquilizer.

Uncle Henry treated Terry, Karen and Greg to dinner at the Turkey Turd Lane Pizza Palace. Karen and Terry both brought friends home from college to prove there really was such a place! The land on which it sat was once a turkey farm, thus, the name. It amazed Terry how easily Greg fit in. It was as if he was always a part of the family. Of course, Terry was so nervous during dinner that she accidentally dumped a pitcher of ice water on poor Uncle Henry. She turned bright red and Karen flopped her head into her hands. Terry was pretty sure that at that moment, Aunt Rose caught on and remembered Terry's high school crush on Greg. Rose glanced quickly at Greg and back to Terry. Then she calmly said, "Oh my goodness. Last time, I did the exact same thing! I think they wax these tables."

Henry started to contradict her, but seemed to be silenced by a swift kick under the table from Rose. "Rose, you never—yeeow!—never wax our tables, do you?"

Rose smiled sheepishly and fluffed her hair a bit. "Oh, no, Henry! See what can happen?"

About nine o'clock, the sisters and Greg returned to the teahouse. As they opened the door, Mr. Tea greeted them with, "Welcome home. Don't spill the beans! I know! I know!"

Terry and Greg glanced at each other and blinked in surprise. "Okay," said Greg with a clap of his hands. "Show me this shelf."

Terry turned on the light in the main room and pointed to the shelf. "It's the one in the corner with the two teacups on it," she said.

"Hmmm. Okay, is this blue cup sitting here on the table the one that might be your mother's?"

Terry nodded. "I guess I left it there last night."

"Okiedoke, let's get another cup for the middle shelf. No need to put this one at risk. I'm not expecting anything, but let's be safe."

Karen, who was in the kitchen, called out, "I'll get one!" and she brought out a small pink teacup decorated with roses and ivy.

"One more down. Look out, hottie!" called Mr. Tea.

"I hope you both don't think I'm rude, but after last night, I'm exhausted. I'm going to bed," Karen said with a yawn.

"Actually, I'm beat, too. I'm sorry we're so boring, Greg," Terry said, looking at the teacup on the middle shelf. "I hope there's no excitement tonight. I need a good night's sleep!"

"You two go to bed and relax. I'm sure nothing is going to happen. I'm going to roll out my sleeping bag right here so I can see both entrances to this room."

"I have a blow-up mattress upstairs, if you want to use it," Terry offered.

"Naw, I was a Boy Scout. I'm fine. Don't worry about me."

Terry was getting ready for bed when Karen came into her room. She held up a red and black lace, skimpy teddy. "Okay, Ter, here's the plan. You put this on. I'll wait about five minutes, run out into the hall and scream, 'Fire, fire! Everybody out!' Then you run out of your bedroom, downstairs and jump into Greg's arms."

Terry laughed. "And what happens when he discovers there's no fire?"

"Hmmm. Okay, I'll wait half an hour instead and then I can claim I was sleepwalking. I think he'll buy it!" Karen didn't even crack a smile.

"If you wait half an hour, I'll be fast asleep. Thanks, but…no."

"Spoilsport," Karen said as she theatrically turned her head, flipped her hair and flounced out of the room.

Terry smiled. That was quite a teddy, she thought. I wonder if Karen really wore that thing? I don't own anything like that. Dang! What if something happened during the night? What if she did have to go downstairs? Terry panicked and ran into Karen's room.

"Karen," she said in a whisper, "what if there is a fire…or something? What should I wear?"

Karen started to laugh. "You just asked me what to wear to a fire."

Terry was too panicked to be amused. "You know what I mean. Tonight! What if he sees me tonight?"

Karen stared at her. Terry knew she was trying hard not to laugh. She saw that look before. Once, when Terry was ten years old, Karen and Shannon explained to Terry what sex was. Terry handled it well until the second she realized that, because Terry and Karen weren't adopted, her parents had done this disgusting, horrible thing. Terry remembered looking wide-eyed at Karen. Terry was sure Karen had not figured out this mortifying bit of news. "Karen...do you...well...Mom and Dad..."

"Yeah, Ter, they did it. Get over it!" Karen replied nonchalantly.

"I swear, I cross my heart, I will never, *ever*, do such a disgusting thing!" Terry informed her. Karen looked then as she looked now. She was clearly ready to burst forth with laughter, but, out of loyalty to Terry, held it back.

"Okay, maybe it seems a bit silly," Terry forged on.

"Just a tad," Karen said calmly.

"Well, I just couldn't sleep knowing that, at any moment, I might have to race downstairs in...my shorts and a tee-shirt."

"Would you prefer naked?" Karen asked.

"*Karen...*"

"Relax, for heaven's sake." She walked over to her dresser, rummaged around a bit and held up a short, but nice pink negligee. "Will this do? It even has a nice pink robe to match. Sexy, but conservative." She pulled the pink robe out of her closet. "I think it's what all the women are wearing to nighttime fires these days."

"Why, yes. Yes, it will do quite nicely," Terry said, holding her head up with dignity. She walked over to Karen, snatched the negligee and robe out of her hand, said, "Thank you kindly, madam," and took her turn flouncing theatrically out of the room.

Four pillows fluffed, Karen took out her journal and began to write:

It's really good to be home. Terry seems to need me, and that takes away some of the pain that Todd caused. It's nice to feel needed and appreciated. Watching this possible romance bloom between Greg Mullins and Terry is hard. It reminds me of Todd and me. It reminds me of how innocent I was. Innocent is nice. Terry is innocent. How she made it this long and still kept it is beyond me. So many women our age treat sex as a recreational sport. It isn't something special. To Terry, it is. I guess it was for me too. Cheating on Todd never crossed my mind. I still feel that anger inside whenever I think about what Todd did. And her! How could she have sex with another woman's husband? She knew me! Man, I hate her. I hate him too. Wow, I went from contemplating innocence to hatred. I hope Terry can stay innocent. I would give anything to have my innocence back.

This teacup thing is eerie. I don't want Terry to know how freaked out I am. I'm glad Greg is downstairs. It's nice to feel...protected. Even if it is only for one night.

Karen snuggled into her pillows and drifted of to sleep.

Terry reached under her mattress and pulled out her journal.

I hope I can sleep knowing that Greg Mullins is downstairs. My feelings for him scare me. I remember crying myself to sleep at night in high school when I knew he was dating other girls. I don't want to go through that again. A part of me just wants him to go away. I'm not as strong as Karen is. She doesn't take things as personally as I do. I really love having her back. She's my touchstone. I wish I could have protected her from what Todd did. Of course, I couldn't. No one could. Every life has pain. Two weeks ago, Pastor Bob did a sermon about the consequences of sin. He said that we never sin in isolation. Our sin hurts ourselves and the people around us. I never thought about it before, but he's right. Todd's sin crushed Karen. I wonder if he cares.

I'm falling asleep as I write. I have on Karen's negligee. I wonder if I'll need to run downstairs tonight. I really hope Karen doesn't yell "fire."

Terry tucked the journal back under the mattress. Then, smiling as she remembered Karen's dance that afternoon in the bathroom, Terry fell asleep.

In the silence of the house, the ticking of the clock seemed to echo. Greg lay in his sleeping bag, thinking about the events of the day and the mysterious letter. He wondered if there really was a treasure. Wouldn't it have been discovered by now? How deep were the woods behind the house? It wasn't long until the monotonous ticking of the clock lulled him to sleep.

Suddenly, he was jolted awake. He lay still, trying to figure out what woke him. His heart was hammering. He took slow, deep breaths to quiet his heart so he could listen.

"Hello, ladies. Nice to see you again! It's been years. It's been years," came Mr. Tea's voice.

Greg frowned. Was Mr. Tea talking to Karen and Terry? What a great lookout I am, thought Greg. I didn't even hear them come downstairs. He climbed out of his sleeping bag and went into the parlor. No one was there. What an idiot, being startled awake by a dumb bird! What a pathetic cop I make, he thought to himself. He chuckled, climbed back into his sleeping bag and prepared to go back to sleep. A moment later, the rose and ivy teacup smashed to the floor. Mr. Tea called, "Timberrrrrrrr!"

At that moment, Greg jumped up. Tangled in his sleeping bag, he toppled forward. Ugh! He fought back hard and managed to free himself. That teacup flew off that shelf, he thought, pulse racing. That was no coincidence and no one else is in this house. It's gotta be a ghost. Whoa...I think a ghost just threw a cup at me. With his heart slamming against his chest, he ran up the stairs. As he got halfway up, he remembered that he was the police. What am I doing? he thought as he came to a dead stop. Police detectives don't run in fear to wake up those they are trying to protect, especially when those people are girls. Terry'll think I'm a dork! Dang! Down the stairs he ran and into the parlor. Coming to a halt in front of Mr. Tea's cage, he stared at the bird and the bird stared back.

"Boo!" squawked Mr. Tea.

"Very funny!" Greg's whole body shook. He put his hands on his hips and took a few deeps breaths. Why, oh, why did I give up smoking? Okay, Greg, man, you gotta get it together. Deep breaths. I hate ghosts, he thought. You can't shoot a ghost. You can't tackle a ghost. Who ya gonna call? He smiled for a moment. I need one of those vacuum things they used in that movie. Wow, this is scary.

"I have a secret," replied Mr. Tea.

"Is that supposed to be blackmail?" Greg shook his head. "I'm talking to a bird!"

"Smooth move, Exlax!" Mr. Tea said as he rocked from leg to leg.

"Greg, is everything okay down there!" Terry's voice called from upstairs.

"Heck, no!" squawked Mr. Tea.

"C'mon down, Terry, and...um...could ya hurry!" Dang! Stupid. Now she'll know you're unnerved. Greg clenched his fists in frustration.

Still tying the pink silk robe, Terry padded quickly into the parlor. "Greg, what happened? Is something wrong?"

"That flippin' teacup came flying off the shelf out of thin air and smashed on the floor." Greg gave up the pretext of bravery as he rambled on. "The bird woke me up. I thought you and Karen were downstairs. So I walked in here, saw no one and went back to lie down. I no sooner get comfortable than the cup, Terry, I swear to you, just flew off the shelf and shattered. It didn't topple, it flew! C'mere! " He grabbed her arm and pulled her into the doorway of the tearoom.

"Oh, man," Terry said as she stared at the pieces of the teacup.

As Greg pulled her a foot or two into the room, he said, "Look, if the cup just toppled, it would have landed right beneath the shelf, but it didn't. That sucker flew off the shelf, Ter.   I'm sorry, but I'm, um...baffled." He caught himself from saying scared to death.

"Terry? Greg?" came Karen's voice from the stairs.

"Get down here, Karen. You aren't going to believe this!" Terry's voice shook.

Greg didn't think as he put his arm around Terry and pulled her to him. As Karen came rushing down the stairs, he realized what he'd done. He gave Terry a quick hug and let go. Bird's right, smooth move, he thought to himself.

Terry looked at him, smiled and blushed and tightened the belt to her bathrobe.

Karen looked at the two of them and then her eyes focused on the cup. Her mouth dropped open. "What the fffff– " She stopped and looked around.

"That cup!" Greg pointed to the shards on the floor. "That cup... flew off the shelf," he said. "It didn't topple, it flew." He paused a moment. "Damn it! It flew!"

"That's creepy," Karen said, adding a few curse words.

"Potty mouth!" hollered Mr. Tea.

"Shut up!" Karen and Greg yelled back.

"Get the soap, get the soap," was Mr. Tea's reply.

"I think we need to go in the kitchen and sit down for bit. We're all stunned." Terry said.

This is gonna be one long night, Greg thought as he followed the sisters into the kitchen. I gotta check eBay for a ghost gun!

CHAPTER 11

Henry shook his head as he plodded up the steps to the Historical Society. He got a kick out of Rose. She was on the phone first thing in the morning, getting the scoop on the events from the night before. He tried to get her to wait until the girls called her. Rose paced for twenty minutes, yapped at Henry until his head was dizzy, drank two cups of coffee (as if she needed more adrenaline), and finally, when he could stand it no more, Henry bellowed, "Rosie, for-the-love-of-pizza, call 'em already!"

"I don't want to bother them too early," she said innocently. "Do you think it'll be okay?"

"If you don't call 'em, I'm gonna wake the whole neighborhood when you drive me nuts! You might as well call 'em before the wagon comes to carry me off to the nuthouse!"

"Henry, don't be so dramatic! If you're that worried, I'll call them now." Rose bustled off to the phone, leaving him staring at her, dumbfounded. Somehow, she always turned the tables on him. It was one of her many charms.

Of course, Rose couldn't understand why Henry was so set on getting to the Historical Society as soon as it opened. Since he wasn't at liberty to tell her about the letter they found buried in the yard, he let her spit and sputter at him until he left. She'd get over it. Besides, it was no use sitting around, stewing over the toppling cup. Henry couldn't help wonder if one thing connected with another. But it made no sense for old man Hamilton to be knocking teacups off shelves, especially now. If he haunted the house, things would have happened long before this. Henry was sure Madeline would have told Rose if she thought the house was haunted. Maybe the events of the last few weeks were all independent of each other, but then again...

Being president of the Historical Society had its advantages. Henry knew where everything was in the building and who in town to ask if he needed more information. He started with the files. Opening the drawer marked 'H,' he thumbed through until he found the file marked 'Hamilton.' Inside was a list of items held by the society and where they could be found. Item number seven:

invitation written by Beauregard Hamilton Sr. inviting town members to Christmas Party. Original in artifact file located in library. Also found in town journal dated November 21, 1933. Journals on microfilm in library.

Henry went into the library and got the invitation from the file. Pulling the handwritten poem from his shirt breast pocket, he put the two side by side. The writing seemed identical. Not only were the letters shaped the same, but both had their *t*s crossed with a slanted line. Of course, it was possible that someone wrote the letter as a prank. Yet, it was highly unlikely that person would try to copy the writing so perfectly. He'd have to have Greg take a look at it. Perhaps he'd sign out the letter and show it to Greg.

Henry stared around the room, not really looking for anything, just thinking. When was it that Thurston died? Hmmm, maybe forty-three years ago. Yeah, he was about the same age as Carl, so.... Henry went to the microfilm files and pulled out the appropriate reels. After a few minutes of looking, he found the headline:

THURSTON HAMILTON FOUND SHOT TO DEATH NEAR FAMILY VACATION PROPERTY.

Thurston Hamilton, only child of Beauregard Hamilton, Jr. was found by his two friends, Carl Despard and Samuel Brinker . It appears to be a hunting accident. Family and friends are in shock.

Henry's hand slipped a bit and he hit the rewind button. He stopped it quickly and began to slowly fast forward. His eye caught the blurry image of another headline. He stopped and focused the image.

ELDERLY WOMEN MISSING—NO SIGN OF FOUL PLAY.

Relatives and friends are unable to determine the whereabouts of two sisters, Eloise and Mary Gutherie. They were last seen five days ago. Although their car remains on their property, there is no sign of foul play. If anyone has information about their whereabouts, please contact local police.

Henry looked at the pictures accompanying the story. One picture showed Mary and Eloise posing in front of their house. It looked as if it was taken in the spring, perhaps on Easter. The women were dressed up, wearing pearl necklaces and white gloves. In another picture, the women hosted a Christmas party. The sisters were in front of their Christmas tree, raising their glasses in a toast. The room was filled with people from town that Henry remembered.

Then Henry caught his breath. It was impossible, it couldn't…well it could, but…. He grabbed the nearby magnifying glass which was kept on hand for situations such as this one. Carefully, he examined the photo. He pushed the button to enlarge the image and examined the photo with the magnifying glass again. Hmmm.... Henry stood and reached into his pants pocket and pulled out his cell phone. He thought for a moment, trying to recall the number. He dialed.

"Detective Mullins," said the voice on the other end of the line.

"Hello, Greg? It's Henry Sanders. Do you have time to come over to the Historical Society? I have something to show you that's pretty interesting."

"Is something wrong?"

No, not at all. I have something just pretty darn interesting I want you to see."

"How's twenty minutes, Mr. Sanders?"

"Henry, please. Twenty minutes? Sure, see you then."

Henry sat down and looked at the picture again...maybe, just maybe. Could the bird, whose cage sat on a table in the Gutherie's house, be Mr. Tea? The woman standing to the right of the cage looked like Silvia Nitmeyer. Curiouser and curiouser, thought Henry.

As Greg left the station, he wondered what Henry found. Greg assumed it was related to either the letter or the teacup. He smiled as he realized that this little mystery was the most interesting case to come his way in years. Once upon a time, in his late twenties, he imagined that being a police detective would mean lots of excitement and intrigue. However, in this small section of Maine, not much happened. There were a few burglaries involving the jewels of the very wealthy, but those seemed to be the perks of an otherwise routine fare of petty thefts from tourists at local hotels. Once it looked as if a child, Robert Smyth IV, of a wealthy hotel owner, Robert Smyth III, was kidnapped. Fortunately for the family, but unfortunately for Greg's want of excitement, the child was hiding out in a friend's treehouse, pouting over being refused a new pony. Yep, Greg admitted, the case of the tumbling teacup was livening things up.

Eighteen minutes later, Greg walked up the steps to the Historical Society. Henry greeted him at the door.

"C'mon in. Wait 'till you see what I found!" Henry sounded quite excited.

"Is it a match on the letter?" Greg asked.

"Well, yeah, that too. However, there's something that may shed some light on the events of last night." Henry practically dragged Greg into the library. He took him over to the microfilm machine. "Greg, this is a picture taken of the two women that disappeared, the ones who lived in the Dindle's house—the Gutherie sisters. Take this magnifying glass and look in the corner here."

Greg scowled in confusion. What could this possibly have to do with the teacup? He squinted at the image. "Hold on...you aren't thinking...there's no way. Do you think that bird is Mr. Tea?"

"Heck, yeah! Look at the bird's eye. See that little black dot next to the right eye? Mr. Tea has that. Look at the cage. It's got to be the same one."

Greg smiled. "Henry, this is a picture in a newspaper. That black dot could be newsprint...anything. I'll give you the fact that the cage looks similar. However, plenty of people could have a cage like that for a parrot."

"Plenty of people have a wooden platform like that? That's one fancy cage! Now, look over here. Do you know who that woman is?" Henry pointed to a woman wearing a long dress. She stood to the left of the cage.

"No, not a clue."

"It's Silvia Nitmeyer, the psychic! She knew those women! I think Mr. Tea was their bird! This type of bird can live to be well over one-hundred years old. This picture is only forty-three years old. I think it's the sisters who are haunting the house. That's why Mr. Tea said, 'Hello ladies.'"

"Whoa there. I don't think the bird was talking to anyone. I think it was coincidence. Yes, the cup thing was freaky, very freaky, but let's not get ahead of ourselves." Greg shook his head and ran his fingers through his hair.

Henry looked at Greg. Greg noticed how hurt he seemed. "Well, Henry, I'll tell you what. We can ask around and see if anyone knows where Mrs. Nitmeyer got the bird. I could be wrong. Maybe that is Mr. Tea."

Henry seemed to perk up a bit. "Now, come look at the handwriting sample I have. Looks similar to me."

He led Greg over to the filing cabinet and, taking the original letter from the file, Henry put the two samples side by side on top of the cabinet. "Looks like a match to me. Whaddaya think?"

"Yeah, could very well be. Enough of a match that my curiosity is aroused, anyway," Greg said.

"I'm gonna make copies of the things I found. I want to show Rosey and everyone else the pictures. I won't show 'em the letter yet. I'll wait until we can tell 'em about the poem."

"Good idea. Why don't we see if his son is still alive? He might know something. Of course, we could be opening a can of worms, but a hidden treasure is pretty intriguing. This is the kinda stuff little boys dream of!" Let alone slightly bored detectives, thought Greg.

"Any chance to feel like a kid again is okay by me! At my age, every opportunity is worth taking. Hey, wanna hear about my pranks on Dottie Dindle?"

Laughing, the two men made the copies, returned the materials and exited the building. As Greg got into his cruiser, he noticed his sides hurt. He realized that, although he worked out at the gym at least five times a week, his laugh muscles needed more of a regular workout. He needed more people like Henry in his life, or perhaps just more of Henry.

CHAPTER 12

"Where've you been?" Tom O'Hara asked when Greg was back at his desk. "You left me a note saying you have a freaky story to tell me, and then you go AWOL. Don't do that to me!"

"Well, buddy boy, it just got better. I've a bunch to tell you," Greg said as he whacked Tom on the back. "You won't believe it." Greg glanced at his watch. "It's lunch time. Wanna go AWOL with me to the deli down the street? I'll buy."

"Sounds good to me," Tom said.

As they walked out the door, Greg said, "I never believed much in ghosts. Angels, yeah, not ghosts, but I'm inclined to change my mind!"

Greg smiled as Tom O'Hara sat back in his seat and sighed. "Wow, that is one incredible story! I would've needed a change of underwear when that cup flew off the shelf! How are Terry and Karen Sutter doing? Man!"

"I think they're numb like I am. It was freaky, waiting for them to get up this morning. I didn't sleep a wink after they went back upstairs to try and get some rest. I hit the kitchen pronto and made coffee." Greg finished his soda.

"Do you think the break-in could be related to all this?" Tom asked

"I really don't know what fits where. To begin with, what's the scoop on the teacup? Why knock a cup off of shelf? None of it makes sense. Of course, it's possible there is no reason involved. I don't recall a rule that ghosts have to be reasonable."

"What about the treasure note? Are you gonna do something with that?"

"I want to see if the son is still alive. He might be able to offer some insight. I'm pretty sure I heard Henry say something about them having a house on the shore." Greg took out his wallet and left money on the table.

As they headed back to the office, Tom said, "It certainly won't hurt to check our data base. By the way, it sure would be a hoot if that was the same bird!"

Back at his desk, Greg sat, tapping his pencil on the blotter while he stared into space. He couldn't put the toppling cup out of his mind. Why was this happening now? Why only knock cups off the middle shelf? Was it Madeline Sutter or someone else? Could it be the elderly sisters who disappeared? Was he nuts to be thinking about ghosts? His grandmother's story of an angel was one thing, but ghosts… Greg took a sip of coffee and stretched. No, the cup flew off that shelf. There didn't seem to be any other logical explanation. Logical? Greg shook his head. He understood how Terry felt. As logical or illogical as it might be, the ghost theory seemed to fit. He shrugged. Ghosts it was, until something proved otherwise. He continued to turn things around and around in his mind. Was the cup Rose found Madeline's cup? Flipping through his Rolodex, he found her number and dialed.

"Hello," said Rose's cheery voice

"Mrs. Sanders? This is Greg Mullins. Ma'am, can you tell me where you got the teacup that Terry thinks was her mother's cup?"

"Oh…sure. I got it at the Goodwill store in town. Why?"

"I want to see if I can find some more," Greg white-lied.

"Well, dear, I looked that day. The woman said that was the only one. Henry and I are planning to do dinner here again tonight for everyone. It seems the least we can do with all that's going on. I hope you'll join us. You seem to fit right in."

"I'd love to come for dinner. That's really nice of you. Same time as last night?"

"Yes, see you then, dear."

After hanging up, Greg felt himself smiling. He really enjoyed their company. He felt a twinge of sadness as he realized the mystery couldn't go on forever. Taking his keys, he headed out the door.

"More ghost busting?" Tom O'Hara called after him.

"Maybe. I guess this is considered background checking." With a wave, he was on his way to the Goodwill store.

The store was in a small strip mall. It had a white brick facade. As he walked in, Greg was shocked at how small and cluttered it was. There were household items in the front and clothes in the back. A small woman with graying hair pulled back in a ponytail stood behind the counter. "Can I help you, officer?" she asked in a gentle voice.

"I hope so, ma'am. I'm trying to track down the origins of a teacup that was purchased here on Saturday. It was white and blue..."

"Oh yes, I think I know just the cup. The woman said her sister had one just like it."

"That sounds like the one I'm talking about. Do you know where it came from?"

The woman smoothed her dress and smiled. "Why, yes, I do. Sort of. It was in a box that was left by the back door. It contained the cup and a few dresses. As a matter of fact, see that pink and white dress I've put on display over there?" She pointed to a dress tacked up on the wall with coordinating shoes and a purse on the shelf directly below it. "That dress was in the box. I think the others have been sold. That's all I know. I have no idea who left the box. I just know that cup was in it. I remember because it seemed odd to me that there was only one. Most people drop things like that off in sets. I didn't really expect the cup to sell. The woman who bought it was one of the happiest customers I've had in this store. She was so thrilled, she almost cried. I mean that literally. Her eyes teared right up."

Greg looked at the dress on the wall. It seemed vaguely familiar to him. Where had he seen it before? He realized the woman was looking at him...waiting. "Well, thank you, ma'am. At least it's something. If you think of anything else, here's my card, please give me a call."

The woman looked at the card and frowned. "Is there something wrong? Was the cup stolen?"

"Oh, no, nothing like that." He thought quickly. "I'm a friend of the family. I just wanted to try and get more like it. Thank you for your help."

"You're welcome, officer. I'll call you if any more come in like that one. Have a nice day." She waved as Greg left the shop. He was sure he saw that dress before...but where? He turned around and went back in the store.

"Ma'am, I'd like to buy the dress that was in the box with the cup." You never know when something like this might come in handy, thought Greg. If not, I'll just give it to my grandmother.

Terry sighed. It was a long day. She was grateful for the fact that the shop was busy enough to keep her from thinking about the cup, but not so busy, she was stressed out. As the last customers left, Terry took some peanuts and headed for the front door. She turned the sign to 'closed' and locked the door.

"Pooped parrot!" called Mr. Tea.

Terry smiled. Bringing him home turned out to be a great idea. She noticed people around him or talking about him all day. He was quite a conversation piece. Like her, people where amazed at some of the comments he made. It really seemed like he understood. Of course, he didn't, but it sure seemed that way. She walked to his cage. "Oh, poor Mr. Tea. People have been ogling you and talking to you all day long. It's tough to be the mascot, huh?"

"Polly want a cracker? Polly who?" said the bird.

Terry burst out laughing. She heard people say that to him repeatedly. "Sorry, buddy. I put a sign right here that says 'Mr. Tea.' I tried. I guess people think every Macaw is a Polly."

The bird blinked.

"I have an idea." Terry took off her apron and folded it over her arm. Opening the cage door, she put her arm next to the bird like the woman at the convalescent home. When Terry and Karen went back to get Mr. Tea, one of the nurses showed her how to handle him. The woman was amazing with him and Terry wanted to try.

"Step up," she said, her heart pounding. Mr. Tea stepped onto her arm. Carefully, she moved her arm out of the cage. "There you go! Look, I've got a treat for you!" She reached into her pocket and took out a peanut.

"Hot diggity!   Kisses for peanuts, kisses for peanuts," Mr. Tea said, rocking from foot to foot.

Just like the nurse, Terry put the peanut in her mouth and leaned toward the bird. He gently took it from her mouth. She held her free hand under his beak. He cracked the peanut and let some of it fall into her hand. Then, he ate the pieces she held for him. When he was done, he leaned his head forward. Terry did the same. Very gently, he gave her a peck on the cheek. "Kissy, kissy," he said.

Terry was delighted. She put her arm up so he could move to her shoulder. She heard Karen come into the parlor.

"Wow, you're braver then I am. He looks so cool, sitting on your shoulder."

"Handsome dude," he squawked.

Both girls laughed. "Okay, you're one handsome dude sitting on her shoulder, Mr. Tea. Ter, Aunt Rose is insisting on drinks and dinner again. She says she talked to Greg today and invited him too. After last night, I'm surprised he wants to come within ten yards of this place."

Terry carefully lowered herself onto the sofa. Mr. Tea stepped off her shoulder onto the sofa back. He stayed right next to her. "I have a secret," he said.

Terry turned her head and looked at him. "I'm sure you do," she said. Looking back at Karen, she said, "Greg told me this morning he wants to try putting Mom's cup on the shelf. I don't think I want to take that risk. I guess I don't know what I want to do."

"I have a secret. Kisses for peanuts," Mr. Tea called out. "Buried in the sand, greedy, greedy." He rocked from foot to foot, then climbed back on Terry's shoulder. "Ding Dong Dell."

"Do you ever give it a rest?" Karen snapped.

"Kiss the tail feathers," replied Mr. Tea.

Terry stifled a laugh. "Okay, my pooped parrot. Time to put you back in your house. I'll give you some peanuts. You're such a good boy!"

"Good boy? He's gonna be parrot soup pretty soon," Karen said, putting her hands on her hips.

"Yakkity yak," was Mr. Tea's response.

Terry gave him a peanut and shut the cage door. "He really was quite a hit today. He behaved well, considering more then half the visitors insisted on calling him Polly."

Karen smiled. "Yeah, he is a cute little guy. He does grow on ya."

"Pucker up, buttercup," Mr. Tea piped in.

"Yoooohoooo," came Rose's voice from the kitchen. "Anybody here?"

"Gotta remember to lock that door," Karen said, smiling at Terry as they headed toward the kitchen.

Terry winked and added, "At least we can put Mr. Tea in a cage."

Karen sat staring at Mr. Tea who calmly stared back. She glanced at her watch again; it was almost six o'clock. She despised waiting. She always tried to dawdle so she could be the last one ready and thus avoid doing exactly what she was presently doing. In the past few months, silence became her enemy. It gave her time to think and reflect and those were things she didn't want to do.

"Penny for your thoughts," squawked Mr. Tea.

"I'm afraid you'd lose on that deal, buddy. My thoughts aren't worth much these days." She winked at the bird and was surprised when he winked back. She giggled.

"I'm your man," said Mr. Tea.

"Well, you would certainly be an improvement over the old one," said Karen with a sigh. "You're in a cage, so at least you can't cheat. You're definitely a better listener." A wave of sadness caught in her throat. My goodness, she thought. I've begun talking to a bird.

"Loyal friend. Loyal friend," added Mr. Tea.

"Thanks, I need one." Karen got up and went to the foot of the stairs. "Ter, what's the hold up?"

"I'm coming. Give me a break. I'm having trouble deciding what to wear."

Karen rolled her eyes. "For Pete's sake, Terry Ann. This isn't the prom. Throw on some shorts and a top and get down here!" Karen reflected that Terry never did have a grasp of how pretty she was. She was always insecure around men. It was probably her insecurities that kept her single all these years. One the other hand, mused Karen, maybe I should have taken a few lessons. I would have saved myself some heartache.

"Patience is a virtue," piped Mr. Tea.

"Well, not one of mine! Who asked you anyway, you nosy bird?"

Mr. Tea rocked from foot to foot, stopped and looked in his mirror. "Pretty bird. Handsome dude. Full package."

Karen laughed and sat back down. She wondered what Todd was doing. Was he with *her*? Perhaps there was another *her*. Did he even know Karen left? He knew she quit her job and was planning on moving. Did he think about her? Did he even care that their marriage was over? Did it even matter?

The flip, flip, flip of Terry's shoes on the stairs brought her mind back to the present. Man, she thought, I have to quit doing that. It doesn't help. Out of sight, out of mind. At least, that was the plan.

"Hey, cute outfit, toots," she said to Terry. "I like that shade of blue on you. Wow, even your flip-flops match. You got it goin' on, girl!"

Terry laughed. "Ya know, I sort of wish Rose didn't invite Greg over. I like 'im, obviously, but I get nervous around him. My stomach can't take much more."

"You need to relax. You can't, and shouldn't even try, to be anything other than who you are. Be yourself and if something happens, then great."

"If not, I cry myself to sleep like I did in high school," Terry chimed in. "No, thank you. I promised myself when I went to college that I was never going to do that again."

"So....what? You don't date, don't take a chance?" Karen asked, locking the back door.

"I guess that's pretty much it." Terry looked sadly at Karen. "I really loathe pain."

Karen shrugged. She was the last person who should give advice about men. Still, she hated the thought of never loving again. It was certainly safer, but was it wiser?

As they reached the gate between the houses, Karen saw Greg standing next to Henry on the porch. His eyes lit up and he smiled when he saw Terry. Had Todd looked at her that way, once? What made one marriage a success and another fail? Don't go there, girlfriend, she said to herself. Don't go there.

Rose came out the sliding door as the girls came into the yard. Karen looked sad for a brief moment and then, as if a mask were applied, her expression changed. She wasn't happy or sad. Karen seemed, despite her smile, stuck in neutral. Oh, Maddy, thought Rose, what are we going to do without you? You were such a natural mother. It came so easy to you. I feel so…inept.

"Hello, my darlings," cooed Rose. She thought they looked exhausted, but she caught herself from saying so. "I hope you're hungry! Henry cooked a chicken on the grill's rotisserie. I made summer squash casserole, baked potatoes and ice cream cake for dessert. The Dindles are coming, too. They should be here momentarily."

As if on cue, Shannon and Dottie came through the gate. "Hello, hello. Long time, no see," said Shannon.

"Aren't you sick of us yet?" Dottie asked.

"Oh, of course not. Don't be ridiculous," Terry said, pouring a margarita and handing it to Shannon.

Rose watched Dottie settle into a chair. Shannon poured lemonade for her. In the past few months, Rose noticed that Dottie seemed slower, easily tired…older. This frightened Rose. After all, they were the same age. Maddie's death made Rose more aware of her own mortality. She had friends that were in Fair Meadows, either convalescing or in the apartments. She tried not to think too much about it, but sooner or later….

"Earth to Rose, come in." Henry chuckled. "You enjoying your trip? Got room for passengers?"

"I didn't go anywhere!" she snapped, embarrassed. "I was just reflecting on Dottie's dress. It's such a lovely shade of yellow."

"Why, thank you, Rose. It's nice to be admired every now and then." Dottie glowed from the compliment.

"Hey, speaking of dresses," chimed in Greg. "I brought a dress I want you all to see."

"Whoa there, sonny," said Henry. "I can't deal with that kinda stuff!"

Greg laughed. "Not for me, Henry! I stopped at the Goodwill today and the clerk said this dress was in the box with the cup Rose bought. Hold on." Greg went over to a corner of the porch and pulled the dress from a bag. "Does this look familiar to anyone?"

Nobody said anything for a few moments. Finally, Rose said, "I swear I've seen it before. I just can't place it. It isn't Maddie's. It's too big for her. Dottie, do you recognize it?"

"I can't say. For some reason, I think whoever wore it, wore a hat with it."

"Yes!" Rose pointed her finger in the air. "It was a white hat with small flowers that matched the dress."

"Exactly! Now where did I see it?" Dottie frowned in thought.

"How can you possibly remember something like that?" Karen laughed. "I couldn't tell you what any of us wore yesterday!"

"I guess we don't get out much." Dottie shrugged. "I can't remember what I wore yesterday, but for some reason, that dress and hat are familiar."

"Gosh, it's going to bother me until I remember." Rose put her hands on her hips. Hmmm, it was a special occasion. Was it on someone I knew, or did I just admire it? Is it a dress that only looks similar to one I've seen?"

"Aunt Rose, don't think about it. Think about something else and it will come to you." Terry stood up and poured herself another margarita.

"Greg, I'll have Rosie call you when she remembers at four a.m." Henry opened the top to the grill and basted the chicken.

"We were all up last night, tonight can be Aunt Rose's turn," Karen said with a yawn. "Which reminds me. Have we decided what to do about our problem teacup tonight? Personally, I say take all the cups off of it, at least for tonight."

"What if you brought the teacup over here?" Rose asked.

"Cups were falling off that shelf before you found that one," Terry said.

"Oh, dear, I guess they were. I forgot about that. Well, I guess I have to agree with Karen, then. The only problem has been the teacup on the middle shelf, right?"

"As far as I know," Terry said. "Anything more and I would be having a breakdown. Actually, that's not true, about the cup on the shelf. When I put the cup that might be Mom's on the top shelf, it moved to the table. That happened two days ago. After last night, it seems like a millennium.

"Chicken's ready, folks," Henry called, interrupting, as he removed the chicken to a platter.

Rose went in to get the rest of the food; the girls and Greg followed her. Dottie Dindle attempted to get up, but Rose told her to stay put.

Terry looked around the patio table. Everyone was momentarily in a silent reverie. Terry remembered her mother making the squash casserole. Anytime there was a picnic, people asked Maddie to bring it. Summer always meant squash casserole. The casserole without her mother seemed…out of place and wrong. The dark empty place inside of Terry seemed to expand. She put her fork down and took a gulp of her margarita. Her appetite seemed to get lost in the darkness inside. Terry didn't know how to handle the moment. She didn't want to hurt Rose's feelings, but she didn't want to eat, either.

"Where did Mom get this squash recipe, Aunt Rose?" Karen broke the silence.

Great minds think alike, thought Terry. Isn't it funny how food can trigger a memory?

"From Emily Landick's mother. By the way, I got a card from her the other day. She asked how we were all doing. Even though she lives two hours away, she and Maddie talked at least twice a week. I think you girls should call and invite her to the teahouse. She'd love to see it." Turning to Dottie, Rose said, "Dottie, do you remember Emily Landick? Her married name is Hammer. She and Maddie were inseparable as kids. Her sister, Bessie, was in our class."

"Oh, yes, I'm pretty sure I remember Emily. She had pretty gold curls, if I remember correctly."

"Yes, that's her. Right after Maddie got married, she called Mrs. Landick and asked for the recipe. The funny thing is that Bessie and Emily hated it. Our family loved it. Mrs. Landick was thrilled to know someone enjoyed it. I think she got the recipe from her mother."

"Wow, I love it, too," Greg added.

Terry felt, irrationally, that she wanted to throw the casserole at the wall. It reminded her of her mother— her smile, her voice, her touch, her laugh and even her smell. She felt tears welling up in her eyes. Mortified, she faked a coughing fit and excused herself. In the kitchen, she took a deep breath. The tears wouldn't be held back. It was as if they had a mind of their own. She put her hand on the counter and closed her eyes, trying to shove the grief back down inside. Suddenly, she was aware of someone else in the kitchen. She stiffened.

"Awe, kiddo, grief is hard," Henry whispered as he put his arms around her. Terry buried her head in his shoulder and let the tears flow.

Greg couldn't help but notice Terry's eyes as she returned. Henry came out a few moments before, announcing that she seemed to be okay, "just a coughing spasm," he said. As she sat down, her eyes lowered, Greg ached for her. He lost his father six years ago and the memories were still fresh. He felt like an intruder, yet at the same time, he wished he could comfort her.

"We never did settle on what to do with the teacup. I think it's best to remove all the cups from the shelf for tonight. You can put them back on in the morning. Perhaps, if we give it a few days, the mystery will solve itself." Greg hoped he was comforting Terry, not upsetting her more by bringing up the cup.

Karen smiled. "Okay, we all seem to agree. The cups come off the shelf for tonight. If anyone has a problem with that, speak now or forever hold your peace."

No one spoke.

"Done!" Karen said, gently hitting fist on the table.

"Henry," Dottie said, "I've been meaning to ask you since our conversation the other night. Was it ever proven that Beauregard Hamilton, Sr. was really a bank robber or was that a rumor?"

"I'm not really sure. I think it was unsubstantiated, but, as kids, we took it as fact. I think I'll go to the library tomorrow and dig around. That's an interesting question, Dottie. It'll be fun to see what I can find."

There was a rustle by the bushes at the side of the porch. Greg turned and saw Carl Despard.

"Hello, all. I hope I'm not interrupting dinner. I was in the neighborhood and I thought I would stop by and see if tomorrow would be a good day to bring my mother to the teahouse. I want to pick a day that isn't too crowded. She moves a bit slower these days."

"Tomorrow is fine. It'll be fun to have her," Terry said.

"Carl, please sit and have some dessert with us," Rose said as she and the girls began to clear the table.

"Oh, that's very nice of you, but I want to get to Fair Meadows and see my mother. I'll take a rain check, though."

Greg watched as Carl, with one leg on the porch step, turned to leave. Greg noticed a flash of fear cross Carl's face. Following his gaze, Greg swore he was looking at the dress that was hung over the white rocker. Greg sat forward, preparing to ask Carl if he recognized the dress, but Karen interrupted.

"Carl, can you bring your mom in around one o'clock? That seems like a good time, huh, Ter?"

"Perfect."

"Would tomorrow be a good time to bring my grandmother, too?" Greg asked. He wanted to have time to watch Carl some more.

"Sure, the more the merrier," Terry said.

Greg watched as Carl took another quick glance at the dress before he left. Things around here get curiouser and curiouser, thought Greg.

A few hours later, after the cups were all safely put away for the night, and Greg checked all the windows and doors before he left, Terry sat quietly propped up in bed. She took her journal and began to write.

Dear Mom,
I need to tell you how much I miss you. If I don't write it down, I think I'll implode. We had your squash casserole tonight. I know that Rose has made it many

times over the years, but tonight, it really upset me. I felt for a moment as if I could touch you and I ached that I couldn't. I expected to see you sitting there with us.

Mom, I don't know what to do about Greg. You and Daddy, Rose and Henry were all happily married. I'm not saying I'm going to marry Greg. I just wonder if the pain of unrequited love is worth the try. This is the kind of stuff you were good about answering. Karen's divorce shocked and scared me. She and Todd seemed so devoted when they got married. I used to like Todd, but now all I feel is hatred. I hate him because he betrayed my sister. Did you hate him? It's funny, you and I never talked about it. Did you and Karen talk about it? I know I could ask her, but I don't like seeing the pain in her eyes. So, anyway, I'm confused. I miss you and all the wisdom you had. I don't think I can ever get over losing you. I know I've written that before, but it helps to tell you again.

-Terry

p.s. If it's you knocking the cups off the shelf, I wish you'd find another way to get your point across. Whatever your point may be, I'm not sure. I hope you don't mind me taking all the cups down tonight. If it isn't you, could you tell whomever it is to knock it off?

Terry giggled to herself as she remembered her ninja act from a few nights before. She turned off her light.

In the stillness, she heard Mr. Tea squawk, "Sleep tight."

"You, too," she called out.

"Goodnight, John Boy," Karen yelled out.

CHAPTER 13

Henry, his curiosity in high gear, was up and out early in the morning and walking through the doors of the library when it opened at eight. His goal was to dig up every bit of information he could find on the Hamilton family. He hoped by using the Internet to search and the archives of the local newspaper, which dated back to 1850, he could get enough information to either support or refute the theory that the Hamilton family fortune came from bank robbery.

"Good morning, Henry, what brings you here first thing?" Marilyn Niles, the town librarian, asked. Now in her fifties, Marilyn had been the town librarian for the last thirty years. She knew everyone in town and everything about them as well. Henry knew she wasn't one to repeat gossip. She just soaked in whatever she heard and saw. Whenever there was a need in town, from casseroles for new mothers to holiday baskets for the poor, Marilyn Niles made sure everyone was cared for. It was as if she considered herself the guardian angel of the town. Henry thought she was one of the kindest people he ever met.

"Good morning, Ms. Marilyn. I'm just here to do some research. My nieces are curious about the history of their house, tourists have asked some questions, and I decided I wanted to dig around and see what I can find. Any ideas?" Henry knew Marilyn was as bright as she was kind.

"Hmmm, let me think a moment. That house has been here since the 1800s. I'm quite sure you know the gossip about bank robberies being the origin of their money. I could be mistaken, but I'm pretty sure the state library photograph collection, that you can get to online, has some pictures of it just after it was built. Of course, we have the archives of the newspaper as well, but the historical society has them, too. Have you gone through those?"

"I was at the Historical Society yesterday and did a bit of digging. I confess an article on the disappearance of the Gutherie sisters, the elderly women who lived next door, sidetracked me. I ran out of time there. I decided I'd try here today."

"Oh, those poor women. You know, my mother was a friend of theirs. She was just sick when they turned up missing. She still swears something must have happened to them. They weren't the kind to just up and disappear."

"The article in the newspaper said there was no sign of foul play." Henry hoped she could give him more information than the paper.

"I don't care what the paper said. My mother says that she talked to them just the day before and they didn't say a word about going anywhere. Besides, they had a pet parrot that they adored. They never would have left him behind."

Bingo! thought Henry. "What happened to the bird?"

"Mrs. Nitmeyer took him. She swore he was psychic. Hey, didn't I hear that your nieces took him from Fair Meadows?"

"That's the same bird?" Henry asked, trying to sound totally surprised.

"Absolutely, isn't that funny how life works out? That macaw is living right next door to where he started out."

"You don't happen to know what they called him, do you? The girls have named him Mr. Tea, spelled 't-e-a,' get it?"

"How adorable! No, I don't remember what they named him. If you're going to be here awhile, I'll call my mother and see if she remembers. I can't wait to tell her what your nieces named him. By the way, Mother and I went to their teahouse a week ago. It was splendid. Terry is such a talented artist."

"Thank you, yes, she is. I should be here for a while. I guess I'll try looking at the photographs online. I confess, though, I'm not really good at the computer. I guess I'm showing my age."

Marilyn smiled. "I'll be happy to help you. C'mon over here to this computer and I'll get you started."

An hour later, Henry was pleased with himself. He knew he had quite a bit to learn about computers, but he did understand the concept of a search engine. Henry thought Google was one of the most amazing things he ever came across. First, under the direction of Marilyn, he started with the online photos. There, he found a picture of old Mr. Hamilton with his father, Rochester Hamilton. Mr. Hamilton, Beauregard Sr., looked to be around ten years old. They were standing in front of the house as it was being built. Henry couldn't tell where the photograph came from. It simply read,

Rochester Hamilton and his son Beauregard watch as their new home is built. The Hamiltons originally came from Connecticut. Photograph circa 1890.

Henry thought for a moment, and then he remembered Marilyn showing him how to use Google. Henry went to the site and typed, "Connecticut bank robberies."
Voilà, up popped pages of entries. Henry carefully

looked them over. At first, it didn't look promising. Then, on the third page listing of sites was one that caught Henry's eye. Someone had actually created a site noting various bank robberies that occurred in Connecticut prior to the 1900s. It also contained information on bank robbers, some known and some unknown. It contained photographs and drawings that dated back to around 1850. Henry was so intrigued that he momentarily forgot why he was at the site to begin with. Then, a piece of information caught his eye. A series of well-planned robberies occurred in central Connecticut from approximately 1870 until 1890 when they mysteriously stopped. Using various methods, the group robbed a number of banks. Interestingly, all of the robberies occurred within half an hour of the bank's closing. The last robbery occurred in May of 1890. A hat was found sitting in the middle of the floor of the last bank. A wood engraving showed a man placing his hat in the middle of a bank floor. The engraving was entitled "Farewell." There was a photograph of the hat. It was simply an old and battered cowboy style hat with part of the brim missing. Henry's heart beat faster. He stared at the computer. Then he turned and called, "Marilyn, how do I print a photo?"

Within an hour, Henry was headed home with two photographs: one of an old battered cowboy hat, and another of the Hamiltons watching their house being built. In Rochester Hamilton's hand was a hat...with part of the brim missing.

As Henry walked by the checkout desk on his way to the front door, Marilyn looked up from checking out a book and smiled. "Henry, I just talked to my mother. The women called the bird Ladies' Man because he was fond of saying, 'hello, ladies,' whenever they entered the room."

Henry smiled and with a wave, he called out over his shoulder, "He still is, Marilyn, he still is."

Terry heard the front door chimes jingle. Wiping her hands on her apron, Terry looked at the clock, 1:00. As she walked through the teahouse, she could hear the chatter of Karen, Mrs. Despard and some other senior citizens. Terry felt a ripple of excitement. She looked forward to this for weeks, a chance to share her precious teahouse with people like Mrs. Despard who were such a special part of her childhood.   As Terry walked into the parlor, she heard Mrs. Despard saying, "...all grown up and successful business women to boot, my, my, my."

"Hello, ladies," said Terry.

"Oh, Terry, what an incredible job you've done. Your parents would be so proud of both you girls. Let me introduce you to some of the ladies from Fair Meadows. This is Clair Granger; I think her children are a little older than you girls." A small plump woman with dark gray hair reached out to shake hands with Terry and Karen.

"Of course we remember Mrs. Granger. Who could forget the high school principal's secretary who kept a jar of butterscotch candies on her desk? It's so nice to see you, isn't it, Karen?" Terry shook Mrs. Granger's hand, purposely avoiding remarking about her children. Pamela and Samantha Granger were the loosest girls in the school. Pam was in Karen's class and Samantha graduated two years earlier, but her reputation was well known. If a guy couldn't get any from the Granger sisters, assuming he wanted some, he would either have to remain a virgin forever or pay for it.

" I do believe my daughter Pam was in your class, wasn't she, Karen?"

"Yes, she was in my graduating class. How is she?"

"Oh, just wonderful," Mrs. Granger beamed. "She's a lawyer in Vermont. She's up for partner. I'm so proud of her. Samantha married a plastic surgeon and lives in Kennybunk. She has three children who are just the dearest things!"

"How wonderful," Karen said, turning to the other woman with Mrs. Despard. Terry knew Karen well enough to know that she was trying to avoid encouraging Mrs. Granger to pull out pictures of her grandchildren. Karen probably didn't want to be reminded of her own lack of children and failed marriage.

"And I know who this lovely woman is," Karen said. "I'd never forget my fourth grade teacher, Mrs. Hosey." The short woman with white hair and penciled brown eyebrows smiled.

"Karen, you've become such a lovely woman!" Mrs. Hosey gushed.

"Wasn't I a lovely child?"

"No, dear, you were a pill with pigtails that rivaled Pippy Longstocking's," Mrs. Hosey said in a loving tone and a smile on her face. Everyone laughed, but Terry knew it was the truth. The teacher continued. "I still remember you giving Josh Clover a bloody nose."

"Well," Karen smiled, "he never pulled my pigtails again, now did he?"

"Carl, it was so nice of you to bring these wonderful ladies," Terry said. Poor Carl, she thought, he looks bored to tears.

"No problem. I've been away for almost two weeks. My mother really needed a day out. What place better than the talk of the town?"

"Remember me?" Mr. Tea squawked. Everyone looked over at the bird.

"Oh," said Mrs. Granger, clapping her hands. "Silvia Nitmeyer's macaw. We miss him over at Fair Meadows. He certainly livened things up."

Terry noticed Carl frown, and she wondered why.

" I have a secret," said the bird.

"And what might that be?" Mrs. Despard asked the bird.

"Move it, ladies, we haven't got all night," Mr. Tea said, rocking from foot to foot as everyone laughed.

"Well," said Carl, "I guess he's sick of our company. Shall we, ladies?" He gestured toward the doorway.

Karen led the way and Terry brought up the rear. "Oh, my goodness! Who did the incredible artwork? Is this your work, Terry?" Mrs. Granger asked.

"Well, yes," Terry said, blushing.

"I got to watch her do it," Carl said. "Amazing."

"I have a secret," called Mr. Tea. Everyone ignored him.

Terry was glad there were no other customers at the moment. It allowed the women to browse through the room at their leisure. As they examined and gushed over the artwork, Mr. Tea squawked, "Finders keepers, sonny. Finders keepers. Nasty boys, nasty boys. I'm telling, I'm telling." Oh, I wish he'd shut up, Terry thought.

She heard the door chimes again. She turned and saw Greg, his grandmother and two other women walk in. She assumed the two other women were his mother and sister. His sister was younger than Terry by at least four years, so their paths hadn't crossed.

As the front door shut behind Greg and his entourage, Mr. Tea said, "It's the coppers. It's the coppers. Now you've had it." Greg leaned back and looked into the parlor. "Hey, buddy," he said, waving to Mr. Tea. "Whoa...easy there, pal!" Terry heard Greg say, "Hold on a sec," to his grandmother. Letting go of her arm, he went into the parlor.   Concerned about Mr. Tea, Terry excused herself and followed Greg, smiling at the women in the foyer as she walked by.

"Is everything…hey, what got into him?"   Terry asked.   Mr. Tea's feathers were ruffled and he was hopping around his cage like he was crazed.

"Hey, Ter. Our pal seems to be having a fit."

"He was fine a minute ago, we were all just in here. Maybe he's feeling lonely."

"Dangerous, nasty boys, nasty, nasty," he repeated. Then, he stopped and looked at them, blinking as if he was waiting for something. Terry and Greg looked at each other. Greg shrugged. "Hey, come meet my family." He motioned her toward the foyer.

"Idiot," said Mr. Tea.

"I say that to him all the time," Greg's sister remarked, winking at Greg and looking into the parlor at Mr. Tea.

Terry laughed. "That's Mr. Tea," she said, pointing. "He's our new addition.   It was really busy here yesterday, and he got lots of attention. I think he's lonely at the moment because he isn't the main attraction."

"Terry Sutter, this is my mother, Sandy Mullins, my sister, Anna Mullins and my grandmother, Hattie Mullins, whom you met yesterday."

"Why, hello, Hattie," Mrs. Despard called from the other room. "I didn't know you were planning on coming today. You could have gotten a ride with us, dear."

"That's sweet of you, Maude, but my grandson is treating us today. He says it's his way of making up for all the time we don't see him because he's working." She patted Greg's arm.

As Greg's party entered the main room, his sister and mother commented on the artwork. The other women walked over. They all chatted and ooohed and ahhhed over the stenciling, pointing out details to each other. Terry felt uncomfortable. She still wasn't used to the attention. She'd taught school where she'd been "just the art teacher." Yes, she'd received attention in high school, but in college, there were lots of other talented people. Now, coming back to her hometown, she was a small town wonder of sorts.

The door chimes jingled again and in came Aunt Rose with Mrs. Dindle. "Hello, everyone. Please don't start the party without us," Rose said, waving to everyone. Another set of introductions and another round of discussions about the stenciling followed.

Terry, Karen, Shannon and the other waitresses talked with the ladies for a bit. Terry didn't want to interrupt, but she wanted to get them all settled. "Ladies, why don't you let us seat you?" she finally said.

"Oh," said Maude Despard, laughing. "We're so busy chatting, we seem to have forgotten ourselves."

"We can put you all together or in groups, whichever you would prefer," Karen said. "You're in luck, the place is at your disposal."

No one said anything for a moment or two. They seemed to be deliberating. Finally, Greg's grandmother said, "Well, personally, I would love to sit as one big group, if that's okay with everyone. It would be so festive!"

The tables were pushed together and everyone picked their seats. Terry found it interesting how people grouped themselves. It was no real surprise that Greg and Carl sat opposite each other at one end. Men seemed to need each other in a teahouse. They grouped together here the way women usually do in public.

Although, she admitted to herself, she never saw them group together to find the bathroom. However, if one left, the others looked very forlorn. Aunt Rose and Mrs. Dindle sat at the other end. Next to Rose was Mrs. Mullins and across from her was Anna. Mrs. Hosey and Anna seemed engrossed in conversation. Mrs. Granger sat next to Greg. Terry felt a twinge of jealousy as she overheard Mrs. Granger regale Greg with anecdotes about Pam. She seems more of a dumb blonde than a lawyer, thought Terry. Oh gag, here come the pictures. Terry positioned herself so she could look out of the corner of her eye and see over Greg's shoulder. Terry caught herself before she gasped. Man, that girl got a boob job! Terry glanced down at her chest and sighed. I got lots of talent, but no boobs, she mused. Thanks, Mom.

She watched Greg hand the picture over to Carl. Carl put on his half-glasses and gazed at the picture. Terry almost laughed out loud at the expression on Carl's face. He cleared his throat a few times, took a sip of water and said, "Wow, I haven't seen her since she was in high school."

Terry was floored to hear Greg say, "Yup, she sure grew...ah...up, didn't she?"

Carl looked over the rim of his glasses at Greg, smiled widely and said, "Absolutely! You must be very proud, Mrs. Granger."

"Oh, I am!" she said as Carl handed back the picture.

Then Carl reached in his pocket, took out his wallet and retrieved a piece of paper that he handed to Greg. "Hamiltons' number," he said with a nod.

"Thanks," Greg said and put the number in his pocket. Terry wondered how the Hamiltons would react to the information about the poem.

"Helllooo, earth to Terry," she heard Karen say.

"Oh, I'm sorry, I was, umm, lost in thoughts of the past." Terry said, embarrassed.

"Well, Anna asked if you had any firm plans as to how you want to expand the water garden."

Looking over at Anna, Terry said, "Not yet. Mrs. Dindle gave me a lovely book about them. There are so many fascinating ideas. I'm still tossing options around in my head. Now, let's get you ladies some tea!"

"I think these blueberry scones are the best I've ever had," Mrs. Hosey commented. "Does anyone mind if I take the last one?"

The rest of the ladies shook their heads. "I stuffed myself on those seafood tea sandwiches," Anna said. "I came thinking I would have a light lunch, but I'm afraid I made a pig of myself."

Mrs. Mullins patted her lips with her napkin. "The strawberry soup was incredible. I thought it might be too sweet, but it was just perfect."

Terry came out of the kitchen to visit with her special guests. There were a few other customers, but they were already served. She could afford a short break. She wished she could spend more time with these special ladies, but, being chief cook and bottle washer, the minutes she wasn't needed in the kitchen were rare. The sadness inside her reminded her of childhood Christmases. It was the same feeling she got when she realized the day was almost over. All the dreaming, planning and preparing were over. It was both a moment to savor and a bittersweet letdown. When she was five years old, she dreamt that she held onto the hem of God's voluminous white robe, begging him to make time stand still. Terry could still recall the agony she felt in the dream as she realized time wouldn't stop, no matter how much she begged God.

This was a moment she desperately wanted to freeze frame, to grasp and cherish for just a while more.

"I'm so pleased you all enjoyed yourselves. Most of these recipes were ones my mother used. My Aunt Rose can tell you countless stories about tea parties we had." Terry looked over at Karen and giggled. "When we were little, Aunt Rose played the part of a queen visiting from a far off kingdom. Uncle Henry and my father came home from work and dressed in mismatched outfits. Then they made balloon animals and did some magic tricks. They were wonderful court jesters."

"The perfect part for Henry, without a doubt," Mrs. Dindle commented. "Madeline's tea parties were legendary. Whenever Shannon was invited, she came running home, telling me she needed to 'dress for tea with the queen'!"

"It was a treat to be the *visiting* queen," Rose said. "Madeline usually let one of the girls be the queen. Maddy played the part of the maid, social director as she called it. She served the tea and advised us on manners. Oh, Karen, I dreaded it when you played queen. You took the part to heart. You were such a bossy thing. You made sure everyone remembered to *bow* to the queen. Any slip-ups, like calling you Karen instead of Your Royal Highness, meant we had to kneel down and kiss your hand. I can still hear you now: 'Down, slave. Kiss the Royal hand.' Once, I made the mistake of reminding you that I was another queen and not a slave. Goodness, what a mistake that was! I thought I was going to be beheaded. Now when Terry was queen, we were ordered to feed the birds and help clean up. She even made a Royal Decree that the kingdom was to eat ice cream for dinner. Personally, I liked visiting better when Terry was queen." Rose winked and everyone laughed. Terry felt another wave of grief mingled with her own biological clock issues. Would she ever have a child? Would she ever get the chance to have a tea party with a daughter of her own? If she did, how empty it would seem without her mother. She used to imagine her mother as a grandmother having tea with her grandchildren. Terry felt a heaviness in her chest. Not now! she told herself.

"Well, I hate to break things up, but I really need to get back to the station," Greg said with a sigh. "I confess I had no idea that a tea party could be so...well...good."

As Carl and Greg started to take out their wallets, Terry said, "No, please, this party's on the house. It's our pleasure to treat all of you."

The last of the other customers were getting ready to leave. Terry went over to cash them out and see how they enjoyed their tea. Carl gestured to her that he was going to use the restroom and would be right back. From the register, she glanced over and saw the women beginning to stand up and collect their purses. Mrs. Granger seemed to be trying to list Pam's marvelous attributes to Greg one more time. Terry wandered back over for one last chat. It was another half-hour by the time people hugged, shook hands, and said their thank yous. Just as they were leaving, Uncle Henry arrived. Terry saw him whisper something to Greg. Greg frowned and nodded.

Now what? Terry thought. Karen obviously noticed it as well. Turning to Terry, Karen said, "If those two are whispering, something's up."

Terry nodded. "Right now, I don't want to know!"

"Amen," said Karen. "Amen!"

CHAPTER 14

Back at the station, Greg pondered Henry's remarks about the Hamilton's fortune and wondered if it really mattered, as far as the break in, that is. Then, of course, there was the issue with Mr. Tea. Could the bird possibly know something about the disappearance of his original owners? It seemed impossible that the bird could remember anything, even if he had seen something. Did it matter?

"Wow, you look lost in space," Tom remarked as he handed Greg a cup of coffee.

"Thanks." Greg took the coffee and stared at Tom. He might as well run all this by him, even if it was extremely bizarre and disjointed. "Have a seat. I want to run some more really weird stuff by you. I need a sounding board."

"Does this have to do with things that go bump in the night?" Tom smiled as he turned a chair around and sat, straddling the back posts and leaned both arms on the back support.

"Sort of and maybe not. Here's the deal. Henry Sanders told me that he found proof that the Hamilton fortune was gained through bank robbery, which substantiates the long time rumors. I couldn't talk when I saw him. I was leaving the teahouse. He pulled me aside and said he's sure the original Hamilton, Rochester Hamilton, was a bank robber. I told him I'd call him from here to find out the exact facts, but I am, for now, assuming he's right. By the way, Carl

Despard gave me a number and an address for the Hamiltons. He's still in touch with them."

Tom nodded.

"Henry also says he's now sure that Mr. Tea is the bird that belonged to the ladies who disappeared over thirty years ago. I'm not sure that means anything, but the fact that I heard the bird say, "Hello, ladies," certainly sends a chill up my spine. Finally, I'm wondering if these are all separate issues or if they somehow tie in together. Am I nuts?"

"I've always thought of you as a bit odd," Tom teased, "but this set of circumstances could make anyone question their sanity. It seems a stretch for any of this to be related, however, it's not impossible. Call Henry and get the specifics. Why don't you see if he minds being on speaker phone? I'd love to hear what he's got."

Greg took the cell phone out of his shirt pocket, pressed a few things, picked up the phone and dialed. "It's ringing."

"Hello?"

"Henry, it's Greg, can you talk?"

"Yeah, I was hoping you'd call. I sent Rosey out grocery shopping. This mystery is costing me a fortune in food! Dang! You people can eat. You're all invited here *again* for dinner. The preparations distract my wife and the shopping gets her out of the house. Meanwhile, I'm headed for the poor house!"

Greg smiled. "I'd be more then happy to pick up some things. You make me feel guilty. You're as good at the guilt thing as my mother!"

Henry laughed. "Don't sweat it. Like I said, it gets Rose out of the house. Besides, once this is over with, I'll probably miss you. Isn't that a scary thought! Anyway, I wanna tell you more about what I found."

"Okay, but hold on a sec. I want to know if it's okay to put you on speakerphone. I have another officer here, Tom O'Hara, I think you met him the other night. I want him to hear this. Is that okay?"

"Sure, sure, go ahead."

Greg and Tom sat and listened with intensity and amazement as Henry described the pictures he found and the hat with the missing section of rim. When Henry got to the part about Mr. Tea originally being called Ladies Man due to the phrase, "Hello, ladies," Greg jerked his body backward from shock, almost tipping over his chair.

Tom reached out and grabbed the chair to keep it from falling. "Whoa, man. Need a change of underwear? How creepy is that! Hold on a second, Mr. Sanders."

Taking a deep breath, Greg shook his head. It could just be coincidence, a phrase from his past the bird uttered at the moment. Assuming they're dead, why would those two women haunt the teahouse? What significance would a teacup have to them? It makes no sense, not yet anyway.

"Everything okay there, boys?" Henry asked.

"Oh yeah, just a bit rattled. Considering, the other night, just before the cup crashed to the floor, I heard Mr. Tea say, 'hello, ladies.' That's rather…unsettling."

Before Henry could respond, Tom said, "I think you should talk to the Hamiltons, the librarian's…what was her name, oh yeah, Ms. Nile's' mother. Can't hurt, might help."

After a few seconds of silence, Greg sighed and said, "I guess you're right. However, I wonder if they'll feel entitled to the money. We never did ask Terry and Karen about what to do with the money if we find it. Heck, Karen doesn't even know about the note yet."

Henry piped in, "I know my nieces. I can tell you right now that they'll hand over the money in a second. Neither of them will want the drama of a court fight over it. Karen'll swear about it loud and clear, but she'll hand it over. Terry'll treat it like a hot potato, no question about it. Trust me on this one. Go ahead and set up an appointment with the Hamiltons."

"Wanna go too?" Greg asked.

"You betcha, young feller!"

"I'll call ya back when I have a date. Any days bad for you?"

"I'm wide open. At my age, no matter what I have going on, I can move it. Call me later or tell me tonight. Gotta go, I think I hear Rosey."

"Okay."

"Can I go, pretty please? Can I, can I? Huh, pretty please?" Tom whined, smiling as he grabbed onto Greg's arm.

Greg chuckled and shook himself free. "Of course, why should I get all the fun?" Taking the paper Carl gave him out of his pocket, Greg began to dial.

"Hello?"

"Is this Mr. Hamilton?"

"Yes? Who's calling?"

"Sir, my name is Greg Mullins. Some friends of mine live in the house that you sold to the Sutter family. Actually, my friends are Sutters. They found a letter that seems to have been written by your father. It indicates there may be money buried on the property. We'd like to come to your house and talk with you about it. Would that be possible?"

Silence for a moment. "Buried money? That's just a silly rumor. It must be some kind of prank."

"We did a bit of research and the handwriting seems to be that of your father. Would you mind taking a look at it?"

"Young man, with all due respect, I'm now over eighty and that house and its horrible memories are in my past. That is where I would like to keep them. Is this really necessary?"

"Sir, I wouldn't have called if I didn't think it was. Please, just look at the letter."

"How did you get my number?"

Greg wasn't sure, but he thought he heard something odd in Mr. Hamilton's tone. "Carl Despard, he knows the Sutters as well, gave it to me. We also found some old photographs we thought you might want. They were apparently left in the attic."

"Oh, heck, for heaven's sake. When would you like to come? Might as well get it over with!"

"Is tomorrow night, around six, convenient for you?"

"Yes, yes. As I said, I'm over eighty, I don't go far. I don't think I can be of any help, but come along. Six o'clock tomorrow, you said?"

"Yes, sir."

"Alright then, goodbye." An abrupt click from the other end signaled the end of the conversation.

"Well?" Tom asked.

"Well, we're in. I can't say much more than that. He isn't happy about it. He said he wanted to put that house and the bad memories behind him. I'm not sure what that means."

"Wasn't his son murdered? Maybe that's it."

"Could be, but I don't recall the murder being in that house. I think he was found somewhere. I know, I know, but I can't remember the details at the moment. At any rate, we'll find out tomorrow night. How about I call Henry Sanders back and ask if you can come to dinner tonight, too? Hey, wanna stay over with me? I could use some company."

"Do I want to stay over in a haunted house? Hell, no! But I will. I admit this is the most interesting thing to happen around here in...forever. After this, it'll be boring. Might as well jump at the chance to have fun now."

"Fun? That isn't how I think of it. However, it is the most excitement we've had around here. In a teahouse, who would've thought?"

Picking up the phone, Greg dialed Henry. When this was all over, he'd miss Henry, too. Greg really didn't think of this as fun, but it definitely wasn't in the category of bad. At least, spending time with the people involved was great. The ghosts he could live without, but the people were gonna be hard to part with.

Rose was fit to be tied. Henry was on her last nerve. It wasn't that she didn't like having company; she loved it. What ticked her off was the strawberry shortcake. She returned from shopping and was unloading the bags when Henry strolled in and looked around. "Oh," he said, sounding disappointed.

"What's the matter, dear? I thought we decided on barbeque chicken and grilled vegetables." Rose's feet were starting to ache, so she was a bit cranky.

"Hmmm, um, nothing," he said in that whiny tone he used when he wanted something, but didn't want to come right out and ask her.

"Henry, for the love of pizza, what's the problem?" Rose felt a headache beginning over her left temple. If he changed the menu and thought I would read his mind, I'm going to crown his balding head, she thought.

"I just thought we decided on strawberry shortcake for dessert." He made his sad puppy dog eyes blink at her.

"What? No, we most certainly did not. Strawberries hit their peak two weeks ago. Besides, I'd have to make the shortcakes as well. I usually do that in the morning."

Henry sighed, said, "Oh, okay," again in his whiny tone and left the room.

Rose watched him go. There is no way I'm going out again. Nope, I'm not gonna do it, she fumed to herself. Strawberry shortcake, my aching foot! I don't see him whipping up the shortcakes! He'll just have to get over it. Although, she thought, he really doesn't ask for that much. Maybe if I don't dawdle at the market...No, I don't think I'll have time to let the shortcakes cool. Well, they'll have extra time since they're for dessert. I *really* don't want to go back out, my feet are killing me. I guess it won't take me too long...Dang it! "Henry, you're going to have to par boil the chicken in the barbeque sauce. Don't overcook it this time." She snatched her purse from the kitchen table and stormed out the door to the car.

Phew, thought Henry. I didn't think she was gonna go for it. He whistled Glenn Miller's *Chattanooga Choo Choo* as he started the chicken. When the chicken was cooking and the timer was on, he took out the phone book, looked up Marilyn's mother's phone number and dialed.

"One ringy-dingy," he said. "Two…"

"Hello?"

"Mrs. Brown?"

"Yes?"

"This is Henry Sanders. I was at the library today, talking to your daughter, Marilyn."

"Oh, yes. She told me. I told her that I was completely sure that Eloise and Mary did not just take off. I'm sure there was foul play. I think, even after all these years, that that horrible Thurston Hamilton was behind it. I hate to speak ill of the dead, but he was such a dreadful boy. I don't think Carl Despard and Samuel Brinker would have turned out so well if that boy hadn't died. He was sheer trouble....evil, that's what he was, plain evil!"

"I know they were going to sell their house," Henry said, glancing at the timer. Rosey would kill him if he overcooked the chicken.

"Oh, yes, but they were planning on staying in town. They had lots of friends. Thurston was forever shooting their windows and squirrels with BBs. They loved to garden and they were forever finding dead squirrels, chipmunks and birds in their flowerbeds. Imagine going out to weed and finding animal carcasses. They'd look up and see Thurston staring down at them from the attic window with a smirk on his face.

Wow, thought Henry. If some kid did that to me and Rosey, I'd go over there and tan his hide. That kid was a creep!

"... warned Maude Despard and Nancy Brinker that their sons were hanging out with a maniac," Mrs. Brown continued. "Of course, Maude and Nancy told their boys to stay away from that hooligan, but they seemed to find a way to hook up with him anyway. I think he was just using them. Eloise and Mary told me the boys always seemed to be building something. A tree house, a race cart, bird houses and feeders so Thurston could shoot the birds. At the end, I believe he even had them help him fix up the attic. Thurston would call out orders and the other two would tote, hammer and saw all day. That bully would act like the foreman."

Why didn't Sam and Carl tell that brat to go pound sand? Henry wondered.

"Sarah Hamilton always fed the boys well and Beauregard would take them hunting or fishing, which was nice since both the boys' fathers died in the war. I know Carl stayed close to the family, but after Thurston's death, Sam Brinker seemed to stay away. I can't say why, but I think there was some bad blood there." She laughed. "Well, for someone who doesn't want to speak ill of the dead, I'm certainly doing a fine job of it. I'm sorry. I'm just sure he hurt my friends."

"Well, if I thought someone hurt *my* friends, I would probably do the same thing. I do agree that Sam Brinker went his own way after Thurston's death. I also want to know about the bird. I think he's the bird my nieces just took from Fair Meadows, Mrs. Nitmeyer's bird."

"Yes! That's him. Sylvia Nitmeyer took him. Their niece didn't know what to do with him. The poor bird was alone for days before anyone noticed the sisters were missing. Sylvia said she dreamed he was calling out to her, telling her he needed help. She tried to call Eloise and Mary, but, of course, there was no answer. She finally called their niece who checked the house and called the police. Ladies' Man was his name. Such a smart bird! I'm not sure any of us really believed he was psychic, but he sure gave us a few good laughs. It was uncanny, you know, his ability to say the right thing at the right time. Sylvia swore Eloise and Mary used to visit him. At night, every once and awhile, he would say, 'hello, ladies' and the curtains would ripple a little as if a gentle breeze came by. That gave me the shivers, I assure you."

"It certainly gives *me* the willies," Henry said, pacing the kitchen. "The other night, just before something weird happened, he said that exact phrase. Wait'll I tell the girls. He certainly is no ordinary bird, I agree with you there!" Henry realized the timer was about to go off. "Thank you so much, Mrs. Brown. Please stop in at the teahouse and visit the bird. The girls named him Mr. Tea, spelled 't-e-a'."

A peal of laughter came from the other end of the phone. "What a clever thing to do. I can't wait to come by."

"Again, thank you for the information, Mrs. Brown," Henry said, getting the potholders ready. "It's been a pleasure talking to you." Just as he hung up, the timer went off. Mission accomplished, he thought.

Henry sat down at the kitchen table and thought about the conversation. It could be coincidence that Thurston Hamilton died so soon after the disappearance of the Gutherie sisters. Is it possible that whoever killed Thurston was involved in the sisters' disappearance? It seemed a bit far-fetched, but they were neighbors. Could they have shared a secret? Would Thurston have confided in Carl or Sam? Probably not, because they would have gone to the police. Then again, Thurston never did. If Beauregard Hamilton was good to the boys, why did Sam stay away after Thurston's death? Grief? Maybe. Did his trip to Vermont tie in somehow? Rosey told him Sam said something about blood when she showed him the picture. Had Sam found Thurston? Who did? Did the newspaper article say? Henry would need to check the article again. The timing of it all just seemed too coincidental. Hmmm.

A few minutes later, Rose returned. "Henry, you're just going to have to be satisfied with my ice cream cake. The shortcakes just wouldn't be done on time. Besides, the price of strawberries was outrageous!"

"That's just fine, Rosey. Thanks for trying. You always take such good care of me," he said, giving her a hug. Thank heavens, he thought. I'm sick to death of strawberries! Good ruse, though.

Rose was thrilled to have Greg bring his friend, Tom O'Hara, for dinner. You could tell a lot about a person by their choice of friends. Tom was very polite, a real gentleman. Rose was glad for that. If Greg was interested in Terry, and Rose thought he might be, she wanted to know he would treat Terry well. Rose still wasn't over the shock of Karen's husband having an affair. What a horrible thing to do!

"Tom, how long have you been on the police force?" Henry asked as he passed out margaritas and ice teas.

"Same as Greg, sir. We met and became friends in the academy."

"How wonderful the two of you wound up working together," said Rose. "Where did you grow up?"

"Not too far from here, actually, a small town named Wells."

"Really," jumped in Mrs. Dindle. "My husband grew up there as well. His family lived right behind the Methodist church there."

" No kidding, small world. My friend, Richard Hobart, lived in that house. As far as I know, his family is still there." Tom smiled.

"Yes, they do live there," replied Dottie. "I play bridge there. I belong to a women's bridge league and we meet in that church a few times a year for tournaments. Mrs. Hobart plays for the bridge league at that church. She gave my husband and me a tour of the house a number of years ago. I didn't meet her children, just her and her husband."

"Is the bridge group that meets at that church part of the league?" Tom asked.

"Probably," said Dottie. "I'm pretty sure that's who hosts the tournaments."

"My mother just joined it. Perhaps you'll get a chance to meet her at the next tournament. Watch out though, my mother is very competitive. She plays a mean game of bridge." Tom laughed.

"Well," said Rose, "Dottie was champ two years in a row. This year's tournament may get interesting." Henry mentioned to Rose about Dottie's gas problem. She wondered if it was happening at the bridge games.

"I think it's about time someone else won," Dottie said. "I hope it'll be your mother. Wouldn't that be wonderful?"

"Anyone want another margarita?" Karen asked, standing up. "In case you're wondering, I don't play bridge, but I play a killer game of Uno. Right, Uncle Henry?"

"Oh my goodness," said Henry, with a twinkle in his eye, "you gotta watch that one! I think she cheats!"

"I do not!" hollered Karen. "I'm just extremely brilliant when it comes to Uno."

"She cheats," said Shannon calmly. Everyone laughed.

"Karen, I think I'd like another margarita," Terry said.

"Yeah, please," Shannon said, holding up her glass.

"Here, let me help you," Greg said, getting up and taking Terry's glass. Terry smiled and blushed.

"Dinner's ready," said Henry, checking things on the grill.

"Here, Mom, let me help you up," Shannon said.

Mrs. Dindle stood up and began to walk to the table….putt, putt, putt. Rose made sure she looked down, she couldn't risk looking at Henry, or anyone else, for that matter. As she lowered her eyes, she caught a glimpse of Henry chuckling.

Terry took the seat to the right of Dottie. Henry started to sit next to Terry, but Rose cleared her throat.

Henry looked at her quizzically and then seemed to catch on. He moved to the other side of Shannon. Karen came out of the house with Greg behind her. Instead of sitting next to Terry, she went all the way around and sat next to Henry. Tom smiled and started to sit next to Karen, but Karen jumped up and said, "Oh wait, Rose you sit next to Henry." Karen and Tom each moved one seat over.

"I'm sorry," said Dottie." The sun is going down and it's bothering my eyes. They're still a little sensitive since my cataract surgery." Henry switched with her.

When no putting noises were forthcoming, Rose heard Henry quietly say to Shannon, "Musta run outa gas." Shannon giggled and Rose shot him a look. Honestly, what if Dottie heard him? Men!

Terry stood up and said, "Aunt Rose, do you want to sit here, next to Uncle Henry?"

"No, dear, I'm fine," Rose said.

"Really, Aunt Rose, it's okay," Terry said. Rose wanted to slap her. Didn't she realize they purposely shuffled around so Greg would sit next to her?

"I never get to sit next to Dottie, sit down, Terry."

Terry looked at Rose and seemed to catch on. With a bit of color in her cheeks, she sat down. Greg sat down and wiped his hands on his pants. Rose saw Tom watching Greg. Tom had a slight smirk on his face. Oh, thought Rose, I bet he knows, too. How funny, he enjoys watching his buddy Greg squirm.

Once everyone finally got settled, dinner passed in a buzz of conversation and laughter.

"Are you married, Tom?" asked Dottie, as Rose cut the ice cream cake.

Rose saw Shannon look at Karen in wide-eyed embarrassment.

"No, ma'am. I was engaged once, but the young lady didn't want to be married to a policeman. She was afraid of being widowed early."

"Oh, what a shame," said Mrs. Dindle, "you seem like such a lovely young man."

Oh my, thought Rose. Shannon isn't going to like that.

"Thank you, ma'am," said Tom.

Rose saw Karen start to chuckle as she put her hand over her mouth.

Shannon stood up. "Mr. Sanders, I think I need another margarita. Is there more inside?"

"Sure, sure. I made plenty. Help yourself, Shannon," Henry said. He seemed to sense her mortification.

"Fill up the pitcher and bring it out," Karen called after her.

Shannon half-stomped to the door. It was clear to Rose, Shannon wanted to choke her mother.

After dinner, Henry took charge. When Greg first arrived, he told Henry it was okay to share the information about the poem. Henry knew Tom and Greg were spending the night on the floor at the teahouse. Henry was grateful for that. He didn't know what he would do if something happened to those girls.

"I want to share something with you," Henry began. "Yesterday, when Terry, Greg and I were digging in the area of the water garden, we found this." He carefully took the old, yellowed piece of paper out of his pocket. "It's a poem that seems to indicate there may be treasure hidden around here somewhere."

"Oh, my goodness," said Rose.

"You're kidding, right?" asked Karen.

"Nope," replied Terry. "I've been dying to tell you and Shannon, but I was sworn to secrecy."

"That's right," continued Henry. "Greg and I thought it best if we didn't say anything until we checked around a little more. We decided to tell you now because I found this article on the computer and it coincides with another article in an old newspaper. I think it gives us reason to think the rumors about Rochester Hamilton being a bank robber are true. I'll get to those in a bit. In addition, Tom, Greg and I are going tomorrow night to talk to Beauregard Hamilton."

"Henry, do you think that's wise?" asked Rose. "Could the Hamiltons try and look for the money and somehow interrupt business at the teahouse?"

"No, ma'am," said Greg. "Karen and Terry own the property. Besides, nothing says it's on that piece of land. Remember, the Hamiltons owned about ten acres. It was sold off in pieces. It's possible that the treasure is in the forest the state now owns. When you hear the poem, you'll realize it's kinda vague."

"Well," said Karen, "let's hear it!"

Henry read them the poem. When he was done, no one spoke for a few minutes. They all seemed to be thinking.

It was Dottie Dindle who spoke up first. "The treasure isn't on the teahouse property. It says, 'not mine but their quite worthy estate.' I think that means it's not on his property."

"He could be referring to the fact that his son, Beauregard Jr., would own the property when he died," commented Rose.

"It says something about tree gnomes," said Shannon, looking around. "It could be under a tree."

"Under Heaven, above Hell is a pretty large territory," said Karen with a shrug, getting up to pour herself another margarita.

"What type of tree gnomes peep in each morning?" asked Shannon.

"The idea that they're watching me is kinda creepy," said Terry.

"Uncle Henry, can you make us all copies tomorrow?" asked Karen. "I think we need to ponder this for a bit. There's got to be enough clues there that someone could find the treasure. It must have all made sense to the writer, probably Beauregard Sr., at the time. Maybe Mr. Hamilton Jr. will be able to give you some insight tomorrow night."

"Speaking of the Hamiltons, tell us about what you found on the computer, Henry," Rose said.

Henry explained about the hat with part of the brim missing. When he was done, he said, "I really do think Rochester Hamilton left the hat there on purpose, as a sign he was done robbing banks. He left Connecticut and came here to settle down. Maybe that's why he came all the way to Maine from Connecticut. Who'd go looking for him this far away?"

Karen let out a loud yawn. "Sorry," she said sheepishly. "I'm exhausted. My brain has called it quits for today."

"Mine too," said Dottie Dindle. "Something is nagging at my brain, but I'm too tired to think what it might be."

"Okay," said Shannon, standing up and holding out her hand to her mother. "Up, up and away, old girl."

Mrs. Dindle grabbed onto Shannon's wrist and pulled herself up. A note, somewhere above high C, slipped into the night air.

"On that note," said Henry with a wink in Terry's direction, "let's get you girls home."

"I'm getting you a hearing aid," Henry heard Shannon mumble to an oblivious Mrs. Dindle.

CHAPTER 15

Greg was glad Tom was spending the night with him at the teahouse. He felt more comfortable around Terry and Karen than he did the other night. In addition, ghost busting alone was not something Greg wanted to do ever, *ever* again. Greg was still having a hard time admitting to himself that he really thought a ghost sent the teacup flying. He hoped Tom might come up with another completely logical explanation. However, Tom seemed perfectly at ease with the ghost idea.

The girls were upstairs when Tom and Greg brought in their sleeping bags from Tom's truck. They didn't want to use a cruiser. People might wonder why a police car was sitting at the teahouse overnight.

"Tonight should be quiet," Greg said, "since Terry took the teacups off the shelf and put them away for tonight."

"Spoilsport," Tom said, grinning.

Greg looked over at the book on water gardens. It sat on the table right next to the shelf. "Ya know, Henry is working with Mrs. Dindle to expand the water garden. I looked through the book tonight that Mrs. Dindle gave Terry and Karen. There's some cool stuff in there. I know your mom's been asking you to put one in. It's not all that hard. Next year, I might put one in at my mom's. One thing's for sure, there's a lot less weeding! Man, I hate that. Given the choice, I'd mow the lawn in one hundred degrees over ten minutes of weeding!"

Tom laughed. "I hear ya. One of the things that's hard about aging parents is how much they need ya to do. I don't mind doing a lot of it, but yeah, I hate the weeding. I wish my mom would go for plastic flowers and Astroturf! Speaking of moms, I love Mrs. Dindle. That woman's a hoot. She reminded me of my mom. Once my mom found out those girls weren't married, she would have asked them how many children they wanted. It was tough not to laugh when Shannon got up to get another drink."

"Hmmm, do I detect a bit of interest?" Greg asked.

"Maybe, too early to tell yet. Speaking of interest," said Tom, "I sense some on your part involving Ms. Terry."

"Shhhhhhh," whispered Greg, "she might hear you."

Tom laughed. "Alllllllll righty, then. Ya need to relax. She can't hear me. Obviously, I'm right."

"Yeah, but I don't think she's interested in me. I liked her, *really* liked her, in high school. I don't think she knew I was alive."

"Man, she knows you're alive now. What are ya, blind? Can't you see how she looks at you? The problem is, she's as much of a wreck about this romance as you are. The two of you are pathetic."

Greg shrugged. "Sooner or later, this mystery is gonna be over and I'll have to fish or cut bait. Every time I think about tellin' her how I feel, my tongue seems to gain fifty pounds and stick to my mouth. The other day, after we found the poem, I slipped and called her 'darlin'. I could've died. I felt like Captain Dork. All I needed was a cape, big, black-framed glasses and a pocket protector. And the other night, with the ghost thing, I hugged her, ya know, like to protect her."

"Oh, you cad!" said Tom, sounding like a southern belle.

"Give me a break, man. I was unprofessional," Greg said, lying down on top of his sleeping bag. He didn't want to take the chance of getting tangled up in it again.

"No, you give me a break!" Tom said, sitting up. "What cop do we know who would sleep on someone's floor in case a ghost showed up? Gimme a flippin' break." Tom looked at Greg, clearly waiting for an answer.

"First of all," Greg said, defensively, "I thought someone was breaking in and smashing or moving the cups to freak them out. Secondly—" He saw Tom's eyebrows rise in expectation. Dang! Tom had him on this one. "Okay, the dead-bolt and garden thing were freebies."

"Exactly. Now, let's get some sleep."

"Sleep tight," squawked Mr. Tea.

"What the?" said Tom.

"It's the macaw I told you about. Ya know, Mr. Tea, a.k.a Ladies' Man."

"Finally," said the bird.

Greg got up and went into the other room and looked at Mr. Tea. Tom followed. "Ya know, we were so caught up in the other stuff, Henry didn't tell the girls we think this bird belonged to those ladies. So, Mr. Tea, you were once Ladies' Man, huh?"

Mr. Tea just blinked.

"I wonder what you know, buddy," Greg said.

"Nasty boys, nasty boys," replied the bird.

"Guess he doesn't like us," said Tom.

"Apparently, he's partial to women." Greg chuckled.

"Smart bird," Tom said, heading back toward the sleeping bags.

BANG! Tom and Greg jumped up. Tom switched on the light.

"Hello, ladies," said Mr. Tea.

Tom and Greg looked at each other and then looked around the room. Greg pointed to the book lying on the floor. "That book was in the middle of the table, I swear, Tom."

"Guys?" came Karen's voice down the stairs.

"It's okay," Tom yelled. "The book on the water gardens fell off the table. Everything's okay. False alarm." He picked up the book and put it back on the table, dead smack in the center.

Upstairs, another door opened. "Go back to sleep, false alarm," Greg heard Karen say. Two doors shut.

Tom lay back down. Greg was annoyed. He knew that book didn't just fall. Besides, Mr. Tea said, "Hello, ladies." Was Tom that dense? Now he was going to have a hard time falling back to sleep. Rats! Greg listened to the ticking of the clock, counted sheep and eventually drifted off.

BANG!

"Timber!" squawked Mr. Tea.

Greg was on his feet, but his brain was dizzy. He was in a deep sleep before the noise. He looked at Tom who was staring at the book on the floor. "Any questions?" asked Greg.

Tom stared at him, speechless.

"Now what?" came Karen's voice.

"Coffee time," called Greg.

Another door opened. "Apparently, there's been a visitor," Karen said.

Greg went to the stairs and looked up. Wow, Terry had on a pink negligee thing that caused him to stop breathing, momentarily. She looked at him and flew into her room. Karen looked at Greg, smiled and rolled her eyes. I wonder what that means, thought Greg.

Terry was on her second cup of coffee before the fog in her brain started to clear. No one was saying much. They drank their coffee in companionable, scared silence.

"It seems odd to be sitting in a teahouse, drinking coffee," said Tom.

"It seems to be par for us," answered Greg. "We did it the other night, too. Does that make us...odd?"

Karen looked at him thoughtfully. "You're talking about the people who giggle every time Mrs. Dindle farts. Yeah, I don't know about you, but I'd say we're odd."

Terry was momentarily mortified. She couldn't believe Karen brought up that subject in front of Greg and Tom.

Greg threw his head back and laughed. "I thought I'd bust a gut when Henry said, 'on that note,' when she stood up."

"How come she doesn't react?" Tom asked.

"She can't hear it," the rest of them replied in unison.

"Hey, how did you know that?" Terry asked Greg, relieved he was laughing.

"Henry told me this afternoon. He told me about getting her to stand up the other day. Tom, you gotta hear this story."

Terry listened to Greg tell Tom all about Mrs. Hardy and Mrs. Dindle. He did an imitation of Mrs. Hardy's voice that had them all laughing. Tom wiped tears from his eyes as Greg said, "...you've got a wife. Have her model for you, you old coot!" Greg wasn't offended. He thought it was as funny as she and Henry did. Phew!

Greg finished and there was a brief silence.

"Can we talk about the book?" Tom asked.

"I don't know what to think," Terry said. "I was sure it was all about the teacups. Maybe it is a poltergeist."

"This may sound really weird," Karen said, "but should we try and have someone come and get rid of it, like an exorcist?"

"Probably," said Greg. "Maybe this has nothing to do with the break-in. One thing's for sure, we're not nuts."

"Why now?" Terry asked. "The house wasn't haunted until recently. Karen, I really don't think this has anything to do with Mom. When it was about the teacups and the shelf, I did. Not now. I thought the teacups were Mom trying to tell us something. The teacups fell off the shelf where she kept her cup. When it was her cup, it moved. That stuff made sense; it connected to Mom. Why move a book? Mom has nothing against books."

"How about water gardens?" asked Tom. Everyone stared at him. "I was just kidding," he said.

"Tom, we found the poem by the water garden. Maybe that's the connection."

"Okay," Karen said, "but what does the water garden have to do with teacups or the shelf?"

"I don't know," said Greg, "and that's what so frustrating. There may not be a connection."

"There's a connection," said Tom. "I can feel it in my gut."

"How often is your gut wrong?" asked Terry.

"Never," answered Greg. "That's why I run things by him. Tom has an awesome sixth sense."

"I wouldn't go that far," Tom said. Terry thought he looked…humbled. Obviously, Greg's compliment meant a lot to him.

"I would," Greg said, very matter-of-factly. "I can't think of one time you've been off. Your gut's like a compass; it always points to something important. If your gut feels there's a connection, there is. We don't know what it is, but it's there. Maybe Hamilton will give us something tomorrow...oh, yeah...tonight."

"What time is it?" Tom asked, looking around for a clock.

"Almost five-thirty," said Karen, looking at her watch.

"Wow, it's gonna be a loooong day." Tom sighed.

"Try going through this for weeks," Terry said.

Greg reached out and patted her arm. "It'll be okay, we'll figure it out. We might be exhausted by the time we do, but we will," he said with a smile.

Terry was floored. She felt herself blush. Tom smiled at Greg. I wonder why he's smiling, she thought.

An hour later, Terry was shocked to see Mrs. Dindle at the kitchen door. Greg jumped up, opened the door and got her a chair.

"Would you like a cup of coffee, Mrs. Dindle?" Terry asked.

"Thank you, dear," she said. "Actually, I am not sure this means anything. Probably, it doesn't. I was thinking about the poem and I remembered that when I moved my rose bush to put in my water garden, I found an old wooden box. Actually, part of a box. It was really old. I'm pretty sure it was from the eighteen-hundreds. The poem said something about a wooden box, didn't it?"

"Yes, Mrs. Dindle, it did," said Greg. "Wasn't there an old box in your attic?"

"Yeah," said Karen, jumping up. "I'll get it."

"I'll help," Tom said, following after her.

Terry looked at Greg. "That's where we found that photo album, right?"

"I think so."

"The one that had the picture of Carl, Sam and Thurston? The picture Rose showed Samuel Brinker?" asked Mrs. Dindle.

"Yeah," Terry said. "I feel so sorry for that poor man. I'd give anything to help him. He was wonderful to Karen when we were in high school."

"He also coached the track team," Greg said. "I had him as a track coach. I don't know what he saw, but, yeah, it breaks my heart to see him like that."

Karen and Tom returned with the wooden box that read "Bank Property, 1890."

"Yes!" said Mrs. Dindle. "My box was missing some parts, but I do remember seeing the word 'bank' written on it."

"Mrs. Dindle," Tom asked, "where did you say you found this box?"

"Where my water garden is now. Under an old rose bush."

"Hmmm," said Tom, "that's very interesting."

"Does that information help?" Dottie asked.

"It might," said Greg, "it just might."

CHAPTER 16

To say it was a long day was an understatement. Greg, despite at least ten cups of coffee, was dragging by the time they left for the Hamilton's. He was glad that Terry was sleeping at the Sander's house and Karen at the Dindle's. Of course, Rose wanted them both, but it seemed the girls needed a 'Rose break.' Karen slept at Rose's the other night, now it was Terry's turn. At least tonight, he could sleep. He really hoped nothing happened at the teahouse during the night. At any rate, no one would know about it until the morning. Tonight, they all needed the sleep. He hoped Mr. Hamilton could shed some light on the recent events. Although, given Hamilton's reaction on the phone, Greg wasn't too hopeful.

The door to the Hamilton house opened as he, Henry and Tom walked up the stone pathway. Mr. Hamilton stood over six feet and he filled the doorway. The scowl on his face made it clear he was not happy to see them.

"Gentlemen, only one of you needed to come. Three of you isn't gonna change the fact that there is no hidden money." He continued to stand in the doorway. Greg didn't think the man was going to allow them to come in. It was Henry who spoke first.

"Oh, for heaven's sake, man, you know I grew up in town prowling through your woods at night, looking for hidden treasure. Now I've even got a note that looks one hundred percent legit. Can't you let a man enjoy the thrill of it all? Don't be such a killjoy, Beauregard!"

To his relief, Greg saw the corners of Beauregard Hamilton's mouth twitch into a smile that lasted only a moment, but it was a smile. Greg was sure of it.

Beauregard shook his head as he spoke. "I don't think there was any boy for three counties that didn't have at least one look through our woods. That's another reason I'm sure the note's a fake. If there were treasure to be found, it would've been found long ago."

Henry stepped in front of Greg and held the note out to Beauregard. "This is in your father's handwriting. I'm sure of it. Don't be a stubborn fool, man."

Snatching the note from Henry's hand, Beauregard glowered as he studied it. "My father was not this creative. He couldn't rhyme if his life depended on it. No, I'm positive. This is a fake." He handed the note back to Henry, but Greg was sure Hamilton's hand was shaking.

"Beauregard, dear, stop being so rude and let the gentlemen in." A soft but firm voice came from inside the house. Beauregard looked over his right shoulder and stepped back and gestured for them to enter.

Each man in turn introduced himself to the Hamiltons. Mrs. Hamilton sat in a blue wingback chair. Although she smiled at them, Greg thought she looked a bit afraid... perhaps cautious was a better word. "Gentlemen, this is my wife, Sarah Hamilton." She nodded and glanced down at the needlepoint in her hand. Looking up, she opened her mouth to speak, but was interrupted by the ringing of the phone. Beauregard yanked a portable phone from a table and walked into another room.

"My goodness, we hardly ever get company or phone calls. Tonight, we get both. Can I get you gentlemen something to drink?"   Sarah's soft voice shook as she spoke.

Henry, Greg and Tom each declined the offer as they took their seats. "Mrs. Hamilton," Greg began.

"Call me Sarah, please."

"Sarah, then.   Like I told Mr. Hamilton, we just wanted for him to take a look at the letter."

"Beau is a bit defensive when it comes to the house and the past. He hasn't been the same since...Thurston's death. It was all too much for him...our only child, his son...his heir."

Greg was distracted by the sound of Beauregard's voice in the other room.   He sounded angry.   Greg looked over at Tom.   Tom's frown indicated that he heard the anger as well.   Henry's voice brought Greg's attention back to Sarah.

"...don't want to cause you pain. I just couldn't help wondering..." Henry whispered.

"Oh, it isn't your fault. I probably would have done the same thing.   Actually, Beau even took Thurston treasure hunting when he was small.   I think that was where Thurston developed his love for the woods and hunting."   She heaved a deep sigh.   "I do miss all the activity...Thurston, Carl Despard, Samuel Brinker. They were the three musketeers.   Carl still comes to visit us now and then.   He and Beau will go for a walk in the woods together, or fishing.   At my age, the thought that I don't have much time left is a bit of a comfort. I know it might sound sad, but ...."

Greg spoke up.   "I know that was a terrible time for you.   The Sutter girls turned your old home into a teahouse.   It was broken into recently, that's how I became involved.   You see, I'm also a police detective. I guess I can't resist a good mystery.   That's why the note interests me.   Do you remember the ladies who lived next door to you? The ones that disappeared."

"Oh, dear...of course. They were so...fun. Who would just up and leave like that?" She fiddled with the needlepoint. Greg sensed he hit a nerve.

"You may remember that they had a bird, a macaw, to be exact. Well, it appears the Sutter girls now have him in the teahouse. Can you imagine? What are the chances of that?" Greg paused for a moment as he shifted in his chair. "The interesting thing is that he says things that make us wonder if he knows what happened to those ladies. I'm sure that sounds odd, but it's true."

Greg watched Sarah to see her response. She was white. At that moment, her husband entered the room. "Sorry that took me so long, gentlemen. Honestly, you'd think my stockbroker could..." He stopped and stared at his wife. "Sarah?"

"Beauregard, I was just chatting with these kind gentlemen. Suddenly, I don't feel well, dear. It could be the heat." Then she collapsed.

The ambulance lights flashed in the driveway. The men stood on the walkway, watching the proceedings through the open front door. "I'm sure glad you were here. I could've lost her, too." Beau's voice shook and he didn't look much better than his wife who was being put onto a stretcher. Greg was worried about him. After Sarah passed out, Tom called 911 as Greg worked to resuscitate Sarah. Henry did a great job calming Beauregard down and got him to sit in a chair while Greg worked on Sarah. Finally, she came around, although even now, her pulse was weak. He wasn't sure she was going to live, but he did all he could. "Mr. Hamilton, please let me drive you to the hospital," Greg said. "Is there anybody else you would like us to call?" Beauregard looked dazed, a man in a nightmare.

"No...I can't think of anyone. We have no family. Oh, God!" He choked back tears.

Greg realized the Hamiltons really had no one. How sad to be their age and all alone. Perhaps Carl? Sarah mentioned him; after all, he did visit them.

"Would it help if I called Carl Despard?" Greg volunteered.

Beauregard stared at Greg as if he were an alien. "No, he's utterly useless." Greg was stunned. He didn't know how to respond. Beauregard continued, "I can go in the ambulance with Sarah. It will be no problem to have a cab take me home." Greg nodded; his attention was now on Sarah as she was wheeled from the house. She reached out for Greg's hand on the way by.

"Please come with me in the ambulance." Her soft eyes searched Greg's.

"It's okay, Sarah. I'm going with you," Beauregard said.

"No, dear. I think it will be too much for you. Couldn't one of those gentlemen bring you? I really would feel safer if this young man came. He saved my life."

Greg felt caught in the middle. He shifted his weight and shuffled his feet. Tom, who stood only a few feet away, came to his rescue. "Mr. Hamilton, I think your wife has a point. Henry Sanders and I will drive you to the hospital. We can make sure everything is okay and wait with you for a bit. You don't need to be alone right now." Beauregard let himself be led away by Henry and Tom. He gazed over his shoulder at his wife. It was clear the man was lost.

Sarah, as weak as she was, had a grip on Greg's hand. She was not letting go. Greg remembered their conversation and wondered why she seemed so determined to live. Perhaps, she really didn't want to die. Of course, death wouldn't care what she wanted. "Sarah, I think they want me to sit in the front," Greg said gently.

"No, dear. I want you in the back. There are things I need to tell you. Things that can't wait." Turning to the ambulance medic and driver, she said, "I'd feel ever so much better if this kind gentleman rode with me."

"We don't normally allow that, ma'am. There isn't really room back there. He'll need to ride in the front." The medic nodded toward the front of the ambulance.

"Young man." Despite her weakened state, her eyes blazed at him. "I could *die* on the way to the hospital and if I'm gonna die, this man needs to be there!" She eyed Greg and said calmly, "Show 'em your badge, detective."

Startled, Greg showed the men his badge. They looked at each other and shrugged.

"That's better." Sarah smiled.

Greg sat in silence as the medic asked Sarah questions and took her vital signs. His mind was on her story. If Beauregard took Thurston treasure hunting, why deny the possibility of a treasure? Was it just a game? Greg doubted it. Was Beauregard upset that someone else would find the treasure? That seemed silly. The man was over eighty. How much treasure hunting could he do? He hadn't asked for a copy of the poem. Was Sarah's heart attack brought on by Greg's questions, or was it just coincidence?

Her soft voice spoke to Greg. "Okay, detective. Now you listen to me. That money, if there is any, should stay hidden. It's caused nothing but grief."

Greg didn't respond. Sarah Hamilton was too weak for him to ask questions. He was sure she knew more then she indicated. Was there a link to the ladies next door? Probably not. Still, she lived next door to them. Did she know where they went? Maybe they confided in her? Could she have been their friend?

"Detective, did you hear me?" Sarah whispered.

"Yes, ma'am, I heard you. Your husband seems adamant there is no treasure." He moved to let the medic check the equipment she was hooked up to. "You seem to disagree, or at least aren't so sure."

She was silent for a few moments. The ambulance siren and the sound of the machines hung in the air. She turned her head and looked him in the eyes.

"We're here," the driver called back.

"Let it go, detective! The money's cursed! Let it go!"

That was it. She was taken out of the ambulance and rushed through the ER doors. Why would a woman, who could be uttering her last breath, choose to have him come with her in the ambulance? Why was telling him to forget about the treasure more important than having her husband with her? What did she know, or think she knew? He stared at the ER doors. Would he ever get a chance to ask her?

Tom and Henry pulled up with Beauregard Hamilton. "Thank you, gentlemen. Mr. Mullins, I'm grateful you were there to help my wife. Please, all of you, go home. Let the past rest. Let us live what is left of our lives in peace!" He walked away from them and Greg saw him go up to the triage desk.

It was almost nine-thirty by the time they pulled into Henry's driveway. Greg was exhausted. The Sutter girls and the Dindles were waiting for them. Greg admitted to himself that the prospect of seeing Terry again put a spring in his step. Unfortunately, there wasn't much news to give them, and what news they did have wasn't real good. He followed Henry and Tom into the house.

"So?" Karen asked. "Any treasure?"

"While we were there, Sarah Hamilton collapsed. It was probably a heart attack. So we didn't get much information. We're all pretty sure Hamilton's holding out, but that's about it," Greg said.

"That poor woman," gasped Rose. "What happened?"

Everyone listened as Henry related the story. He praised Greg for his role in resuscitating Sarah Hamilton. Greg realized Henry was really proud of him. That felt good. Greg's father died when Greg was twenty. With his dad gone, Greg didn't get to hear the accolades and respect of an older man. He enjoyed it.

"Well," Rose said, "it isn't important now, but Henry, you forgot the photo album. It's kind of sad she didn't get a chance to look at it. It might have brought back some good memories."

"Apparently not for Mrs. Despard," Karen commented. "The jury's still out on what set off Mr. Brinker."

"What album are you talking about?" Shannon asked.

"We found an old photo album up in our attic the night of the break-in. It must've belonged to the Hamiltons. It has pictures of them and their house," Terry answered.

"And a lot of squirrels," added Karen.

"Can I see it?" asked Shannon.

"Sure, dear. It's right over there on the table," Rose said, pointing.

Shannon went and got it and sat back down on the couch next to Karen.

"I was really hoping for more to go on," said Greg. "We might be nearing a dead end. None of this seems to have anything to do with the break—"

"Squirrels!" shouted Shannon, interrupting.

"What?" asked Tom.

"Squirrels, the little guys that live in trees and eat nuts. Look, this one is peeking in the attic window. I bet squirrels are the tree gnomes!"

No one spoke for a moment. "Think about it," continued Shannon. "They have homes, which could be their 'estate'; they evidently watched the Hamiltons from their windowsill; and they are certainly under Heaven and above Hell."

Greg had to admit it sounded good. He looked at Tom who was nodding his head in thoughtful admiration. Apparently, it felt right in Tom's gut.

"Now all we need to do is figure out which tree held a squirrel's nest over sixty years ago," said Terry.

"Well," Tom said, "we might want to try the vicinity of the Dindle's water garden."

"Why?" asked Rose.

Mrs. Dindle explained to her about the old box, then added, "But everything around there has been dug up over the years. I found that box under an old rose bush."

"Rats," said Tom. "It's gotta be there, somewhere."

"Hold it, hold it, hold it," said Shannon, obviously in thought.

"You're on a roll tonight," commented Karen, who was up and pouring herself another margarita. It amazed Greg how many of those things that woman could put away in one evening.

"What if...." Shannon continued, looking at Tom, "the sisters who lived in our house—"

"The Gutheries," said Henry.

"Yeah," said Shannon, seemingly annoyed that her thoughts were interrupted. "What if *they* found the gold and took off with it?   Maybe Beauregard Sr. is trying to tell us they took his gold."

"Okay, I'm with ya," said Tom.

"But why now?" asked Terry.   "Remember, the house wasn't haunted until now.   And why knock teacups off the shelf?"

"I dunno," Shannon said, shrugging. "Maybe the old girls didn't like tea."

"Wow," commented Henry. "She could be right. Maybe…. Okay, if that's true, does Hamilton suspect it?"

"And why would Sarah Hamilton warn me off? Is she protecting the Gutheries? Maybe she knows where they went," Greg said. "If she makes it through, I'm gonna talk to her again. I think she's the key to some of this. At least she knows more than she said."

"Dang," said Karen, flopping her head back on the couch. "Something else to keep me awake tonight."

"I'm gonna sleep, anyway," said Terry. "I'm so tired, I don't care who took the treasure or where it went."

The discussion broke up, and Greg and Tom walked Karen and the Dindle's home. He and Tom were finally headed home. Greg could hear his mattress calling his name.

"I hope Sarah Hamilton lives long enough to tell me what she knows. I feel like a heel, thinking about leaning on a little old lady, but I really wanna figure this out. What's your gut saying?"

"My gut says we're going in the right direction. There's missing pieces, but we're getting warmer. I think Shannon's right, the Gutheries found the treasure. If they're still alive, which I think is very doubtful, Hamilton may be trying to track them down. Maybe that's why Sarah isn't talking and why Hamilton is denying the treasure existed. I'm with you; I hope Sarah Hamilton makes it."

They drove in silence the rest of the way to Greg's house. Tom dropped him off and headed home.

Greg lay in bed, thinking. He really wanted to figure this stuff out, but then...he really liked spending time with Terry and her family. He sensed Tom was developing "a thing" for Shannon. She was certainly smart; she figured out the tree gnome piece. Still, what did the teacups have to do with this? His mind released the mystery for the night and he fell into a deep sleep.

CHAPTER 17

It was late afternoon before Greg got a chance to check on Sarah Hamilton. The hospital had her listed as "stable." He called Henry.

"Hey, it's Greg," he said when Henry answered.

"Well, hello, young fella! Any news?"

"Actually, yeah. Sarah is listed in stable condition. After work, I think I'll have Tom head out there with me. If her husband's around, he may not let us talk to her. It's worth a try, though."

"Sounds good. If you're up for it, stop by when you're done. I went out and got some beer this afternoon. I'm getting a little tired of margaritas."

Greg laughed. "It's a deal. I'll call ya when we're done and let you know one way or the other."

"Adios!"

"Adios," Greg said, seeing Tom walk in.

"What's the good word?" Tom asked, sitting down at his desk. "I don't think I've seen you all day."

"Yeah, I was helping on a traffic fatality. Two cars with teens barreled into each other. We're trying to figure out what happened. Both had stop signs; both left skid marks. Two dead, five in critical and a couple of body parts on the road. Ugly." Greg shuddered as he thought about it. Being a cop didn't make him immune to the horror of it all.

"Any news on Sarah Hamilton?" Tom sipped what Greg assumed was coffee.

"Actually, yeah. She's in stable condition. I was gonna ask you to go with me after work to pay the old gal a visit." Greg got up and poured coffee into his mug.

"I can, but if her husband is around, you're not gonna get within ten feet of her."

"I know, I know, but I gotta try. I found something to poke at and I'm gonna poke away and see what happens."

"Let's hope what you're poking at doesn't bite," Tom said.

"Hmmm," said Greg. "I hope I can find out what teacups and treasure have in common."

"They both begin with the letter *t*," Tom said, slapping Greg on the back.

By the time four-thirty rolled around, Terry felt ready to drop. I can't wait to close and take a nap, she thought. She was so tired, she was numb. She felt no fear or anxiety. She literally felt nothing at all, except exhaustion. Just then, the door opened and Carl came in.

"Hey," he said.

"Hi, you here for tea?"

"Naw." He smiled. "I wanted to give you and Karen these." He handed her two tickets. "*My Fair Lady* is at the Cabaret Dinner Theater. Rose Filwater, who I think was your art teacher, did the scenery. I thought you and Karen might want a night out. It's last minute. Tonight is the last night it's playing. It's my way of saying thank you for the other day."

"Hi, Carl," Karen said, walking toward them. "To what do we owe the pleasure?"

"Carl brought us tickets for the dinner theater tonight," Terry said. She hoped her exhaustion was not coming through. Rose Filwater was Terry's mentor.

Terry wanted to see her artwork, but not tonight.

"Really," said Karen.

"I'm sorry it's last minute. You certainly don't have to go," said Carl. "I knew Terry's art teacher from high school did the scenery. It's my way of saying thank you for the tea party. I can take 'em back and try to get some for their next production. Although I don't know if Rose Filwater is doing the scenery."

"It's *My Fair Lady*, Mom's favorite," said Terry, feeling a sense of resignation. They were gonna go. They had to. Carl didn't have a lot of money. This gift was a big deal. She looked at Karen and saw the same sense of resignation in her eyes. Terry hugged Carl, who blushed. "You're such a sweet man. You didn't have to do this. We'd love to go."

"Great," said Carl, beaming. "Do ya mind if I use your restroom?"

Terry smiled. "Not at all."

As Carl went down the hall, Terry looked at the tickets. "It doesn't start until seven. At least we can grab a nap."

"Yeah, I really need one," said Karen. "My whole body aches. I feel like I got hit by a truck. A power nap and a dinner show. It sounds fun."

"It's *My Fair Lady*," said Terry. "I hope I don't bust out bawlin', thinking of Mom."

"I'll bring plenty of tissues," said Karen, hugging her sister.

Henry was having a tough time keeping himself amused. The girls were at the dinner show; Greg and Tom were at the hospital; and Rosey was at a quilting bee. He sat down and began to look through the photo album. Maybe he should have asked Greg to come by and pick it up. It might perk Sarah up to see some old photos of her son. On the other hand, it might depress her.

I wonder why she told Greg the treasure was cursed? That really was an odd thing to say. Too bad Thurston Hamilton was killed. I'll bet he knew what happened to that treasure. Hmmmm, maybe that's why he harassed those women. Maybe that's why they just took off. Henry stood up and began to pace. Were they afraid of Thurston Hamilton? He looked at a picture of Thurston, Carl and Sam. Carl and Sam! I'll bet Thurston told them something, Henry mused as he went in to the kitchen to cut himself a piece of ice cream cake. Would it be wrong to ask Sam Brinker? What if he flipped out like he did when Rose showed him the picture? Maybe it was the picture that set him off. Rats, thought Henry. I forgot to check that article and see who found Thurston's body. I really think it said it was Carl and Sam. Yeah, I'm sure it did. Is that what Sam is thinking of when he talks about blood? Man, I love Rosey's ice cream cake, he thought. It's funny how eating helps me think.

Okay, I'll assume Shannon is right. The Gutherie sisters found the treasure. The Hamiltons found out and Thurston began to harass the ladies. If the treasure was found in their garden, it might explain the animal carcasses Thurston left. Henry washed off his dish, put it in the dishwasher, then went outside to pace on the porch. Okay, so the ladies left town in the middle of the night. Wait, it said their car was left behind. That meant someone drove them. Was that someone Sarah Hamilton? Maybe Thurston was tracking them down when he was shot. No, he was killed in a hunting accident. Hey, maybe, just maybe…no…that was far-fetched. Of course, a few weeks ago, ghosts in the teahouse was far-fetched. Henry slapped a mosquito, then lit the citronella candle. What if Eloise and Mary buried the treasure? What if Thurston was looking for it when he was killed? That could work. If Sarah Hamilton was the driver for the ladies, it was possible she took them down by her house on the shore and helped them hide the treasure. If Thurston went to go looking for the treasure, he probably took Carl and Sam with him. Okay, Sam had to know something. However, if I upset him, Rosey and the girls will have my head. What to do?

Henry went to the kitchen and took his car keys. He'd risk his neck. It was better than pacing around. Wait, what if Greg called? Henry took his cell phone. He'd call Greg after his visit with Sam.

"Hello, Sarah," Greg said, smiling. "I came to see how you're doing. This is Detective Tom O'Hara. You probably remember him from the other night."

"Lucky me," said Sarah, sitting up a bit. "I get two handsome detectives to visit me."

Greg cleared his throat. "You certainly gave us a scare. It looks like they're taking good care of you here."

Sarah eyed him cautiously. She seemed to sense this was more than a friendly visit. "I certainly can't complain. All the nurses have been very nice. It's kind of you two to stop by. I should be getting my rest, though."

Greg knew it was now or never. The doctor gave them only fifteen minutes to talk to her. Greg did not feel hopeful. "Mrs. Hamilton, it seems you know something about the rumor or truth of the hidden money. Perhaps you know something about the disappearance of the Gutherie sisters as well. Although you urged me to leave well enough alone, I'm not going to do that. I can't help wondering if the secrets you're keeping are causing your body stress. That may be what got you here in the first place."

Sarah's eyes narrowed. "It's curiosity that killed the cat, detective. A secret never killed anyone."

Tom spoke up. "Actually, that's not true, Mrs. Hamilton. It's been my experience that secrets kill more people than curiosity ever will. There's something about lies and secrets. They keep haunting their owners. It's as if they take on a life of their own and become like the living dead. Their putrid, rotting corpses follow us until the truth surfaces and buries them. If the truth can't bury the lies, the lies bury their owners. It seems to me, ma'am, the lies and secrets you've been carrying around all these years are really starting to stink. Time to bury 'em. Don't you think?" He took a recorder from his pocket and set it on the sliding table sitting in front of Sarah.

Greg watched Sarah for any sign she might give in. They were running out of time. Her face grimaced. In an instant, the sweet gentle persona she carried vanished. Her demeanor changed. Her lips curled into a cruel snarl. She stunned Greg with a short cold laugh.

"My husband and son thought they were slick, but they're no match for me. They were as nasty as my parents. I thought I'd taken care of the evil in my life when I buried my parents. Eloise and Mary Gutherie were my friends. I wasn't going to let Beauregard and Thurston get away with it. Not for money. They'll never get that money, now. Fools.

"On the night the Gutherie sisters disappeared, I happened to look out my kitchen window. It was quite late. I couldn't sleep. Thurston and his two friends were out hunting and Beau was asleep. I was just puttering about. When I looked out the window, I saw Mary and Eloise working in their yard. I thought it was odd they were in their garden at that time of the night. I was going to go outside and see what they were doing, but I decided since I was in my nightgown, I'd better stay inside. Because the boys were out and about, I was concerned they might have done something horrible again. They were often doing terrible things like leaving dead animals in the Gutherie's garden. I wasn't blind. I knew Thurston had a cruel streak. I checked again and noticed Mary and Eloise were bringing something into their house. It didn't seem to have anything to do with the boys, so I went back to bed." She took a sip of water.

"I d just fallen asleep when I heard the kitchen door open. Thurston came to the bedroom door and whispered for Beau. Beau sat up and said, 'Go back to sleep. I'll go see what they caught.' So I rolled over and tried to go back to sleep. I heard them go outside again. I thought they went to take care of whatever the boys killed. I didn't hear anything for a while. Suddenly, I heard voices again and I heard the truck door open. I went to the window and saw Beau with a rifle pointed at Eloise and Mary. I didn't know what to do. They all got in the truck and left. I was so confused. I couldn't understand why he would do such a thing and with the boys, too. Then I decided I must be wrong. Perhaps something happened and he was taking the sisters to the police station. He must have needed the gun for protection. I was so upset that I took some sleeping pills and went to sleep.

Greg didn't like where this was going. The hairs on his arm rose up as he began to realize that the sisters didn't leave on their own volition.

Sarah continued. "Early in the morning, the phone rang. I answered and Beau said he and the boys decided to go to the house on the shore, the one where we live now, and hunt. I thought it was odd, but I decided I'd better not say anything. I got dressed, waited until about 9:00 and went next door. No one was there, but the doors weren't locked. I went in and walked through the house, calling their names. Their bird kept saying, 'Move it, ladies. Finders keepers, boys. Nasty boys. Ladies gone. Ladies gone.' It was over forty years ago and I still can hear that poor bird. Anyway, in the corner of their living room were these wooden boxes with bags. Some of the bags were open. It was filled with all sorts of gold coins and jewelry. I knew it had to be the treasure. Eloise and Mary Gutherie found the treasure! In another corner was a trunk with stacks of bills. Eloise once told me they didn't trust banks. It looked as if they kept all their money in that trunk." She took another sip of water and continued.

"I went home, sat down at the kitchen table and cried. I knew they must be dead. I blame myself. If only I went outside the night before. I don't think Beau and Thurston would have killed me, too. Maybe I could have saved my friends' lives." She took a tissue from the table next to her and wiped her eyes. Then she readjusted herself in the bed.

Greg's mind was racing. Sam Brinker and Carl Despard were involved. Could this be what was tormenting Mr. Brinker? If they found the treasure, what happened to the money? Those men didn't seem the type to be involved in murder. And Mr. Tea! That phrase, 'nasty boys,' hadn't he'd heard Mr. Tea say it the other day at the teahouse? Yes! Mr. Tea said it to him and Terry just before the bird called him an idiot! Did Mr. Tea recognize Carl Despard? Was it possible? His mind refocused as Sarah continued.

"I was sick all day. After dark, Beau and the boys came back. Samuel Brinker looked awful. Carl looked shaken, but Samuel was pale as a ghost. I'm sure his breakdown started way back then. That poor, poor dear. After I'd fed them, I said I was going to bed, but I stood at the window, hidden by the curtains, and watched them move the money into the woods. I knew then what I had to do.

"After a few more days, people began looking for Eloise and Mary. Beau and the boys made themselves scarce, so it was easy for me to have time to look for the treasure. Once I found it, I called my sister, Lucille. She lived down by our house at the shore. We came up with a perfect plan." She smiled brightly, obviously proud of herself.

"I called down to the house at the shore and told Beau I needed Thurston to take me over to my sister's house. My plan worked like a charm. It was fall, you know, and the leaves were changing. We were almost to my sister's house when I told Thurston I wanted to see if I could find some fall wildflowers. I made him pull over. He followed me into the woods. He was so surprised when I took out a small pistol. I told him I knew what he did and I wasn't going to let him hurt anyone again. I raised the gun and shot him. I wiped the gun off, put it in his hand and slipped through the woods to a place my sister was waiting for me. The leaves helped cover my tracks. I also used a pine branch to sweep them away as I walked. The bad seed was gone. Thurston had tormented people for the last time. Beau did what he did for Thurston. Maybe Thurston talked him into it. I don't know. There would be no more children for us, naturally. Beau and I would just have to live out the rest of our lives alone. I could live with that far more than I could live wondering who Thurston was going to hurt next.

"Lucille and I went back to my house, into the woods and moved the bags. We went up into the attic, pried up the floorboards and some of the wood paneling. We hid it behind there. I knew they'd never find it. The snakes even took the money from the trunk! Lucille and I have small feet, you know. We took some children's boots from the Goodwill bin at the church and walked waaaaay around the outside of the woods, and tracked into where the gold was. We even ripped some flannel shirts and left pieces hanging about on small trees and bushes. Kids were always in the woods, so it wasn't too far fetched. The first part of the plan was done."

The treasure was in the attic! The break-in. Greg glanced at Tom who was staring wide-eyed at Sarah. Greg almost laughed. Police detectives rarely stare open-mouthed at someone, but this was one scenario they never expected! This quiet, seemingly gentle woman was a psycho who had killed her own son. Somehow, the Sutter's teahouse got sucked into this.

Sarah closed her eyes as she continued on. "That night, Beau called Lucille's house, looking for Thurston. I told him that he dropped me off and headed back. Maybe the truck broke down. Beau and the boys went looking and they found the truck and Thurston.

"Right after the funeral, Beau and Carl discovered the bags were gone. They knew it wasn't Samuel because he went to stay with his aunt in Vermont. His mother thought the stress from Thurston's death made him ill. I was glad he went away. Anyway, Beau and Carl spent nights and weekends tramping around our woods. After a few months, I insisted we sell the house and move. Beau, of course, wanted no part of it. So, I took to my bed. Finally, he relented. He really didn't have much fight left in him after Thurston died."

She sighed, opened her eyes and looked at Tom and then at Greg. "So, that's the story. I can't say I feel better or worse for having told it. Since I seem to be confessing my sins to you gentlemen, I will also tell you that Lucille and I killed our parents. They were horrible drunks who beat us. One day, we took a shotgun out to the barn and shot them while they were drunk and asleep. We set the barn on fire and went into town to get fabric for dresses. Of course everyone knew they were drunks. They all assumed my parents caused the fire themselves. Everyone felt so sorry for me and Lucille. The people in town even rebuilt our barn for us." She smiled again. "I guess I'm like an avenging angel. I do away with evil." She shrugged. "I still miss Lucille. She died about ten years ago. She was a wonderful sister."

A nurse came in. "Officers, it's time for you to let our sweet patient rest." She walked to the bed and helped Sarah settle back down. Sarah smiled and patted the nurse's hand.

Tom reached out, turned off the tape recorder and put it in his pocket. Greg stared at Sarah, not sure what to say to this woman who personified a wolf in sheep's clothing. "Thank you, Mrs. Hamilton. I hope you rest well," was all he said as they left.

As they walked down the hall, Tom said, "Wow, that was a trip. That was one story I never saw coming. Man!"

"I guess we should stop at Fair Meadows and see Sam Brinker. We can track down Carl Despard too. I'm not sure what to do with this information. Under different circumstances we'd arrest her, but, at the moment, she's not going anywhere. We'd better talk this over with the chief."

As they reached the patrol car, Tom looked at Greg. "Someone knows where that money is. Assuming Sarah is telling the truth and she never told anyone, someone seems to have figured out her secret."

"No," said Greg. "I don't think they know for sure. They're scouting and they're getting close."

"Any ideas?" Tom asked.

"Not really, but Sam or Carl might have a few." Then it hit him. He smacked the steering wheel. "It's gotta be Carl. Sam Brinker is out of commission. Sam might know something, but he certainly isn't breaking into the teahouse."

"Well, Sarah's story explains the book on the water garden falling off the table. It also explains the story Mrs. Dindle told about Shannon's lunch money winding up outside in the garden." Tom smiled and gave a shiver. "Looks like we got ghosts."

"Yeah, but I still don't get the teacup. If it's all connected, we're missing something." He looked at Tom. "Let's hope our stop at Fair Meadows points us in the right direction."

As he entered the convalescent part of Fair Meadows, Henry obeyed the posted sign and shut off his cell phone. He stopped at the desk.

"I'm looking for Sam Brinker," he told the nurse.

"Room two-twenty-one, just down that hall," she said, pointing.

Man, thought Henry, I hope I don't regret this.

Henry peeked in Sam's door. There was a bed, a small nightstand, a dresser with a television on top and two chairs by the window with a table between them. Sam sat in the far chair by the window, working on a puzzle book. It has to be math puzzles, thought Henry, walking in the room.

"Henry, this is a pleasant surprise. How's the golf game? I don't get to do that here. They've got a little chip-and-putt I use, but that's it."

"I'm afraid I haven't played much golf lately. I've been helping Terry get things squared away at the teahouse," Henry said, taking a seat in the other chair by the window.

"It was nice to see Karen the other day," Sam said, looking down at his hands. "I had a rough spell that day, so I feel bad."

Henry thought, well, there's no time like the present. "Sam," he said quietly, "I want to talk to you about the night Eloise and Mary Gutherie disappeared."

Sam licked his lips and his eyes darted back and forth, but he said nothing. "Sam, is this what's tormenting you? If it is, you can't get well refusing to talk about it. I don't think you hurt those women, but I think you know what happened to them. Is that true?"

Sam began to sweat, his hands shook, and again he licked his lips. Henry waited. "I know nothing about that, you're wasting your time," Sam snapped at Henry.

"I think you might," Henry said gently. "The girls found a note indicating there is treasure buried somewhere on the Hamilton's property. Mrs. Dindle, who lives next door to the teahouse, found some wooden bank boxes in her garden. I think the Gutherie sisters found the treasure. I also think that Thurston Hamilton knew they found it. I'm sure he would have told you and Carl." Henry felt nervous. He didn't want to push Sam too hard.

"Why would he say anything to us?" Sam asked, looking down at the puzzle book.

Good, thought Henry. He didn't deny it. He answered my question with another one. I'm getting somewhere. "Sam, you guys were his best friends. Like I said, I don't think you hurt them. I just want to know if they found the treasure and if they left town with it. I'm not accusing you of anything." Henry stopped and smiled, trying not to push too hard. "Sam, it's obvious something is weighing on you. Is it Thurston's death?"

"I don't want to talk about that," Sam said. "Look, Henry, please leave me alone. I can't help you, I really can't."

"Okay," said Henry, realizing it was not a good idea to harp on the poor guy. "Just one more question. Is it that you *can't* help or you *won't* help?" Henry didn't know why, but a thought occurred to him that made him ask Sam one more thing. "I want your word that there is nothing in the past that can hurt my nieces. You don't have to tell me anything. Just promise me they're safe. They mean the world to me and Rosey."

Sam Brinker stared into Henry's eyes. Henry said nothing. It was obvious Sam was debating. Henry stared back. He watched as Sam's thoughts turned inward and traveled back over forty years.

"It was probably around eleven- thirty...maybe even twelve. We were coming back...."

He saw it clearly, as if years had not elapsed, as if that night was suspended in time. Hunting wasn't good that night. He and Carl weren't really into it. Thurston always was. Thurston had a passion for the thrill of the hunt. He couldn't get enough of it. He stalked things in an eerie silence that gave Sam the shivers. Now, Thurston was agitated like an addict needing a fix. It was Thurston who saw them first. He stopped and crouched and motioned Sam and Carl to do the same. Following his pointing finger, Sam saw the two elderly women drag a bag into their house. Even from a distance, it was clear they were dirty and sweaty. Even when they gardened, every hair was in place and they looked as if they'd just stepped from a picture. Perhaps that was why Thurston hated them. Maybe their elegance and gentleness irked him. What were these normally spotless ladies doing dragging something inside at this time of night? Were they gardening at night because Thurston tormented them during the day? Did they not want people to see them dirty? Naw, that seemed stupid.

"The treasure…" came the hiss of the snake. "They found my granddad's treasure!"

Sam looked at Carl. Carl looked from Thurston to the women. Carl seemed as nervous as Sam. Thurston could be dangerous. "No…." Carl whispered. "That's impossible. It's probably some kind of fertilizer…" Carl was silenced by a wave of Thurston's hand.

Sam watched as Thurston belly-crawled toward the women. Sam wanted to jump up and scream, to warn the prey of the hunter, but his own fear paralyzed him. The Gutheries went inside. Maybe they would stay there. Thurston slowly inched toward their garden. It was hard to tell, but in the moonlight, it looked as if they were trying to plant a bush. It sat on the side by a hole. Dang it! The Gutheries came out. As they neared the garden, Thurston stood up. "Whatcha doin', ladies?" They jumped and put their hands to their chests.

"Go away, Thurston," Eloise, the braver and stronger of the two, said. "Get off our property. You're not welcome here!"

"I go wherever I want, Missssss El-o-ise. Right now, I want to see what you've got in that hole you're diggin." He bent and looked.

Sam's heart pounded so loud, he was sure everyone could hear it. He was drenched in sweat. Oh God, he prayed silently, let it be manure in that hole.

"Well, you might have something in there that belongs to me. Let's go have a look inside, shall we?" He leveled his rifle at them. "Move it." He turned, looked over his shoulder, and beckoned Sam and Carl to follow.

Obediently, they simultaneously stood up. "This is bad, Carl, really bad. Maybe we should get Mr. Hamilton."

"He's as loony as Thurston. Where do ya think Thurston gets it from? Let's go. Maybe we can think of something, or maybe they'll just give him the dang bags." Carl led the way as the two boys followed Thurston into the house.

Thurston's voice came from a room to the right as Carl and Sam entered the kitchen. "Well, well, ladies. Looks like you did the work for me. You make good little wenches." He laughed as Carl and Sam entered the room that contained expensive Victorian furniture and a bird in a cage. Sitting next to the cage were four old wooden boxes containing yellowed bags with some type of writing on them. Sam thought he could make out the word 'bank.'

"Finders, keepers, sonny," Mary spoke up.

"Shut up!" barked Thurston.

"Nasty boys, nasty boys," squawked the bird, hopping from leg to leg and flapping his feathers.

Thurston cursed and turned to Carl. "Keep your gun on 'em. Don't let 'em move. I'm getting the old man." He stormed out of the room and Sam heard the kitchen door slam.

"Ladies, for god's sake, just give 'im the bags. Don't make trouble, please," Sam begged. His stomach felt ill.

"Why don't you stand up to him, young man?" asked Eloise. "The two of you seem like decent boys. He's trouble. He's gonna get you in a mess one of these days. Look at yourselves. You both look terrified, standing there."

Sam knew she was right. He looked over at Carl. He was sweating and the rifle shook in his hands. "Ladies, this is bad. He's crazy, give 'im the bags.

Does it really matter? After all, it was his grandfather's money."

"Why should we give in to a bully?" Eloise said, defiantly lifting her head. "We were going to call Sarah in the morning. She's so lovely. What a tragedy her son turned out like...*that*. Why don't you go out the front door and run for help, boys? We'll lock the doors and hold 'em off until you get back. Take one gun and leave one for us."

Before Sam and Carl could answer, the kitchen door slammed again. The authoritative thud of his boots on the floor preceded Mr. Hamilton's entrance. Thurston swaggered in behind him, looking even more bold and nasty.

"Ladies," Mr. Hamilton said in a gentlemanly, but cold and nasty way. "I hear you have something that belongs to my family. We expect you will give it back."

"Why should we?" Eloise asked, standing taller, head up. "It was on our property. The property *you* sold us. I think possession counts for something...Mr. Hamilton." She seemed to outshine him. The tall and broad Mr. Hamilton was dwarfed in the presence of this gracious, strong woman.

Sam watched Mr. Hamilton's face change as if being bested brought out the hate and rage in him. Thurston stood next to him, his face a reflection of his father's. "Let's go for a little ride, ladies," Mr. Hamilton growled, pointing his rifle at them. The ladies looked at each other, perhaps realizing they went too far. "Move it, ladies! We haven't got all night."

Suddenly, Mary grabbed at her chest, her face paled, sweat broke out on her face. "Oh....oh...." she moaned.

"Mary!" Eloise grabbed her sister and held her up. "We've got to get her to a hospital. You stupid, greedy man! You can have the money. For heaven's sake, get her to a hospital, take your damn money."

Mr. Hamilton smiled a sly, smarmy smile. He turned and gestured graciously toward the doorway. The sisters shuffled out, Mary leaning on Eloise.

"I'll take her," Eloise snapped, moving toward her own car. "You can stay here and count your precious, stolen bounty."

Sam felt a wave of relief until Mr. Hamilton said, "Get in the truck, now. Don't argue with me, you self-righteous bitch." No one spoke for a bit. Then, as if in a trance, they all climbed in the truck. The death truck as Sam later came to think of it.

They drove for about half an hour. Sam, Carl and Thurston, sitting in the bed of the truck, heard Eloise begin to scream. They turned and looked through the window into the cab. Mary was slumped over onto Eloise's shoulder. Eloise began to hit Mr. Hamilton with her fists. He smacked her so hard, her head snapped back and then fell forward. Thurston laughed, Sam clutched his stomach and looked sideways at Carl who stared into the night sky.

The truck pulled into the house at the shore. The moon shone on the waves. The ocean looked like the dark, oozy, life-draining hole that Sam felt in his stomach. Mr. Hamilton jumped out of the truck, walked around to the passenger side and pulled Mary's lifeless body out of the truck and carried her over his shoulder as if she was just another dead animal. Thurston grabbed the unconscious Eloise and threw her over his shoulder. He walked back to the truck bed, grabbed his rifle and followed his father to the dock. Tossing both bodies onto the dock, they took the dinghy and motored out to their boat, *Beauregard's Pride*. They climbed aboard and headed the boat toward the dock. Carl and Sam watched from the back of the truck as Mr. Hamilton docked the boat and Thurston jumped onto the dock with his rifle, took aim and shot both bodies. He raised his rifle, threw back his head and howled at the moon.

"Oh…God have mercy on us," Sam said, his whole body shaking. Carl continued to stare speechlessly at the sky.

"Hurry up, boys. We need some help here," Mr. Hamilton called. Carl and Sam walked to the dock. Blood, pieces of bone and muscle were splattered about. The sight and the smell brought Sam to his knees, retching into the ocean. He'd killed and gutted animals plenty of times before, but these were human beings. Women he might have saved, had he not been such a coward.

"Ha, you sissy," Thurston mocked him. Get up and give us some help, be a man!" Sam watched helplessly as Carl and Thurston heaved Mary onto the boat. Thurston picked up Eloise's feet. "Grab her arms, Sam. Don't just stand there." Sam felt weak, drained of all energy. He could barely lift her. Carl nudged him out of the way and took the arms. Carl lost his grip for a second and Sam grabbed her, splattering himself with blood. Wordlessly, they climbed aboard.

Mr. Hamilton motored out a fair distance into the ocean. Then they dumped the bodies, weighted down with anything they could find, over the side. "Here, sharky, sharky. Come get your din din," Thurston called. Sam felt cold hatred engulf him. He knew he would, from that moment on, despise anything Hamilton.

"So, that's the story." Tears rolled down Sam's face. He looked directly at Henry. "I'm a coward. I held the story of that horrible night inside, afraid that

Mr. Hamilton would harm my mother. He swore if Carl or I breathed a word that we and our families would regret it. After what I'd let happen, I figured I deserved whatever happened to me, but I didn't want my mother to suffer for my cowardice. That night, Thurston and Carl took the crates and bags into the woods and hid 'em. I went home. I don't know why they let me go home, but they did. We figured they'd look for the Gutherie sisters sooner or later, so the next night, Mr. Hamilton made us clean their house up and wipe down anything that might have our prints on it. Police scoured the woods, even used dogs. Mr. Hamilton kept us at the shore for over a week. We scrubbed down the dock and the boat. He barely let us out of his sight.

"You wanna know the funny part. They did it all for nothing. The treasure disappeared the day Thurston was killed. Mr. Hamilton went ballistic. He had Carl look all over the woods for the rest of the summer. I made up a story and convinced my mom to let me stay with my aunt in Vermont. At first, I think Mr. Hamilton thought Thurston told someone else about the gold and someone took it and killed Thurston. When I came back from Vermont, Carl told me to be on the lookout for anyone who seemed to have money all of a sudden. Never saw anyone, though. Then, about ten months ago, Carl came to see me. He said that Mr. Hamilton thought Thurston might have hid the gold somewhere else. Maybe Thurston knew he was in danger. Mr. Hamilton thinks the gold might be in their old house."

Henry leaned forward. "Did Carl or Mr. Hamilton hurt Madeline Sutter?"

Sam shook his head. "Naw. She got sick on her own, but Carl used that as his chance. He stole some of his mother's sleeping pills, ground 'em up and put them in her sugar bowl. Every day, he'd go make her tea. He'd search the house while she napped. He felt sick when she fell. She probably made herself a cup of tea and toppled down the stairs. Carl liked her a lot. He loves those girls. Carl does what Mr. Hamilton says for the same reason I kept my mouth shut, to protect his mother. Hamilton's money is paying for Mrs. Despard to be here. Once my mother passed, I wanted to come out with it all, but then Mrs. Despard had the stroke. Hamilton owes us, me and Carl. Once Carl came to see me and told me about Hamilton's theory, I started having nightmares. I kept seeing those poor ladies. It got worse. I started hearing them calling for me to help them, even in the daytime. And that bird! That bird the girls have now is the same bird. He taunted me. I'd walk by and he'd chant, 'Guilty, guilty. Nasty boys. Move it, ladies. Nasty boys. Our secret.' That's no ordinary bird. No way."

Tears ran down his cheeks. "All these years. Thank God it's finally out. I hope Hamilton will take care of Mrs. Despard, but somehow I doubt it. She looked so nice dressed up for the community dinner they had here. Her picture was even in the paper. I hope God can forgive me. I don't think I can forgive myself."

Henry put his hand on Sam's knee. "The new pastor, Pastor Bob, at the church in town, says that we have no right to judge ourselves or others. Judgment is for God alone. To say we can't forgive is to put ourselves in the place of God. God forgives when we ask and repent. It doesn't matter how we feel about it. I hope that helps. I think he's right."

Sam smiled and reached out and shook Henry's hand. "Thank you. I think it does." There was silence as Sam stared into space. Suddenly, Sam Brinker threw back his head and let out a horrible wail. The wail seemed to contain the pent-up pain that grew and festered over the years. "Oh, my God, forgive my cowardice." He wrung his hands, then wrapped his arms around his body. A nurse ran into Sam's room. Henry opened his mouth to speak, but Sam cut him off. "Nurse, get Doctor Howard. I need to talk to him immediately." The nurse looked at Henry who nodded. Doctor Howard was the psychiatrist for Fair Meadows. Henry knew Sam would be okay now. The truth was out; the past had lost its death grip on Sam's mind. Henry once heard a pastor say, "The power of Satan is in the lie, in the unmentionable secret or anything we are afraid to speak of. Once the truth is out, even though there might be consequences, a person is free, Satan's hold is gone." How true, Henry thought. Sam is living proof of that.

An image flashed in Henry's mind. The dress! The dinner, the community dinner, here at Fair Meadows, he, Rose and Dottie Dindle went. The dress was Mrs. Despard's. Oh no! Carl Despard...he gave the girls tickets for the dinner theater tonight. He'd better call the police and get someone out to the teahouse. He ran toward the front door, his cell phone in his hand. The electric doors slid open and Henry ran smack dab into Greg and Tom.

CHAPTER 18

Mrs. Filwater's artwork amazed Terry. She realized she was so engrossed in studying the scenery, she didn't feel any waves of grief over her mother. If I could find the time, Terry thought, it would be fun to help out here. I'll have to give Mrs. Filwater a call. The lights went up for a short intermission and Terry looked over at Karen. She looked pale.

"Kar, you okay?" she asked, touching her sister's arm.

"No, I've got one of my migraines. I feel like hell!" She cradled her head in her hands.

"Do you think you're gonna be sick?" Terry asked, knowing that Karen usually threw up during a migraine.

"Not really. I wish I could, though. It usually makes me feel better."

"I better get you home before it gets worse. We're both staying with Henry and Rose tonight, right?" Terry wasn't sure she was up for another night of Rose's smothering, but they were out of excuses. At least nothing was crashing in the night at Rose's.

"Yeah, but I just wanna go home and lie down for a bit. You know how I get. I don't want anyone near me during a migraine. Aunt Rose means well, but I'd have to kill 'er. Oh man, my head."

Terry took Karen's arm and steered her toward the door. Karen got migraines from stress. The ghost stuff took more of a toll on her than she let on. I wonder if Greg is getting anywhere with Sarah Hamilton? Terry thought. Before they left for the theater, Uncle Henry told her Greg and Tom were heading to the hospital. Terry looked at Karen. She seemed even worse. "I'll have you home in a jiffy," Terry said, hoping Karen didn't throw up in her car.

"Here we are, home sweet home," Terry said, opening her car door.

"Uhhhhh, black spots," Karen wailed.

"Almost there. Pretty soon, you can lie down." On their way home, Terry called Rose from her cell phone and asked her to bring some ginger ale over for Karen. Rose understood Karen needed some peace and quiet in her own room. It was only eight-thirty, so Terry wasn't worried about being in the teahouse. Things didn't go bump until after midnight.

Terry unlocked the front door, switched on the lights and started to help Karen upstairs. Then Terry realized the attic stairs were down; she froze, unable to move or scream.

"Whaaaa?" whined Karen.

Terry's head spun. Not again, she thought.

"Let's go," Henry yelled, continuing to run toward his car. "I think there's gonna be another break-in at the teahouse tonight."

Tom and Greg quickly caught up to him. Before they could ask any questions, Henry's cell phone rang. "Hello?"

It was Rose. "Henry, thank goodness you answered. I've been trying to reach you!"

"What is it, Rose?" he snapped.

"Well, no need to get huffy," Rose said, and Henry rolled his eyes. "I need you to pick up ginger ale on your way home. Terry called, Karen got sick at the dinner theater. They had to leave."

"What?" screamed Henry into the phone.

"No need to worry, dear. They're safe. I saw them come home a few minutes ago."

Henry felt himself go cold. "Rosey," he whispered, "do not, I repeat, do not leave our house. Do not open the door. Hang up and, unless caller ID says it's the girls, do not answer the phone. Greg, Tom and I are on our way. I'm calling the teahouse when I hang up. Don't ask me any questions, Rose. I don't have time. Just do exactly what I said. Goodbye."

They reached the police cruiser and Henry said, dialing as he spoke, "The girls are at the house, guys. I'm riding with you. Put on the siren and go. I'll explain in just a sec." The phone at the teahouse rang.

"This is Madeline's Teahouse. We can't take—" Henry hung up. It was probably safer to not leave a message. Someone else might be in the house.

The siren was on and Greg headed for the teahouse. "Sam Brinker told me—" Henry began.

Greg interrupted. "We got quite a story from Sarah. Henry, why do you think there's gonna be a break-in tonight?"

"Hamilton thinks the treasure is somewhere in the teahouse. He's using Carl as a patsy. Carl gave the girls the tickets for tonight—"

Greg cursed and picked up the police radio. "Dispatch, come in...."

"Good evening, ladies," came an unfamiliar voice from the shadows of the main tearoom.

"Trouble, trouble, move it, we haven't got all night, ladies, nasty boys," squawked Mr. Tea. Terry heard his wings flap as he jumped around his cage.

The phone rang. Shoot, it's probably Aunt Rose.

Karen cursed, then said, "Who're you?"

"I believe you have something that belongs to me and I came to retrieve it," said the voice. An elderly man wearing tan pants and a striped shirt came out of the shadows. He had a gun pointed right at them.

"Not good," came Mr. Tea's voice.

"How'd you get in here?" Karen, bold as ever, asked. Terry wished she would shut up and not risk agitating the man.

"It wasn't hard. You should remember to lock your restroom windows before you go out," the man replied.

A sound from the attic drew Terry's attention upward. She couldn't believe her eyes. Carl.

"Hamilton, I found it. Leave 'em alone. I thought you ladies went to the dinner theater," Carl said.

Karen cursed again and held her head.

"Upstairs, now," growled the stranger, apparently Mr. Hamilton.

Terry was now more confused then scared. Somehow, despite the circumstances, she didn't think Carl was going to let Mr. Hamilton shoot them. Dang it, Aunt Rose and the ginger ale! Please, God, she prayed, don't let her come over here. As she helped Karen up the stairs, she thought, what did Carl find? What could we possibly have that belongs to Mr. Hamilton? There's nothing in that attic. What did they miss? It couldn't be the treasure. Could it?

As they reached the top of the stairs, Carl asked, "What's wrong with her?" pointing to Karen.

"Bad migraine," said Terry, looking around. Some of the floorboards were ripped up and she saw old, yellowed sacks with gold spilling out of them. Was this the treasure? How did it get in the attic? Karen groaned and crouched on the floor, holding her head in her hands. Terry started to squat beside her, but Mr.

Hamilton yanked her up by her arm. She yelped in pain. For an old guy, he was strong.

"Hamilton, I'm warning you," Carl said. "I will not let you hurt them in any way. This is where I draw the line. I was a coward back then and I guess I still am, but it ends here. Take your gold. I'll help you load it in your car, but you touch them and I'll kill you with my bare hands."

Beauregard laughed. It was the eeriest laugh Terry ever heard. It sent a chill through her.

"You always were nothin' but a mama's boy. You and that sissy, Brinker. Besides, Carl, my boy, I'm the one with the gun." Terry heard him cock it. He was going to shoot Carl!

Karen let out a blood-curdling yell and threw her body at Terry who slammed into Beauregard Hamilton. Before they plummeted down the stairs, the gun went off and Carl howled in pain. Terry felt herself bouncing from one step to another, down the attic stairs and then down the main stairs; she saw the blur of stripes as Beauregard tumbled with her. She heard the crash of a door before she felt her body jolt to a stop. A ripple of cool night air passed over her body before blackness engulfed her.

There were voices she could not answer. People were all around her, yet they were far, far away. She wanted to call out to them, but her mouth would not move. She floated upward. She could see them now. Henry cradled her body in his arms, tears streaming down his face. Greg shouted at other policemen who ran into the house. He bolted up the stairs to Karen who was sliding down the attic stairs. He sat down next to her and held her while other officers rushed up into the attic. Aunt Rose and the Dindles appeared in the doorway; they were crying. They tried to get to Henry, but a woman officer moved them outside. Yelling into his radio, Tom stood with his hand on Henry's shoulder. Next to her on the floor was Beauregard Hamilton. Another policeman knelt by him, checking for a pulse. Terry looked around. If she was here, where was he? Was she dead and he wasn't? How unfair was that? Then she saw them. They were in the parlor. Her mother and two women. Somehow she knew they were Eloise and Mary Gutherie. She tried to move toward them. Her mother smiled and blew her a kiss; the women waved. Terry tried to run to embrace her mother, but Terry was…tethered. Her mother shook her head. Terry understood; now was not her time. The three women seemed to slide gradually away, into another dimension. Not up, not down, but simply away into a light.

Terry felt a gentle tug behind her belly button, as if she was a balloon and an invisible cord was bringing her downward.

"Farewell, farewell, ladies," said Mr. Tea.

And then there was darkness.

Every bone in her body hurt. She wanted to end the pain, to slip back into unconsciousness, but it eluded her. She tried her voice and heard a moan.

"Terry," she heard Greg whisper. "Darlin, can you hear me?"

Darlin? she thought. Hold on, I can hear ya, just gimme a sec. She forced her voice again, another moan. She felt a kiss on her forehead.

"It's okay, Terry. If you can hear me, squeeze my hand."

For a darlin', I'll do whatever I have to. Man, I hurt. Shoot, what if I can't move my hand? She felt her fingers move. Ouch, they hurt too.

"Nurse, she's coming around. Nurse? Hello? Nurse? Nurse!"

The was a beep. "Okay, we hear you, we'll be right there, relax, Detective" came a voice.

Am I dreaming? Terry wondered. Wouldn't that stink! Okay, I gotta open my eyes. I can do this; I know I can. The lights hurt her eyes, she squinted. I think I see Greg, she thought. Soft footsteps came into the room.

"Miss Sutter? Can you hear me?" came a woman's voice.

A nurse? A doctor? "Uhhhhh," was all Terry could manage.

"Miss Sutter, can you open your eyes?"

Yeah, but I don't want to, thought Terry. Turn off the lights, she wanted to say. "Uhhhhh."

"Let me turn off the lights," said the voice.

"I've got 'em," came Greg's voice. A click.

Oooookayyyy, here I go, thought Terry. She saw a nurse standing over her. Greg sat next to the bed, holding her hand. She smiled. Tears rolled down his cheeks; he smiled back.

"Your friend here hasn't left your side in two days," said the nurse. "He's quite loyal."

Greg blushed; Terry glowed.

"The doctor says you can go home tomorrow," Karen said. "It's about time. Shannon and I are havin' a tough time without you. Ya need to get off your lazy butt and start helping out!" She kissed Terry's forehead and smiled.

"Hey, I managed for two months without you. You can manage five days." Wow, thought Terry. Five days seemed an eternity ago. Now she had six broken ribs, a concussion, a broken arm and lots and lots of bruises. "How's Carl?"

"He's home. Greg said the bullet missed his heart by a fraction of an inch. He'll need lots of therapy for his shoulder. I guess I should be angry or hate him, but I can't. I talked to him, ya know. He's sick over Mom's death. However, we really don't know if it was the sleeping pills. She could have tripped. I know he was willing to stand up to Mr. Hamilton because of us. Somehow, that counts." Karen shrugged.

"I don't know how I feel. I think the falling teacups were an indication that Mom's tea was drugged. Nothing's happened since, right?"

"Right. Sarah Hamilton died last night. She never knew about her husband's death. I guess I feel guilty about that. I really didn't mean to kill 'im. I thought I would go insane when it looked like I killed you, too. I was in so much pain because of my migraine and all I could see was you lying crumpled on the floor." She laughed. "After the ambulance took you out, I heaved all over Greg. He was a good sport about it. I still feel guilty, though."

"Speaking of guilt...." Terry looked over at a large bouquet of flowers. "I got those from Todd."

"I know. His cousins saw an article in the paper and they called him. He called me. My bouquet is bigger!" She giggled. "I still don't know how I feel about him. Right now, I just won't hang up on him when he calls. That's a big concession on my part. By the way, he told me I broke his office door. I don't know why he didn't tell me that before. Maybe he knew I needed some cheering up. Be warned, Aunt Rose is planning on taking care of you. Henry is dealing with things by fussing on our new water garden. You won't believe it." Karen's face turned serious. "He really thought we lost you. He came in the front door and you landed at his feet. I didn't see it happen, but Tom said he thought Henry was going to have a heart attack. I think you know where you stand with Greg."

"The nurses say he didn't leave my side. He stayed here for two days straight. I guess that speaks for itself." Terry debated, as she had for two days, about telling Karen about Mom and Eloise and Mary, but decided against it. It was something she wanted to keep to herself, for now anyway.

"Well, you're lookin' pretty good," came Shannon's voice from the doorway.

"A lot better then when I last saw you," added Tom. "I'm sorry I wasn't here sooner. I was coverin' for your buddy, Greg. I figured you'd rather see him than me. Shannon tells me you get to come home tomorrow. That's good news."

"Yeah, it is. I can't do a whole lot yet. Greg's sister, Anna, is going to help out at the teahouse for a few weeks. I'm glad it's over. Ya know, I never did ask about the treasure. Actually, this is the first day I haven't been on heavy pain medication. I've pretty much slept since it happened."

"I really don't know what happens now," Karen said. "Greg took it all to the police station. He's gonna help us deal with it. It looks like a heck of a lot of money."

"I don't know the whole story. Greg said he'd tell me when I got home. I can't wait to hear how it wound up in our attic. The Gutheries were murdered, weren't they?"

"Enough," said Tom. "Yeah, it's an ugly story. We'll fill you in once you're home."

"One more question, please," said Terry.

"Just one," Tom said.

"Did Carl kill the Gutherie sisters?"

"No. He and Sam Brinker saw it happen. That's it for now. If you don't rest, they may not let you go home tomorrow."

"Okay, okay. I'll rest. I'll do anything so I can go home and finally hear the whole story," Terry said, settling herself back against her pillows.

The late September breeze rustled through the leaves as the sisters stood by their parents' grave. Leaning on her cane, Terry watched as Karen reached down and placed the spray of purple and yellow mums at the base of the headstone.

Tears streamed down Karen's face. "Being here makes it so real. They're really gone. I still shake when I think how close you came to being here, too."

Terry patted here sister's shoulder. The chill in the air made her joints ache. She was healing…slowly. The doctors said her progress was great, but to Terry, it seemed to be taking much too long.

"Karen, don't focus on that. I'm not there," she said, pointing. "I'm here with you. Do you realize the chain of events that Mom's death set off? It's not just the teahouse, but my relationship with Greg, Mr. Brinker's mental recovery, Shannon's relationship with Tom and you and I finding all that gold."

"I'd give every penny back just to have them back," Karen whispered.

"So would I, but that's not the point. It's all about life and timing. I guess all of this made me realize that things have seasons. As much as we wish we could freeze time, we can't. We were never meant to. Part of me is terrified because I can't hold on to people like Aunt Rose, Uncle Henry and Mrs. Dindle. Still, I find a little bit of excitement and hope in each day because I feel that God really is in control of life's timing." She sighed. "I'm sorry. I guess I'm being too philosophical." She never told Karen about seeing her mother and the Gutherie sisters. Maybe someday she would; she still felt it was something she wanted to keep to herself.

Wiping her tears away, Karen said, "Todd called again yesterday. He wants to come visit."

"What did you tell him?"

"I told him I needed to think about it. I'm still afraid of being hurt again. There is a part of me that's jealous of you and Shannon."

Terry looked at her sister. "The funny thing is that, just yesterday, Shannon and I were talking about how scared we are. I'm terrified and so is she."

"Shannon said she's scared?"

"Yeah, I was shocked when she told me. I thought you and she were the brave ones. Guess not. At least not when it comes to matters of the heart. I wonder if most people are scared."

"I suppose anyone who's been hurt would be scared." Karen shrugged.

Both stood for a few moments without saying a word. Then Terry said, "Do you want me to leave you alone here for a bit?"

"No, I'm fine. How about you? Do you want to have time alone here?"

"No, I don't feel they're here. I know they see us…always."

They turned and Karen took Terry's arm and helped her walk back to the car. As she sat in the passenger side of the car, Terry said, "I can't wait until I can come home again. Uncle Henry and Greg have been great about keeping Aunt Rose under control. She gives me space, but…I just want my life back."

"It'll happen," Karen said, fastening her seatbelt. By the way, I talked to Mr. Watson, the man at the bank. He says the money should be released to us soon. Do you still want to give most of it to Fair Meadows?"

"Yeah, I really do, don't you?"

"Yeah, I do, too. I'm still not sure how much money we're talking about. A few million at least."

"Well, we won't have trouble finding money to do the Bed and Breakfast phase. I guess I'm still in shock over the whole thing. I can't imagine we have that much money."

Karen smiled. "Everything since I got here is still a blur. Luckily, there's no rush."

As they pulled into the driveway of the teahouse, Greg and Uncle Henry came out.

"What are you two doing here?" Karen asked as Terry slowly got out of the car. She hated Greg seeing her crippled and struggling. She knew it was silly to feel that way. Obviously, he didn't care, but she felt bulky and unattractive with her cane.

Greg jogged to the car and helped her. He gently kissed the top of her head. "I'm helping Henry get the water plants in for the winter. Mrs. Dindle's in the house directing. We figured we'd surprise you. By the way, Karen, we got information about our twenty-fifth high school reunion," he said with a big grin. "Shannon brought hers over and went through your mail and found yours."

"She went through my mail?" Karen asked, incredulously.

"Yup, she said she wanted to make sure you had no way of wiggling out. Now you can't claim you didn't know."

Terry looked up at Greg and realized he was really enjoying this. Terry looked over at Karen. She knew neither she nor Karen would care at all if Shannon looked through their mail. However, she wasn't sure how Karen would feel about a high school reunion. She hadn't gone to any of them in the past.

Karen looked...peeved. She glared at Greg and snarled. "Shannon's a brat and I'll do whatever I please." She stalked off.

Terry looked back at Greg. He was laughing. "Wait'll she finds out Shannon and I are volunteering her to help organize it."

Hmm, thought Terry. He's more like Uncle Henry than I realized. She smiled at him, thinking, God help us!

Greg and Uncle Henry helped Terry into the house. "Love birds," squawked Mr. Tea.

Greg and Terry laughed. "You don't need to be psychic to know that," Greg said.

"Triplets," replied the bird.

Terry felt dizzy. "I think I need to sit down... quickly," she said, panicked over Mr. Tea's last statement.

"Triplets, ha, ha," the macaw said, jumping and flapping about his cage.

Greg helped Terry ease into a chair. She could feel his hands shaking as he held her arm. He was extremely pale. "Henry," Greg said, in a half croak, half whisper.

"I know, I know." Henry said as Terry watched him trot for the door. "One pitcher of margaritas comin' right up!"

ABOUT THE AUTHOR

 Leslie Matthews Stansfield is the author of MR. TEA AND THE TRAVELING TEACUP, the first book in the Madeline's Teahouse series. She is the author of a previous book about the town she lives in. She grew up in Delmar, New York, and credits her friends with developing her imagination. Leslie is a graduate of the University of Hartford and recently received her Masters' degree from the University of Phoenix in Educational Leadership. She is a math tutor in a public school as well as the Christian Education Director of her church. She is currently working on her second book in the Madeline's Teahouse series. Leslie has four children and eight grandchildren and lives in Windsor Locks, Connecticut.

If you enjoyed reading *Mr. Tea and the Traveling Teacup* here's the first chapter in the next Madeline's Teahouse adventure by Leslie Matthews Stansfield: *Mr. Tea and the Bobbin' Body.*

Putting on her robe, Terry glanced in the mirror, then stepped into her bedroom. A vision flashed through her mind. She stopped, turned around, and went back into the bathroom. Squinting, she stared at the mirror. A cold shiver went through her. She got closer to the mirror and looked very carefully. OMG! IS THAT A GRAY HAIR? It certainly looked like a gray hair. It wasn't there yesterday. At least she didn't think so. No, no, no! Her boyfriend Greg's high school reunion weekend started tonight. It simply couldn't be. Breathe, she told herself.

Forcing herself to be casual, she walked into Karen's bedroom. No Karen. A humming sound came from the attached bathroom. Terry went to the bathroom doorway and watched Karen putting on her make-up. Karen stopped humming and cut her eyes to Terry's reflection in the mirror. "Good morning," she said. "Are you okay? You look a little pale. I hope you're not getting sick. I'm counting on you to help with things this weekend." Karen scowled into the mirror.

"I think I'm fine. I overate yesterday. I feel a little…whalish."

"Whalish. Nice word for the day after Thanksgiving. I like it. Whalish."

Be calm and breezy, Terry told herself. *Don't give it away.* "Hey, Kar, have you ever had a gray hair? I…um…think I saw one on Shannon yesterday." *Oh, nice, throw Shannon under the bus*, she thought, looking at her own reflection in the mirror. Shannon Dindle was their next door neighbor and lifelong friend.

Karen frowned and studied Terry in the mirror. Then Karen turned and looked at her directly. "Do *you* think you have a gray hair?"

Terry was afraid to speak, to even blink. *If Karen knew, would she tell Greg? Would she make fun of her in order to seem cool this weekend?* Terry felt the tears spill over.

"Oh, honey, don't panic. I am sure it's nothing," Karen cooed at her.

"I'm afraid Greg will be ashamed of me this weekend. I'll look old."

"Oh, please! He's older than you. He's my age, remember. Don't be silly."

"But he's so hunky, still. I don't want people to feel sorry for him."

Karen rolled her eyes. "Okay, you've been told forever how beautiful you are. The fact that you don't realize it is part of your charm. Trust me, really. Now, where is the little devil?" Karen said, stepping forward and studying Terry's head.

"Right here," Terry answered, looking in the mirror and pointing to the monstrosity.

"This one? This little thing. I think it's just blonde," Karen said, separating it from the others.

"Ow!" Terry yipped as Karen yanked the strand of hair out of her head.

"Problem solved!" Karen said, as she let the hair drift to the ground like a fall leaf. "All gone. No worries. We have to get going. We have to set things up for later. I can't believe Shannon convinced me to donate so much time, energy, and food to this shindig."

"I'll get dressed. I think it'll be fun. It'll give us a chance to show off our skills and Mr. Tea," Terry said, rubbing her head. Mr. Tea graced the parlor of the sister's business—Madeline's Teahouse—and charmed their customers with his wit and amazing vocabulary. In his previous home, it was rumored the bird was psychic.

"Crud, I forgot we have to get him there, too. Ugh, one more thing to do."

"Just call Shannon and go over with her. I'll call Greg and he and I can bring over what food you can't and Mr. Tea."

"Fine, fine," Karen said, waving her arms in the air. "I never wanted to go to this thing. I hate these things. I detest them even more now that I'm divorced and childless. Hate, hate, hate. I didn't like half those people in high school, and now I have to pretend to be their long lost buddy."

"What are you talking about? You were popular in high school. You were in the theater group and the cheer squad. All I did was design scenery for the plays," Terry said, heading to her room with Karen on her heels. Terry started to get dressed as Karen said, "That was just it. You had talent. Everyone 'ooohed' and 'ahhhed' at what you did. I just sang in the back of the chorus."

Terry put on her shirt and stared thoughtfully at Karen. "You should count your blessings. Ya know, some people won't be there this weekend because they're dead. Mary Elizabeth died of breast cancer. Terry Weaver was killed by a drunk driver. Donna Wiggins' car went over that cliff. Speaking of the Wiggins, is Rachelle Wiggins coming this weekend?"

"Yeah, I think so. I'm pretty sure she was one of the names Shannon said. I remember Shannon talking about how hard it would be for Rachelle to come without her twin sister. Did you know Terry Weaver's parents donated over five-hundred dollars toward the reunion costs?   I don't think they ever got over that loss. "

"Greg told me the kid that hit him died a year later when his car flipped over in a snowstorm.   He was drunk   again.   Okay, I'm ready.   Are we going together or separate?" Terry asked as they headed downstairs.

"Call Greg and see what he wants to do."

The front door opened and Greg Mullins walked in. "Hello," he said, looking up.

"Right on cue. I think you and I will bring Mr. Tea and whatever Karen and Shannon can't fit in Shannon's van," Terry said.

"Nope, Tom and Shannon have already made two trips this morning. I was sent to collect you and Mr. Tea."

"Secrets," Mr. Tea said, hopping around in his cage and fluffing his wings.

"Yeah, okay. Let's get a move on," Greg said, as he headed into the parlor to get the bird.

Terry, Greg, and Mr. Tea were manning the nametag table.   People mulled about, drinks in hand. Terry glanced at her watch and was stunned to see it was almost seven. It amused Terry to realize that many of the men who were the hairiest teenagers were now bald or balding. She kept looking over at Karen as one woman after another pulled out pictures of children. Karen was always gracious. Terry liked being able to sit back and watch people. She was lost in thought about who was thinner, who was heavier, who was now more well-endowed than in high school, and who, much to Terry's amusement, brought a trophy wife or a boy-toy.

"Did I tell you how proud I am of you and the amazing job you did with the decorations?" Greg whispered in her ear, giving her neck a little nuzzle.

"Thank you," Terry said, feeling a hot rush run through her. "I don't think it's much, though, compared to all the cooking Karen and Shannon did. All those hors d'oeuvres! The waitresses keep running back to fill their trays."

"Well, the first hour is open bar," Greg said. "It's a really smart idea to have food. The doors should open for dinner in about fifteen minutes."

"I liked the idea of cocktails by the pool," Terry said. "I had fun doing the ocean cruise theme. Shannon really wanted the reunion to take place on a cruise ship. I did my best." She loved listening to the comments passers-by made.

"That ocean looks so real, I keep waiting for my feet to get wet."

"The way that mermaid's hair glows, you'd swear it was the sunlight shining on it."

"I had to look at the picture of the captain at the wheel for a few seconds to realize it was a painting. Look at the way his cap seems to catch the light! I heard Terry Sutter did the art work. No surprises there. She was always amazing."

"Well, look who it is!" a woman said, walking up to the table. "The famous set designer. Do you recognize your old friend, the costume designer?"

Terry gasped. Until the woman said, 'costume designer,' Terry didn't have a clue. Now it was obvious. "Wow, have you lost weight! You look great," Terry exclaimed, getting up and running around the table to hug her old friend.

"Gastric bypass and lots, and I do mean lots, of exercise," Sandra Hochberg said.

Terry turned to Greg and did the introductions.

Greg stood and shook Sandra's extended hand. "Honestly, I would never have recognized you, Sandra. Terry is right, you look great."

"Thanks, Greg. That's kind of you," Sandra said. Terry noticed her squeeze Greg's hand. Turning to Terry, she said, "Terry, I don't remember you being in my grade. Were you?"

"No, I was two years behind. I'm helping out. Karen, my sister, enlisted me," Terry said, realizing Sandra held on to Greg's hand a little too long. Old friend indeed, Terry thought. Perhaps at a high school reunion, all bets are off.

"Nice legs, toots," Mr. Tea said.

"Well, isn't he the charmer," Sandra said, winking at Greg.

"Yes, he's our macaw. We call him Mr. Tea, *t–e–a.* Karen and I own a teahouse now."

"I heard that. And I heard it's marvelous. My mother went with some of her friends. I hope to visit it this weekend."

"We'll be open tomorrow from 11 to three," Terry said. "We're keeping shorter hours this weekend so Karen can enjoy the reunion activities. Speaking of which, it's almost time to open the doors for dinner."

"Will you be stuck at the teahouse, holding down the fort?" Sandra asked, her voice sounding a bit hopeful.

"No, we close before the activities start," Terry said.

"Oh, goody. Anyway, Greg, I hope you and I can catch up over dinner and a drink or two," Sandra said.

"I'm sure there'll be room at our table," Greg said. "That would be great. Aren't the decorations Terry did fantastic, Sandra? She outdid herself." Greg smiled broadly. "I'm so proud of her. Have you noticed the details on the murals? Don't the waves look like they're about to break? Did you notice the mermaids on that island scene other there?" Greg asked, pointing.

"What about the waiters and waitresses being dressed as sailors? That was her idea and the caterers loved it. The dining room is decorated like the deck of a ship, with railings and everything."

"Warning! Warning!, Warning!" squawked Mr. Tea. "Anchor's away!"

"That's interesting." Sandra giggled. "He's so precious." Then, with a rather cold look in her eye, she said, "So, are you two...together?"

"Sure are," Greg said. "Oh, I think I see them unlocking the doors to the dining room." He walked around the table and put out both of his arms. "May I escort you ladies to dinner? he asked.

"How lovely," Sandra said, her voice a little flat.

"We'll be back, buddy," Terry said to Mr. Tea.

"Here we go again," he said, hopping from foot to foot.

"That buffet was amazing," Tom O'Hara said. "I didn't think I'd ever want to eat after yesterday, but..."

"You always say you never want to eat again," Shannon huffed. "You're always eating and never gaining. It's downright annoying." She threw her napkin on the table in mock disgust.

"I think it's a man thing," Rachelle Wiggins-Taylor said. "My husband is the same way."

Terry really liked Rachelle. Karen invited Rachelle and her husband, Russ, to join their table for dinner. Greg, Russ, and Tom really hit it off. Sandra seemed to be enjoying talking to Karen and Shannon about recipes.

"Terry, I really can't tell you enough how perfect these decorations are," Rachelle said. "I'd forgotten how talented you were. You and Sandra were so artistic. You made the plays that much better by your work."

"Let's not forget Donna's make-up skills," Sandra said. "She added a lot. I was so sorry to hear about her death."

"Me, too," said Karen.

"I still can't believe she's gone," Rachelle said. "Holidays are the hardest. My mom likes to pretend everything is fine, but there's always an emptiness at the table."

"I feel that way since Karen and I lost our mom," Terry said.

"I think of how magic the holidays seemed as a child." Rachelle sighed. "My children love them. I never thought about how adults feel. It's like we try and put away our memories to let the children have their magic."

"I never thought about it that way, but you're probably right," Karen said. "That's quite insightful..." Karen's voice trailed off as they all turned their heads toward the sound of a commotion. It seemed to becoming from the doors by the pool area. That was when the screaming started.

www.ingramcontent.com/pod-product-compliance
Lightning Source LLC
Chambersburg PA
CBHW050426260626
47156CB00003B/1166